Dawn of the Monsters

EDITED BY DEANNA KNIPPLING AND JAMIE FERGUSON

I0610495

Featuring stories by:

DEAN WESLEY SMITH • RON COLLINS • P. D. CACEK • MARK LESLIE
STEVE VERNON • ANNIE REED • SÈPHERA GIRÓN • REBECCA M. SENESE
MARCELLE DUBÉ • JAMIE FERGUSON • DEANNA KNIPPLING

BOROGROVE PRESS • COLORADO

Table of Contents

Introduction..*1*
   The Editors

Transmogrification...*9*
   Jamie Ferguson

The Ritual of the Drawing..*35*
   Mark Leslie

On a Dark Road to Nowhere...*51*
   Marcelle Dubé

In the Shade of the Slowboat Man.................................*79*
   Dean Wesley Smith

Neck Bolt Lynch Pin..*97*
   Steve Vernon

The Bitch...*123*
   P. D. Cacek

Rites of Passage...*145*
   Annie Reed

Beach Comber..*179*
   Sèphera Girón

Bargain Hunter..*197*
   Rebecca M. Senese

The Grave-Diggers...*237*
   DeAnna Knippling

It Came Out of the Swamp..*271*
   Ron Collins

About Amazing Monster Tales......................................*297*

About Borogrove Press...*297*

Other Collections...*297*

AMAZING MONSTER TALES

Dawn of the Monsters

Introduction

The Editors

In which editors Jamie Ferguson and DeAnna Knippling help usher in the return of the era of pulp monsters!

Welcome to the first volume of Amazing Monster Tales, *Dawn of the Monsters*. We're here because we love pulp fiction and want to see more of it. More monsters…more strange and inexplicable events… more invaders from another dimension. Garish colors, big characters, strange technologies, and wildly improbable events? Yes, please!

Dawn of the Monsters is the first volume of a series. This one doesn't have any special theme, other than "it's the first one, so let's call it DAWN OF THE MONSTERS!!!"[1]

Each volume will focus on the monsters. We might take you to different planets, under the sea, or on a road trip, but we promise there will be monsters, and there will be pulp.

What Are Monsters?

Soooo glad you asked.

Monsters are:

- Outside the realm of stuff that's proven to exist.
- Able to act of their own willpower.
- Not human, or at least not quite.

Human-eating plants? Monsters. Self-willed attack rocks on an alien planet? Monsters. Artificial intelligence with an agenda of its own? Monsters. Sparkly vampires? *Monsters, I tell you! Monsters!!!*

We have some sympathetic monsters, some unsympathetic monsters, and some monsters who simply don't have time for the human world. And who can blame them?

What Is Pulp?

The pulp era was a time when many, many stories were written and published in flimsy newspapers and cheap magazines. Pulp was printed on a cheap grade of paper that was nicknamed "pulp" paper, for how lumpy it was. (The other stuff was called "glossies" or "slicks.")

The era ran from the 1890s to the 1950s and started with *Argosy* magazine. Other pulp magazines included *Spicy Detective*, *Thrilling Wonder Stories*, *Weird Tales*, *Black Mask*, and *Astounding*. Pulp writers included Ray Bradbury, H.P. Lovecraft, C.L. Moore, Tennessee Williams (no, really!), Mark Twain, Louis L'Amour, Rudyard Kipling, and Joseph Conrad.

If it sold, it was fit to print!

Pulp writers wrote fast. Sometimes they wrote to formulas the magazines demanded they follow. Other times they took risks on stories that only the pulps would publish. Sometimes the work was ridiculous and improbable. Other times a story might turn into one of the classics of a generation.

So what *was* pulp? What were people reading, when they read pulp?

More to the point, what are we talking about when we say we want to see it return?

From our point of view, pulp fiction is about:

- Unbelievable situations.
- Told in the most believable fashion possible.

Some of you may disagree with this as a definition, which is fair. The pulp era was a big chunk of time, and a broad selection of genres, to define with strict accuracy. But this is what we'd like to bring back: detectives who aren't crushed underneath the systems they buck; sheriffs who can ride off into the sunset instead of dying of hypothermia out on the prairie; evil masterminds too clever to be caught and the improbably intelligent journalists who catch them anyway; and our favorites, the monsters who are really, seriously, just misunderstood.

Our Cover Artist

A moment of applause and appreciation for our cover artist, Paul Roman Martinez. We basically handed him a couple of rules and said to have fun with it.

First, that nobody on an *Amazing Monster Tales* cover should appear helpless. One thing we didn't care for on pulp covers were characters who were terrified, trapped, and unable to act. More action! Second, we also asked for no bare nipples (which were typical of the era) so we didn't get banned from retailers. C'est la vie.

Paul handed us back this (pardon, I have to say it) *amazing* cover. He is a pulp-era artist extraordinaire, and I recommend both his art, at *https://PaulRomanMartinez.tumblr.com*, and his board game *Adventures of the 19XX*, for which he also writes and illustrates graphic novels.

Our Stories

We start with a tale from editor Jamie Ferguson, "Transmogrification." Many, many, *many* pulp magazines included stories from their editors and house writers under various pen names, often packing in several stories from the same author in each issue under different pen names! We decided on keeping our names. Jamie's story is the bright and cheerful tale of a mad scientist, his secret lab, and the terrible invention that he inflicts upon a species other than his own. This story sums up where we're coming from with our pulp monsters: sometimes it's the monsters who are the bad guys...but often it's the humans involved!

Next comes Mark Leslie's story, "The Ritual of the Drawing," a tale about an upstanding citizen of a *very* fine community whose existence revolves around an agreement that is not one-sided and biased in any way, and of course it's just what we all wanted, wasn't it? Humanity often tries to accommodate its monsters rather than fight them...

After that story, "On a Dark Road to Nowhere" was supplied by Marcelle Dubé, an atmospheric tale of isolation, cold, and terror! When the monsters come out, how can we defend ourselves? Outclassed and outgunned, how can we possibly survive? *Maybe we don't!*

Then take a long, slow breath into Dean Wesley Smith's "In the Shade of the Slowboat Man," in which the monster shows its humanity. What makes us human, you ask? Is it in never having done anything cruel or unforgivable? Or does the essence lie in another direction?

Author Steve Vernon contributes his story, "Neck Bolt Lynch Pin." A Canadian Mountie meets...*FRANKENSTEIN.* There may be a beer or two involved, eh? When the monster meets the law, the question becomes not just what is right, but whose right it is to decide.

Then we do a little slide over to the dark side in P. D. Cacek's story of love and obsession, "The Bitch." Sometimes the real monster is people who only *think* they love you...

If you're looking for a tale about fighting back against the forces of evil, check out Annie Reed's "Rites of Passage," in which the stakes are a cosmic invasion. How can we stop the unstoppable? A secret superpower might be involved: the power of admitting that maybe, just *maybe*, our first instincts might be wrong!

Then comes Sèphera Girón's story, "Beach Comber," in which another character makes a mistake...dragging everyone into a situation with much higher stakes than she could have ever anticipated!

Rebecca M. Senese contributes a story, "Bargain Hunter," that is in some ways a companion piece to Mark Leslie's "The Ritual of the Drawing." But where in Mark's story the characters have agreed to the situation they have found themselves in, in Rebecca's story, none of the characters realize what they've gotten themselves into. Maybe they should have read the fine print...if there *was* any fine print, that was!

Our other editor, DeAnna Knippling, brings a tale of horror that spans the generations in "The Grave-Diggers." Should the sins of the fathers be visited upon their sons? Or the sins of the great-great-great grandmothers upon their grandsons? Another deal gone bad, it seems: people should read the contracts they sign a little bit closer!

Finally, we wrap things up with Ron Collins's[2] story, "It Came Out of the Swamp." In the end, after the monsters have been defeated, after everything has been said and done, after the stories have been told and retold and retold again, what's left? What clues remain to be followed? What does it all mean? And where should we go from here? The narrator arrives at a theory...

In the end, we hope we've left you with some good stories. A few dark stories, a few funny ones, a few ironic twists. A few laughs, a few tears, a few jumps of fright, and a little bit of hope that we can learn to be a little more human, whatever our backgrounds.

—DeAnna Knippling

1 Working on this project has consumed a major portion of my lifetime supply of exclamation points, let me tell you.

2 No relation to Barnabas Collins of *Dark Shadows* fame.

Transmogrification

Jamie Ferguson

Lester hated his job.

He enjoyed the work itself—and really, who wouldn't enjoy spending their days in a laboratory analyzing the properties of different organic materials and experimenting with incorporating them into robots?

But the job itself was a different story. His boss, Dr. E. E. Humphreys, was a slave-driver, a micro-manager, and a know-it-all. And to make matters worse, the tall, well-coiffed man insisted on wearing a cologne made of patchouli and spruce that tickled Lester's nose. Looking at things through a microscope was rather difficult when you kept having to sneeze.

Today, however, was a Saturday, and the fragrant doctor had headed to the Denver airport early yesterday for a conference in Sweden, so he wouldn't be in the office. Lester shouldn't be either, but he'd left his phone at the office the day before and was getting behind on Robotznik, the game he'd been playing on his phone every day for the past few years.

He pulled his electric car into his usual spot in the large, empty parking lot—three rows from the entrance next to a clump of short, stout juniper bushes. He pushed open the door and stepped out into the warmth of the beautiful Colorado evening. The summer solstice was a little over a week away and the days were long. Even though it was just after six o'clock, the sun hung high in the sky. Sunlight glinted off the reddish-brown sandstone on the top of the foothills that stood just west of town, the sky was bereft of clouds, and bits of cottonwood fluff floated by on the light June breeze.

Lester headed for the glass doors of the office entrance, glancing over his shoulder at the coffee shop across the street to see if he could spot Petra, the barista he'd had a crush on since she started working there last fall. He didn't think she worked weekends and wasn't sure the shop was even open this late, but maybe he should stop by afterward, just in case.

Not that he intended to speak to her. Just the thought made his heart race. Fortunately, at this point she knew his order. When she saw Lester she'd look up at him, one dark eyebrow raised, and ask "Dry cappuccino?" He only had to stare at her greenish-brown eyes and nod. He'd breathe in the scent of her vanilla perfume—at least he thought she smelled like vanilla, although it could have been the smell of the syrup the shop used in Italian sodas—and would stand silently at the counter and fiddle with a pen or a straw or something, hoping he didn't look as awkward as he felt. While Petra prepared his drink, he'd sneak glances at the wisps of dark hair that had slipped out of her ponytail, or the silver earrings that hung from her delicate ears, or her slim, muscled shoulders, trying to watch her without appearing creepy. He wasn't entirely sure he succeeded. Finally, she'd draw a picture of a flower or a cat or something equally charming on the surface of his coffee with latte foam, and would set his cup on the counter in between them, giving him a quick smile. He'd mumble "thanks," but by the time he got the word out of his mouth, she'd be busy helping the next customer.

A cappuccino at six in the evening later tonight would almost certainly mean he'd be awake all night, but it would be worth it to see Petra. Maybe he'd even try to talk to her for once.

Maybe.

Lester passed the empty bike rack and reached the entrance. He swiped his badge in front of the reader. The doors unlocked with a loud click, and he slipped into the cool, air-conditioned, empty office building. He walked past the reception desk, up the stairs to the second floor, and began to wind his way through the maze of cubicles. The sunlight that trickled in through the windows on the front side of the building provided enough illumination that he didn't mind that the overhead lights had been switched off. Other than the dimness, everything looked exactly the same as it always did, but the building felt eerily quiet without its normal hustle and bustle. Even the tiniest sounds seemed louder than normal: the scuffing of his sneakers on the thin, gray carpet, the hum from one of the air conditioning vents in the ceiling, the beating of his heart. The back of his neck tingled. It felt almost as though someone was watching him. But of course that was ridiculous. The entire building was empty except for him.

Lester tried to ignore the odd feeling and marched on until he reached his own tiny cube. He wrinkled his nose as he realized his phone wasn't where he'd thought it would be. His desk was empty except for his mouse, an empty mug that smelled faintly of coffee, and a small collection of action figures. He wheeled his chair back and crawled underneath his desk, looking through the dusty jumble of computer cables, but his phone wasn't there either. Great. He must have left it in the lab.

He sighed and pulled himself to his feet. He passed the last few rows of cubicles, then walked down the wide, open hallway that led to the laboratories. The large, spacious offices of the executives lined the west side of the building. They were all situated against the exterior wall so they had windows and a view of the mountains, unlike the cubicles lowly research scientists like

Lester sat in. He glanced at the closed door to the last office, which belonged to his boss. The gold letters on the polished mahogany nameplate read *Doctor E. E. Humphreys, Celebrated Scientist and Head of Research.*

Lester rolled his eyes. Doc—his private term for Dr. Humphreys, which he would never, ever use in front of the other man—had a knack for making himself sound important, whether or not it was justified. The doctor went out of his way to look the part of a brilliant, respectable scientist. He wore an immaculately groomed beard, perfect for stroking when he wanted to look deep in thought; his shirts were always ironed; he got manicures every other Friday morning; and, while Lester couldn't prove it, he was pretty sure neither Doc's coal-black hair, nor the distinguished silver streaks that ran through it, were natural.

He reached the interior wall and opened the door to the long, tiled hallway that led to the research labs. The lights flickered on, triggered by a motion sensor. Lester glanced up at the small, round globe on the ceiling that contained the security camera, gave his usual wave, then headed down the hall. The soles of his sneakers made little rubbery squeaking sounds as he walked. When he reached the door for Laboratory 207, where he did most of his research, he swiped his badge across the reader. The door unlocked with a loud click that echoed down the empty corridor. He pulled open the door and paused for a moment to wait for the fluorescent lights inside the room to flicker on.

The lab was about twenty feet wide and forty long. A large stainless-steel refrigerator stood against the far wall, next to shelves lined with glass beakers, petri dishes, metal tongs, and a variety of metal instruments. Several robotic arms jutted up out of the long metal track that ran through the large table in the middle of the room. Three wide monitors took up most of the surface of the small desk in one corner; the computer itself sat on the floor underneath the desk. High, white tables laden with equipment—an electrophoresis chamber, a compound light microscope, several centrifuges and microcentrifuges, a chromatograph, and, covered with a plastic sheet, a magnetometer—stood against one wall next to a tall, wide, closed door.

Lester couldn't prove it, but he was pretty sure the opaque window at the top of the door was made of one-way glass and suspected Doc used it to spy on his employees. He certainly seemed to have a knack for showing up in the lab whenever Lester took too long of a break.

Neither Lester nor anyone else he'd ever talked with knew what was really behind that door, and the one time he'd asked the doctor he'd gotten an icy stare but no actual explanation. His pet theory was that it led from Dr. Humphreys' office directly to the lab. Not that the doctor came into the lab all that often, which was just fine. Lester tended to make a ridiculous number of mistakes when his boss was around, and it didn't help that he appeared to be allergic to the doctor's spruce and patchouli cologne. Fortunately, Doc didn't stop by very often these days. He claimed to be heads-down on a robotics project so secret that he had to work on it in his office instead of in one of the company labs, although Lester doubted that was really the case because there wasn't any equipment in the doctor's office.

He shot a glance at the glass window. If Doctor Humphreys really did use it to spy on his employees, he certainly wouldn't be able to do so from Stockholm. Lester walked over to the desk in the corner, but his phone didn't appear to be there either. He gritted his teeth. He had played Robotznik for 437 days straight, and if he didn't find his phone soon, his streak would be broken.

He pushed his chair aside, crouched down to look under the desk. He sighed with relief as he spotted his phone lying on the grayish-white tiles next to the wall. He grabbed it and stood up. He'd just check in on his game. Besides, it wasn't as if he had anywhere to be. Well, maybe staring tongue-tied at Petra if she was working, but even that could wait thirty seconds.

He pressed the button on the side of his phone and grimaced at the red text telling him he only had two percent of battery life left. He navigated to his game. Then the screen went blank as his phone shut itself off.

Lester scowled. That had been more like two seconds than two percent. At least he'd finally found his phone. He'd plug it in when he got back to his car. It would only take a few minutes to charge up enough for him to keep his streak going.

He jammed it into his pocket and headed toward the hallway, then paused in mid-step as he realized the mysterious door with the glass panel wasn't closed after all. Lester stared at it for a moment. Not only had he never seen it open before, every time he'd surreptitiously tried the handle, it had been locked. This was his chance to finally find out what lay on the other side.

He walked across the room to the door, took a deep breath, and pushed it open.

The hinges made a tiny creak as the door swung inward, revealing a small, darkened room. He took a step forward, squinting in the dim light, then spotted a light switch.

He flipped the switch and lights hanging from sconces on the walls flickered on, illuminating the narrow little room. It was roughly ten feet long and maybe six or seven feet wide, had the same grayish tiled floor and white-painted walls as all the laboratories, and contained nothing but two closed doors. One stood in the middle of the wall to Lester's right. The other was at the far end.

He stepped inside the room, which smelled faintly like chlorine, then glanced back over his shoulder at the door to the lab. His guess had been right. The window was made of one-way glass. That meant the doctor really did spy on the researchers in the lab. Or maybe someone else did, but who other than Doc would care about what his employees did? What a jerk.

Lester shook his head and walked over to the closest door and turned the handle. The door swung inward, opening without a sound. His breath caught as he realized it opened into Dr. Humphreys' spacious, high-ceilinged corner office. He walked through it, his shoes making soft scuffing sounds on the thick gray-and-white checked carpet.

The early evening sunshine streamed in through the tall glass windows on the south and west walls. The view of the pines and sandstone outcroppings of the foothills was magnificent. A large mahogany desk took up one corner of the room; two dark-blue upholstered chairs sat in front of it. From personal experience, Lester knew the chairs weren't as comfortable as they looked; Doc had probably selected them for that very reason. Two sofas, a few cushioned armchairs, and a low glass table took up a big chunk of the room. Framed degrees and awards and news articles hung on the walls, and bookshelves lined two of the walls, including the side of the room Lester had come through.

On this side of the wall, the door he'd opened was part of a bookcase.

No wonder he'd never noticed another door in Doc's office. He crouched down and inspected the shelves. In the back corner of the lowest shelf, behind a four-inch wide dictionary, he found a tiny button. That must be how Doc controlled the door from this side.

He stood up and peered around the shelf/door into the small room he'd come from. If this door led to Doc's office, where did the *other* door lead?

He went back into the hallway, pulled the secret door closed behind him, then walked over to the third door. Did the other executives know about the secret room? They had to. Didn't they? Was Lester violating some company rule by investigating?

If he was, he'd already broken the rule, so he might as well keep on going.

Lester reached for the handle of the third door and turned it before he could think too much about his questionable logic.

The door opened onto a wide, tiled hallway that sloped gently downward, curving around a wall. More sconces hung from the walls and illuminated the space.

Where did the hallway go? Maybe it led to a room on the first floor? There were labs down there as well. If Doc used the one door to spy on Lester and his co-workers, maybe he spied on some of the researchers in one of the other labs as well. But the first-floor labs were used for chemistry work, and weren't set up for the experiments with organic materials or robotics that Doc's team's focused on.

Lester's breath caught as he realized that if Dr. Humphreys really was working on a super-secret project like he'd claimed, this hallway might lead to a hidden laboratory.

He took a step forward, then stopped. If a secret lab really stood at the end of the mysterious hallway, he could probably get in serious trouble if anyone found out he'd been here. Who knew who Doc's customer was? What if it was a government agency? What if they figured out Lester had learned about their project and decided to send him to jail? Or worse?

Prickles ran down the back of his neck. He'd done enough exploring for one day. He should forget about all of this and go home, charge up his phone, order a pineapple and jalapeño pizza, and play Robotznik for the rest of the evening. He didn't need to investigate a mysterious hallway that he hadn't even known existed.

Although...this might be his only chance to find out what the doctor was really doing. The door in the lab had always been locked; he might never have this opportunity again. Lester had endured enough scrutiny from the pompous, egotistical doctor, and was tired of the man getting all the credit for the work his employees did, even though he himself flitted off to swan around at conferences and barely did any of the actual research.

Besides, it was Saturday evening. No one would even know he'd been here. There were no security cameras around other than the one he'd passed earlier at the entrance to the laboratory section. He had a perfectly legitimate reason for his presence in the lab, since that's where he had left his phone. And not only was the building empty, Doc wasn't even in the same country.

Lester took a deep breath and headed down the sloping tiled floor.

The sounds of his sneakers on the tiles echoed as he wound his way down the curving ramp. The hallway probably sloped to make it easier to wheel equipment around, although it might have made more sense to have put in an elevator. He walked down, and down, and down. He had begun to wonder if the passageway would ever end. Then the floor began to flatten out.

The hallway ended at another tall, wide door. Lester rested a hand on one wall while he regained his equilibrium after walking around the turning hallway for so long. He looked up at the ceiling, but there were no security cameras in sight.

He crossed to the door, pulled it open, and then stared, open-mouthed, at Dr. Humphreys' secret laboratory.

It was at least five times the size of the one he worked in, if not more, and it was chock-full of all kinds of state-of-the-art equipment. The chromatograph in the corner was the model that Dr. Humphreys had claimed was too expensive for the company's budget. The centrifuge was larger and more powerful than the one Lester and his co-workers used. Even the stainless-steel refrigerator was twice the size of the one in Lester's lab. Every piece of equipment he'd ever dreamed of working with was here—plus a few things he didn't recognize.

He walked into the lab and wandered around, admiring the things he recognized and trying to puzzle out the things he didn't. A chair upholstered in a bright orange and red flower print sat in one corner; something that looked like an old-fashioned metal hair dryer from a beauty salon hung above it from a cluster of cables attached to bolts on the ceiling. Tall shelves held large glass jars filled with pebbles and boxes of different kinds of clay. A collection of robot arms reached down from a metal track suspended above a long, low table, hanging motionless just above a collection of glass beakers containing different colored liquids that all smelled like mint and rubbing alcohol. A low hum emanated from something that looked like a cross between an air conditioner and a big ball of twisted copper wire.

What was all of this stuff? What kind of research did Dr. Humphreys do here anyway?

Lester reached a hand out to touch what looked like a piece of green velvet stretched over a wire frame in one corner of the room. The material felt springy and buoyant against his fingers—more like grass or moss or something living than like fabric.

He froze as the sharp sound of metal on metal came from behind him.

A hairy, eight-foot-tall monster stood in between Lester and the door to the hallway.

The monster glowered at Lester. Its thick, bushy eyebrows looked like giant caterpillars crawling across its face. It wore tattered jeans and a black T-shirt several sizes too small with the words *I Love Rocks* emblazoned across the chest.

Behind the creature Lester could see a large metal cage. The door of the cage hung askew and the bars nearest the door were bent.

The creature took a step toward Lester, and then another, its bare, hairy feet making thumping sounds on the tiled floor. It moved slowly and appeared to be favoring one leg. The thing seemed almost human, but its features were thick and blocky, as if it had been carved out of sandstone that had then turned to a reddish-brown skin. Streaks of something dark red were smeared down one side of its face and along its left arm. They looked suspiciously like blood—not that Lester had ever seen that much blood in real life, but he had watched plenty of movies.

"Hi," Lester said. "I, uh, I don't know what's going on here. But I'm definitely not part of it. I work upstairs. I just found the door by accident."

The monster continued toward Lester. It passed the flower-patterned chair, then stopped and swung a giant hand at the strange hair dryer-like thing, pulling it loose from the collection of cables that had suspended it from the ceiling. The metal crashed to the floor, sparks flew from the cables, and the smell of ozone filled the air.

"I don't know what Dr. Humphreys was doing down here," Lester said. He took a step backward. "I swear. I just work for him. He's a terrible manager. And his cologne makes me sneeze."

The monster paused and stared at Lester for a minute, its head cocked to one side.

Lester swallowed as the monster began walking toward him again. He backed up until he ran into a cold, metal table. His stomach flipped as he realized he'd managed to trap himself in between the table, the monster, and a wall filled with empty glass beakers and vials. He looked around, frantically searching for something to protect himself with. The monster was now so close that Lester could smell its earthy scent.

"You're not going to get me!" Lester yelled. He pulled a wheeled stool out from underneath the table and pushed it at the creature as hard as he could. It slid across the tiles and hit the monster in the leg. He grabbed an empty beaker from the shelf and threw it, completely missing the monster. He threw another beaker, and then another, finally managing to hit the monster in the side of its head. The glass broke as easily as if it had been thrown against a boulder.

The creature made a loud sound like a combination of a growl and a groan, and limped toward him, apparently oblivious to the broken glass that crunched under its bare feet.

Lester climbed up on the metal table and pushed the shelf of glassware toward the monster with all his strength. The shelf toppled and then fell with a crescendo of breaking glass as the beakers and vials hit the tiled floor.

Lester leapt off the table and sprinted around the room to the open doorway. He ran through it and dashed up the sloping, curving hallway, moving faster than he'd ever run before. The monster grunted as it followed behind him, the thumping of its footsteps echoing off the walls. Lester reached the open door at the top of the stairs, ran through the doorway, and then plowed into someone so hard he knocked them both over. They fell on the tiled floor in a jumble.

He scrambled up from off of the other person's left arm. The calm, soothing scent of vanilla filled his nostrils.

"Who are—" he began, and then he gasped as he realized he'd run into Petra, the barista he had a crush on. What was she doing inside the building, much less in a secret room he hadn't even known existed an hour ago?

Petra pushed herself to her feet and glared at him. She adjusted the spaghetti straps of her black tank top, then wiped her hands on her denim shorts.

A snort echoed up the hallway from behind Lester. Whatever Petra was doing here could wait.

"There's a monster coming," he said. "Let's go! It's going to get us!"

He grabbed Petra's left arm, dragged her over to the door to his lab, and turned the handle and pulled.

The door didn't budge.

He tugged at it for a moment, but it was locked. He'd left it open, he was sure of that. It must have swung all the way shut after he'd gone through it earlier.

Or had someone else closed it?

Petra shrugged out of his grasp and crossed her arms. He stared at her greenish-brown eyes. His fingers tingled where he'd touched her skin, and his heart raced—and not completely because he'd just run away from a monster.

"I thought you were a nice guy," she said. She tilted her head to one side, making her dark ponytail bounce.

"I am," Lester said. He felt as though he were watching himself from far away. He couldn't really be talking to Petra. Not for real. This was some sort of dream. She stood so close to him that he could see the tiny smattering of freckles that ran across the bridge of her nose. Her full lips were as beautiful as if they'd been made of rose petals. Tiny silver hoop earrings hung from her delicate ears. A lock of dark hair had escaped her ponytail. He wanted to reach out and brush it back behind her ear, to breathe in her sweet vanilla scent, to run his hands along her—

A low grunt came from the passageway that led up from the strange laboratory below them.

Lester blinked as he remembered he was supposed to be saving Petra. And hopefully himself as well.

He dashed over to the door to Dr. Humphreys' office and pushed it open. A ray of evening sunshine shone through the windows and into the little room he and Petra stood in.

"Come on," he said. "I need to get you out of here."

"I'm not going anywhere," Petra said. She glared at him, her hazel eyes narrowed. "And to think I always worked so hard on making foam latte art in your cappuccinos."

"The foam drawings are awesome," he said. He reached out to grab her arm, but she stepped back out of his reach. He could hear the sound of the monster breathing as it huffed and puffed its way up the ramp. It was almost too late! "But we have to get out of here *right now*. I don't know what that thing is, but it's big and it's scary and it's dangerous. Come with me, Petra—please!"

His voice trailed off as the giant shape of the monster appeared behind Petra's petite form.

Lester grabbed her shoulders, pushed her to one side, and then stepped in between Petra and the monster.

"Run!" he said to Petra. He clenched his hands into fists and held them up. The monster looked down at him, and then tilted its head to one side. Lester took a deep breath and met the creature's big, brown eyes. He clearly wasn't going to make it out of this himself, but at least he'd saved Petra.

The creature moved one arm. Lester braced himself for the coming blow.

The monster scratched behind one of its ears.

"Here I am," Lester said. "Go on, kill me, or eat me, or both. But I won't let you hurt Petra!"

He swung a fist at the monster. It grabbed his wrist in its giant, warm, strangely solid hand. Lester struggled for a minute, trying to pull his hand free, and then stopped. It was like having his fist stuck in a crack in a rock face.

"Okay," Petra said from behind him. "I believe you now. Sigurd, you can let him go."

Sigurd?

The creature released its grip. Lester pulled his hand back and rubbed his wrist. Behind Petra and the monster the door to Dr. Humphreys' office beckoned, the evening sunlight now a golden-red.

"What's going on?" Lester asked.

Petra glanced at the monster, and then back at Lester.

"Sigurd is my brother," she said. She walked over to the monster and laid a tiny hand on its giant, hairy forearm. "We have troll lineage through our mother's side. Your boss captured him and was doing experiments on him to make him stay in between his human and troll forms. Sigurd is stuck in between being human and being stone. I just hope we can figure out how to undo this."

"I, uh…what?" Lester ran a hand through his hair. He could believe the monster—*Sigurd*, he reminded himself—was a troll. But *Petra*, the girl he'd dreamed of since last fall, was a troll? "I don't understand. What exactly is a troll? You can turn into a *rock*?"

"I'll explain it all later," Petra said. She jerked her head toward the door to Dr. Humphreys's office. "Let's get out of here first."

Lester followed Petra and her brother through the open doorway into the doctor's office. The sun had just gone down behind the tops of the foothills and it was beginning to get dark. Sigurd took a few steps toward one of the windows that faced the mountains and stopped, his big mouth hanging open.

"Longgg," he said. His voice was deep and low. Something that looked suspiciously like a tear trickled down the side of his face. He rubbed his eyes with the back of a knuckle.

Petra reached up and patted his shoulder. "I know, you were trapped in there for a long time. Let's get you back home."

Lester pressed the button he'd found earlier and watched as the secret door shut. It probably didn't matter if he shut it, because Doc was going to figure out what had happened when he got back from his conference. There might not be security cameras in the secret lab, but he could get the footage from the camera by the entrance to the research laboratory section of the building. It wouldn't take a genius to figure out that Lester had been involved in helping Sigurd escape from Dr. Humphreys's lab—especially since all three of them were going to have to pass that same camera on their way out of the building.

But leaving Sigurd would be untenable. Even if he weren't Petra's brother, he didn't deserve to be kept captive and experimented upon.

Petra had stopped to look at the blood on Sigurd's left arm. Lester took a deep breath and walked around them, heading across the gray-and-white checked carpet to the door.

He was about five feet away when it swung open and Dr. Humphreys walked in, bringing with him his ever-annoying scent of patchouli and spruce.

The doctor wore white trousers that were mysteriously wrinkle-free, a baby blue polo shirt with a navy collar and navy trim on the bottom of the sleeves, and a pair of wing-tipped shoes that probably cost more than a month of Lester's salary. He held a strange, metallic contraption out in front of him, a stick made of chrome with a flat disc and a bunch of small holes on one end. It looked like a fancy showerhead.

But Lester had seen the lab downstairs. Whatever the doctor held wasn't a showerhead, but a weapon.

Lester sneezed.

"I'm surprised to find you here, Lester," Doctor Humphreys said. He set his briefcase down on the floor, careful to keep the strange weapon he held pointed in front of him. "I do, however, appreciate you catching a second troll to help with my experiments. I've been hoping one of his kind would attempt to rescue him. I'd give you a raise, except of course you now have to mysteriously disappear and will never be heard from again."

"I just came here looking for my phone," Lester said. He eyed the showerhead-like thing. "I didn't know you had a secret lab. And why aren't you in Sweden?"

"The conference was a ruse," the doctor said. He chuckled. "There is indeed a conference in Stockholm, but I wasn't about to leave a creature like this magnificent beast here unattended. I knew someone had been skulking outside the building for the past few weeks, so I made a point of announcing that I'd be out of town in order to catch him. Or her. I see she's a relation. You can't see the family resemblance now, of course, but I saw him before I began my experiments."

"Let my brother go," Petra said.

Sigurd made a strange, grunting sound and shook his head.

"I'm not letting anyone go," Doc said. "Lester, isn't this creature fascinating? I injected him with transmarurinan-zeplaphonic acid, an innovative, revolutionary substance I invented. It caused him to change into something in between his two natural states, and to stay there."

"I don't understand," Lester said. Maybe if he played along he could buy them time to...to do something. He just wasn't sure what. "What are his two states? I thought he was a troll, or a human who turned into a troll, or something like that."

"Don't you get it?" The doctor let out a high-pitched giggle. The sound made the hairs on the back of Lester's neck stand on end. "Trolls look like people, generally large people, unlike your petite lady friend over there. But when they choose to, they take the form of rocks. Like this."

The doctor pointed his strange contraption at Sigurd. A bolt of bright blue zapped through the air and hit the giant creature.

Sigurd's arms and legs were sucked into his core as he turned into a large gray and black boulder.

"No!" Petra cried. She wrapped her arms around the stone shape that had just been her brother.

"I see," Lester said, his heart thumping. He stared at the boulder. It stood about four feet tall and maybe three feet wide. He wondered how much it weighed. "You really meant *rocks*."

"Yes, rocks," the doctor said. He raised an eyebrow at Petra and waggled his weapon. "If I use this on you, young lady, you'll turn into one as well. And, unlike what your kind does normally, you won't be able to change your own shape. The only way to reverse the transformation is with this controller."

Petra turned toward the doctor and clenched her hands into fists. "You had no right to imprison my brother and experiment on him. Turn him back."

Lester realized with a start that she did, in fact, look remarkably like Sigurd, or at least before he had become a boulder. Her features were much smaller and far more delicate, but the resemblance was there nonetheless.

If Sigurd really was Petra's brother, that meant...

Lester took a deep breath. He'd fallen in love with a troll.

He set his jaw. No matter what kind of creature Petra was, he loved her, and he had to save her. He stifled another sneeze and tried to come up with a way to accomplish this challenging goal.

"Just imagine how this will transform the world of robotics," the doctor was saying. He waved a hand in the air. "Our company has been researching incorporating organic materials into robots. Now, thanks to my ingenious experiment, we can include rocks as well. I've been studying how this gentleman functions when he's in a form that's both part human and part stone. A few more studies, and I'll be ready to start combining nanorobotics with rocks. We'll be able to make mountains move—literally!"

Robots made from stone? Walking boulders?

Chills ran down Lester's spine. He had no idea what else the weapon in the evil doctor's hand could do, but anyone who could figure out how to cause another being to change form was surely competent enough to be armed with something that didn't just work on trolls. Who knew what it would turn Lester into?

But what could he do? The doctor was brilliant. Resourceful. Dangerous.

Egotistical…

"Doctor Humphreys," he said, keeping his expression curious and calm. Or at least he hoped that's how he looked. "I had no idea you were researching such an interesting area. I am, of course, not an expert in trolls, like you clearly are. I'd love to hear more."

The doctor narrowed his eyes and looked at Lester.

"Don't you get it, Lester?" The doctor waved his weapon in Lester's direction. "This isn't something you can learn about and live."

"I completely understand," Lester said. It was, unsurprisingly, challenging to act nonchalant when he felt as though his insides were tied in knots. "But since I'm here, perhaps you'd consider allowing me to work in your laboratory as your assistant? I'm nowhere near as accomplished a researcher as you, of course, but it would be an honor to work for you and learn from you, even if I never see the light of day again."

Doctor Humphreys stared at Lester for a minute. Out of the corner of his eye, Lester could see Petra's mouth drop open.

"I could use someone to repair a few of the robot arms," the doctor said finally. "I'm a busy man, and only have so much time. I'll think about it."

"Thank you, sir," Lester said. He turned toward Petra and met her eyes, then looked at Sigurd's stone shape standing next to the desk, then back at Petra. He held her gaze and raised his eyebrows, hoping she'd get the message. She scowled at him.

He tried again. "I'll miss seeing you at the coffee shop. Well, and going to the coffee shop, since I won't be doing that again.

Did you know some people drink coffee before going *running*? They say it can make you move faster."

Petra blinked at him, then turned and ran toward the doctor.

Dr. Humphreys zapped her with his weapon. The bright blue light turned Petra to stone in mid-step. She transformed into a smaller version of the gray and black rock that Sigurd had become.

But unlike Sigurd, she'd been transformed while in motion. Petra the boulder rolled across the floor, straight toward the doctor.

Doctor Humphreys leapt to one side, easily jumping out of her way, but Lester was ready. He tackled the doctor while the boulder plowed into the wall next to them. A cloud of bits of paint and plaster filled the air as he grabbed Doc's wrist and wrestled the weapon from the madman.

Lester leapt up, holding the thing out in front of him as he backed across the room. Petra the boulder was now embedded in the wall. He hoped it hadn't hurt.

And he hoped he could figure out how to turn her back.

"Give me that," the doctor said. He pulled himself to his feet and began walking toward Lester.

"Stay right there, or I'll use it on you." Lester sneezed and scurried behind the mahogany desk.

"That won't work on me," the doctor said. "I'm not a troll."

"Are you sure?" Lester asked. "How do you know your great-great-great-grandfather wasn't a troll?"

He tried to inspect the weapon while keeping an eye on the doctor. Even close up the thing looked like a fancy showerhead. It had two buttons, one labeled "on/off" and the other "transmogrify."

"Because he wasn't, of course," the doctor said. He took another step toward Lester, and then another, until he stood directly on the other side of the desk. "Now give the transmogrifier to me."

"As we just saw, a troll can be indistinguishable from a human," Lester said. He pointed the weapon at the doctor and switched the thing on. It began to make a soft but audible hum. "But you're sure you don't have any troll heritage, so let's give this a try just to see."

The doctor swallowed and eyed the transmogrifier. "I'd rather not."

"Put your hands on top of your head and go stand in front of the bookcase," Lester said. He waved the transmogrifier toward the shelves that hid the secret door.

"Don't you see how important this research is?" The doctor lunged across the desk, reaching for the transmogrifier.

Lester pressed the button on the weapon. A ray of blue light hit the doctor square in the chest.

Dr. Humphreys froze and became translucent, fading and shrinking, until all that remained of him was a cloud of white cotton fluff about three feet in diameter. It floated a few inches off the floor.

Lester looked down at the cloud. He had no idea what the doctor had transformed into, but apparently Doctor Humphreys had been right about his lack of troll heritage. At least his cologne seemed to have transformed as well, since the scent appeared to have dissipated.

He shook his head and aimed the gadget at Petra, took a deep breath, and then pressed the button. Petra transformed from her rock shape to her familiar, pretty, dark-haired human form. She looked around the room, her hazel eyes wide.

"Where is he?" she asked.

"Right there," Lester said, gesturing to the little cloud puff. She walked over and stood next to Lester. They stared at the cloud for a moment.

"What do you think that is?" Petra asked.

"I don't know," Lester said. He shrugged. "If your family is tied to stone in some way, maybe his is to air? Or water, since clouds are made of condensed water droplets? Let's get your brother back, and then we can figure out what to do about the doctor."

Petra nodded and laid her hand on his arm. Lester's skin tingled where she touched it. He smiled at her, and then pointed the gadget at Sigurd's stone form and pressed the transmogrify button.

They watched Sigurd transform back into his human shape, his real human shape, not the odd mix of human and rock that Dr. Humphreys had forced him to take. The human Sigurd stood a little over six feet tall, not eight, and while his hair and beard were just as unkempt, he no longer looked like a monster. Petra raced over to her brother and hugged him.

Lester smiled back, and then looked down at the puffy little cloud that floated a few inches off the floor. Maybe there were notes in the doctor's secret laboratory that would explain this. And if not, maybe Petra and Sigurd knew someone who would know more.

Maybe.

Petra released her brother and smiled at Lester, her eyes wet. "Thank you, Lester."

"Yes, thank you," Sigurd said.

"My pleasure," Lester said. He turned the transmogrifier off.

The sun had set and the stars were twinkling. He'd clearly missed his twenty-four-hour window for Robotznik, and his 437-day streak had finally come to an end.

He grinned as he realized that he didn't care. He'd finally spoken to Petra.

Lester, too, had been transmogrified.

About the Author

Jamie focuses on getting into the minds and hearts of her characters, whether she's writing about a saloon girl in theAmerican West, a man who discovers the barista he's in love with is a naïad, or a ghost who haunts the house she was killed in—even though that house no longer exists. Jamie lives in Colorado, and spends her free time in a futile quest to wear out her two border collies, since she hasn't given in and gotten them their own herd of sheep.

Find out more about Jamie at:

jamieferguson.com

The Ritual of the Drawing

Mark Leslie

Everybody in Birks Falls knows that Mr. McNeal didn't want to kill those children.

All he wanted was a peaceful existence. We all know it was the town's failure that led to the tragedy; that, and in the end he just couldn't fight his own nature.

You see, Mr. McNeal is a vampire.

And, under the proper circumstances, a vampire is a wonderful thing for a town to have. After all, we'd been living in peace with one for generations. Our crime rates were low. People respected authority and the community. And, up until those neighbourhood children started disappearing, things had been just fine.

Perhaps I should explain a little bit about how things work here in Birks Falls.

To do that, I guess I should start at the beginning, when the people of this town first found out about Mr. McNeal.

It was well over a hundred years ago when we first suspected that the newcomer named McNeal was a vampire. At the time, little was known about vampires. They existed as a part of myths and legends, vague tales told about undead beings stalking the night to drink people's blood.

It didn't take long for the townspeople to put the facts together.

Of course, it was a different world back then.

Back then, newspapers regularly included articles about ghostly encounters, demonic possessions, and other paranormal phenomenon. Newspapers, and people, weren't as closed-minded about such things as they are today.

What they knew was that not much longer than a month after the mysterious gentleman named McNeal had arrived, a vagrant had been found dead near the railyard, his body completely drained of blood. The dead tramp wasn't known to any of the townspeople, and, based on his clothes and the location of his body, they assumed he was a hobo who had been riding the rails into town. In addition to this, McNeal had never set foot in the local church, and nobody had ever seen the newcomer about town during the daylight hours, with his claim of having a sensitivity to light.

It was obvious, to them, that he must be a vampire.

And, naturally, they wanted to be rid of such a monster living in their midst.

More than a dozen men, led by Mayor Farnsworth and Sheriff Appleton, gathered in the town square that fateful spring morning, armed with clubs and knives, crosses and holy water. They waited until at least an hour after the sun had risen in the sky before heading to Mr. McNeal's home.

The story of the encounter has been shared and passed down through various oral versions through the generations. Especially vivid are the details about how they arrived at the door and prepared to break it down, rush inside, and thrust a white oak stake, one specifically crafted by a local woodworker named Wainwright, through the creature's heart while he slept.

But the moment Sheriff Appleton placed a single foot onto McNeal's porch, the front door opened.

"Sheriff Appleton," Mr. McNeal's voice called out from the shadows inside the home. "Mayor Farnsworth. I have been expecting you."

"You have?" Appleton said.

"Indeed, I have, Sheriff. Won't you and Mayor Farnsworth please step inside so we can discuss our situation? I am afraid to say I do not have enough chairs to accommodate your entire party."

The mayor and sheriff looked at one another, then back at the men behind them.

Obviously, they were confused. They knew you weren't supposed to invite a vampire into your home. But the protocol for letting a vampire invite you into their *own* home was not known.

"I assure you, gentlemen, that I do mean neither you, nor this town, any harm. I have a proposal to discuss with you. All that I ask is that you leave your weapons and holy instruments outside."

Mayor Farnsworth handed his club and cross to the sheriff. "I'm the leader," he said. "I'll go. You stay here, and if something happens to me..."

"Such melodrama is not needed," McNeal said.

As Mayor Farnsworth stepped up onto the porch and under the full shadow of the verandah, he could make out McNeal's figure just a few feet beyond the doorway.

"Okay, McNeal," he said. "I'm coming inside to talk with you."

"I mean you no harm, Mr. Mayor. I am at my weakest state right now. I couldn't harm you even if I were to try. Let's make quick with our discussion so you can get on with your day and I can get my much-needed sleep."

Mayor Farnsworth stood in the doorway for a moment and turned to nod at the sheriff before stepping inside.

The door closed behind him.

When the mayor came out, less than half an hour later, he informed the sheriff and the men gathered there that a deal had been struck with McNeal.

As mayor Farnsworth recounted, McNeal had explained his condition, his need for the blood of a single adult human once per month. He had also reminded the mayor that he had purposely not taken the life of a single townsperson. He had, specifically, selected a homeless traveling vagrant once his hunger had gotten to a point he could no longer bear.

Farnsworth had never shared the specifics of his conversation. But he managed to convince Sheriff Appleton and the townspeople that the agreement he'd made with Mr. McNeal would be beneficial to the town.

The deal was that Mr. McNeal would stay in Birks Falls but would never kill any innocent townspeople. Instead, the people of the town would provide him with one adult-sized human at least once a month. Mr. McNeal couldn't *not* drink blood—but he could at the very least let *them* decide whose blood he would consume. He suggested that vagrants or criminals be among the ones he should feed on, and that it would be another way to keep order in the community.

The townspeople came to see his offer as a unique way to dispose of society's unwanted—the criminals, the insane, the unproductive. The mere thought of what might happen should one cross the line into crime would act as a deterrent. Legend has it that the crime rate dropped dramatically that next year.

It's funny when you think about it, but, having grown up in Birks Falls, it's hard to imagine growing up without a vampire in town. I still remember my mother prodding me to get my school work done.

"C'mon Elsie," she would say. "Get cracking at that homework or else I'll send you to see Mr. McNeal."

Sometimes, all that a teacher would have to do was make a sucking noise, and all of the children in the classroom would snap to attention.

The fear, of course, grew when everybody became exposed to the now famous vampire novel *Dracula*. Bram Stoker put into words and horrific images the very fears and whispering the townspeople had engaged in. By then, the threat of "vampire" had an image everyone could appreciate. I'm certain that back in the late 1890s the crime rate must have plummeted even more dramatically.

All that good for so simple a task.

I mean, look at all the benefits we've reaped from this situation by offering up nothing more than twelve people per year. Take a look at your own town. Even if your population is as low as six thousand like Birks Falls, I'm sure that you could come up with at least one person every month whom you'd like to send to Mr. McNeal.

Perhaps you could come up with two people every month.

The townspeople were able to orchestrate an annual assembly wherein the elders of the town provided the vote as to who was to be selected as the donated. It then came to be that every New Year's Eve, the entire population of the town over the age of sixteen would gather in front of the town court and participate in the ritual of the drawing.

All the participant names were written down on slips of paper and placed in a large steel drum. One of the elders would draw twelve names during the final twelve minutes before the stroke of midnight. Those twelve people drawn would be that year's chosen and would be responsible for delivering one of the donated to Mr. McNeal, for one month each.

Most people considered it an honour to be among the chosen. Children grew up longing for the day they turned sixteen so that they too might have a chance at being one of the chosen. But times are changing, as they often do.

Now there are those who see the honour as some sort of curse. They feel they have better things to do than deliver the donated to their rightful fate. They claim it is a barbaric chore they shouldn't be forced to do. Little do they recognize it is a very civilized custom that maintains order and respect. It is a custom that has made this town a very safe and peaceful place to live and raise a family.

Like most customs, nobody is actually forced to participate. There are no written laws about the ritual of the drawing. It is merely a tradition which has always been strictly adhered to.

But the fact that it is never enforced and that it relies on mutual trust is probably why this whole mess came about.

You see, just this past year, a teenager named Jed Stevens was drawn as one of the chosen for the month of May.

Jed is my only son.

His generation has the attitude problem I have already mentioned. Yet, despite his attitude, nobody suspected that he simply wouldn't feed Mr. McNeal. Such a thought was…well, it was *unthinkable* at the time. People had protested in the past, but before Jed Stevens came along, nobody had ever *not* performed their duties as the chosen.

Some might suggest that, had Jed had a decent male role model in his life, and not the drunken father who got himself killed when Jed was merely a toddler, that things may have turned out differently.

But I have nobody, of course, to blame for this, other then myself.

If I had been a better mother and spent as much time as my own mother had at raising me right, perhaps Jed would have turned out differently. If I had used my husband's death as an example of what happens when you follow the wrong path, that might have made a difference. But it's too late now. I failed Jed. Just like I had failed my husband. And like I had failed the town.

Jed had decided he would let that month's donated go free rather than deliver the criminal to his fate. The result of this "act of mercy" was the loss of several neighbourhood children.

Having not been fed for an entire month, Mr. McNeal grew hungry. Ravenous, in fact. The diet of one adult every month was a considerable cutback for him as it was, so, when even that stopped, he was far beyond his limit of self-control.

It wasn't Mr. McNeal's fault that he wasn't being fed. I mean, he *had* been keeping up with his half of the deal. It was our own fault for not forcing the chosen to perform their duties.

Combine Mr. McNeal's understandable hunger with the presence of the neighbourhood children playing on his lawn after sunset, and the results are obvious.

Such a tragedy had been avoided for well over a century with our annual ritual of the drawing. I guess the people of the newest generation, like Jed Stevens, just don't listen, just don't see the necessity of the tradition. They only see that they don't like it, and they rebel.

This time, the rebellion cost the town several innocent children, may their souls rest in peace.

Once it was discovered that Jed had shirked his duties and was responsible for the lives of these children, a meeting of the elders was held. It was rapidly decided that I should be the one to take responsibility for Jed's actions. We had to make sure that an example was made of him so that such a thing would not happen again.

The next day, I lead him, tranquilized, gagged, and handcuffed, to the door of Mr. McNeal's home. It was dusk and the church tower threw a long shadow that grew slowly along Mr. McNeal's front yard as the sun sank. I shuddered, thinking about how the shadow traced a path across the very yard where those children used to play. Such a shame, I thought, wanting to point this out to Jed, but I couldn't look at him. Instead, I continued to stare at the growing shadow until the sun sank completely below the horizon. Then I counted to one hundred for good measure before I knocked.

This was, of course, quite an honor. Nobody except the chosen ever got to see Mr. McNeal in person.

Mr. McNeal greeted me at the door with a pleasant smile. I was amazed with how attractive he was. He was a handsome man, even though his hair was thin and speckled with grey. His face looked like it was carved from a soft wood, delicate and smooth to touch, yet his eyes were sharp and bright. His smile revealed a perfect set of pearly white teeth. Human-looking teeth, not the sharp, blood-stained incisors out of vampire movies.

He wore a pale grey dinner jacket with a red ascot about his neck and navy-blue Ivy-League-styled pants. On his feet he wore what looked like penny loafers. I was perplexed. Despite his so-phisticated manner, his dress was of a combination I'd never seen thrown together before. But despite the collage of style, it was pleasing to look at just the same.

His eyes never left mine as his smile straightened, then threat-ened to become a frown. He knew why we were here. For a mo-ment I thought he was going to turn us away and say that it was too late. No more ritual of the drawing. No more mercy. No more peaceful co-existence.

Then he smiled again, and I realized I had been holding my breath. I breathed again, appreciating his smile. He was very

becoming and looked to be in his mid-fifties, just a few years older than me. I'm certain, also, that I caught a look in his face that
moment which reminded me of my late husband. I felt a pang of
loss and shame at that thought, but quickly pushed it aside.

Silently, Mr. McNeal gestured for us to follow him, and turned
to lead us into the living room.

I paused for a moment. As far as I knew, nobody other than
Mayor Farnsworth had ever stepped foot inside Mr. McNeal's
home, during that legendary agreement that had been brokered
between the two.

I took another deep breath, then stepped inside, ignoring
Jed's low whimpering through his gag as I pulled him across
the threshold. Jed stumbled forward, reminding me, again, of
my husband, his father and the many times I had witnessed his
drunken stumbling into our own home. My son might have been
tranquilized enough to not try to resist, but he was still aware of
the fate he was being led to.

I had no time to really admire the premises, for my eyes remained mostly on Mr. McNeal. He was fascinating. It was as if
I could not look at him enough.

I sat down on a rocking chair while Mr. McNeal took Jed by
the arm and sat with him on the sofa. He offered me a cup of tea,
which I accepted.

Mr. McNeal left, and I tried to keep my eyes from Jed's. He
attempted to speak but the gag prevented it. I was glad of that. It
was better not to hear what he had to say to me.

I felt awkward being alone in Mr. McNeal's living room with
Jed, the cause of all the trouble. It was an honour to be invited
into Mr. McNeal's home, but the reason I was here, of course,
was shameful indeed. After all those decades of tranquility, I was

a part of the era that had failed to uphold our end of the deal with Mr. McNeal.

I half expected that Mr. McNeal would take my life that night along with Jed's. I wouldn't have tried to stop him if he did. After all, we did fail him. It was our duty to restore the peace.

When Mr. McNeal returned, bearing a silver tray with my tea and a bowl of sugar, he offered me a reassuring smile. He apologized that there was no cream, but, as he explained, he rarely had guests who drank it, so it went bad rather quickly.

I pondered over that last statement. Were there other vampires like Mr. McNeal living in neighbouring towns who came to visit him from time to time? Did he, or could he, have such things as *relatives*?

I wanted to ask him so badly, but I was in no position to interrogate him.

He was an extremely polite host. He did not begin to drink his beverage until I had completely finished mine. During that time, we engaged in small talk. It was a rather pleasant time, despite the circumstances, but for the life of me I cannot remember exactly what it was that we talked about. Just the sentiment. I can only remember that I had actually been enjoying myself and completely forgot that Jed was sitting there with us.

When I finished my tea he offered me more, but I politely refused.

He smiled and then looked longingly over at Jed.

Jed's eyes widened and he attempted to leap from the sofa. Mr. McNeal's hand shot out and held him back..

Then Mr. McNeal shifted closer to Jed, calmly reached his other hand over, and snapped his neck. He quickly opened a vein on Jed's neck with a fingernail and placed his mouth there to catch the flowing blood.

I was very surprised, of course, but also honored. Nobody that I'd known or heard of in all the legends had ever observed Mr. McNeal drinking blood. I'd always thought that the donated would still be alive and that the vampire would sink his teeth into their neck like in all those vampire movies. But instead, Mr. McNeal drank the blood from Jed's neck the way someone would put their lips around a water fountain.

I listened to the noises of the feast in amazement. There was nothing scary or painful about the experience, like we had always thought. The legends had described the donated as writhing in pain while their lifeblood was sucked from them. But this was nothing like those tales. Certainly, Mr. McNeal was drinking blood from a human's neck. But he was doing it in a dignified and distinguished manner, the way Queen Elizabeth might drink her tea.

When he finished, his lips were coated in deep crimson. He plucked a cloth napkin from the silver tray and diligently wiped the blood away. He then thanked me for the offering and we agreed that such a thing was an unpleasant necessity. It should never happen again. Nor would it, I suggested, for we had learned our lesson. Now that we'd had a fitting punishment, actions such as Jed's would be very unlikely.

He led me to the door and bid me a fair evening.

Then, as if reading my mind as I stepped outside, he passed me a handkerchief from his inside breast pocket. I used it to dab at the tears that suddenly began to flow.

As he closed the door, the spell I had been under faded even more.

Grief flooded over my soul as a tsunami of tears suddenly spilled from my eyes.

I walked down his sidewalk, again past the lawn where those unfortunate children had once played, and the reality of the event I had just participated in took effect.

I had sat there with not a single protest to make as a vampire killed and consumed the blood of my only son. Not only had I concurred with the event, but I had observed it without any emotion, as if I were a scientist recording data from a routine experiment.

And why?

Because I had been under some sort of spell?

Perhaps. But I believe it was also because I was part of the example being set for the better of our entire town. Now that the example existed, parents would take the role of instructing their children in the importance of tradition more seriously. I had obviously failed somewhere down the line.

I had lost two people I loved to the ritual of the drawing and the traditions and customs which surrounded it. Seventeen years ago, my husband had sunk deeper into his drinking problem than ever before. Wandering the streets all hours of the night in a drunken manner, Earl had spent the better part of a year in the "drunk tank." He was no longer there for myself or our baby. He neglected his job. His alcoholism got worse and worse as the days passed, until finally the elders decided that he was no longer of any use to society and was slated as one of the next year's donated.

I had been forced to bring up Jed by myself. That wasn't easy, living in the shame of my husband. And I don't think I can use it as any excuse. If there's one thing I've learned living in Birks Falls, there's no such thing as a good excuse to shirk your civic duties. I had failed as both a wife and a mother.

I clutched the handkerchief that Mr. McNeal had handed me tightly as a reminder of the mistakes made and the tears spilled. I planned on bringing it to the town elders so they could hold onto it as a reminder of what happens when one shirks their responsibility.

Perhaps parents will use my example for generations to come to teach their children the importance of responsibility to one's community.

Hopefully, they will learn the reason why tradition is sacred.

And ultimately what happens when you shirk both your duties and tradition for some smaller personal cause.

Hopefully.

Only time will tell.

For now, though the streets are still safe, the unwanted dregs of society are not a threat to our peaceful haven. So long as we have Mr. McNeal and the ritual of the drawing.

About the Author

Mark Leslie would be the first person to admit he's still afraid of the monster under his bed, and he continues to channel that fear into most of his fiction. Mark's dark fiction is often compared to "Twilight Zone" or "Black Mirror" in terms of style, but he usually just adopts the term "horror" when describing the types of tales that he writes. He also writes non-fiction true ghost story tales.

Find out more about Mark at:
markleslie.ca

On a Dark Road to Nowhere

Marcelle Dubé

As near as Maggie could tell in the moonlit winter night, the creature didn't have ears. Or eyes. It barely had a head.

It had teeth, though. Lots and lots of teeth.

Her breath fogged out in front of her, capturing the glow of the moon before dissipating. She pressed her bony cheek against the rough bark of the lodgepole pine, breathing in its astringent cat-pee smell and hugging the tree as if to keep it from escaping. She held the rifle loosely in her free hand, ready.

She had yet to get more than a glimpse of the creature, in spite of having trailed it through the snowy woods for the last twenty minutes. She'd left her damned bifocals on the kitchen table of the cabin, but she'd seen the thing silhouetted a couple of times against the starry sky as it sailed from tree to tree.

In full sail, it looked like a square of black tinfoil, six feet by six, with pinpricks of starlight shining through what seemed to be thin, squared-off, membrane-like wings on either side of a thicker, cigar-shaped body. It had appendages at each corner and a tiny knob in between the two upper appendages. That was probably its head. If it had ears, they weren't visible.

It had been perched on an aspen tree for the past few minutes and she couldn't figure out what it was doing. Searching? Listening?

Suddenly it threw itself through the air, its wings spread wide in the cold air like some kind of demonic flying squirrel.

Just as suddenly, the wings folded in on themselves, turning the rectangle into a cylinder that hit the top of a spruce tree.

There was a mad scramble and the thunk of dislodged snow hitting the ground before the creature finally came to a stop. The spruce tree swayed slightly under the thing's weight.

It might have been funny if she hadn't seen what it had done to Rupert.

The only sound in the forest was the creaking of trees in the cold. No owls. No voles scurrying under the snow. No coyotes or foxes padding quietly, looking for dinner. Even the wolves seemed to be holding their breath.

What the hell did it *want*?

She'd been making her way back to the cabin from visiting the outhouse when she saw its ship, such as it was, streak over her head. She had ducked automatically and Rupert, her Samoyed, had barked wildly. Then she'd heard the thump and felt the landing through the soles of her mukluks.

It was close. Rupert barked a mad warning and took off into the trees, and Maggie took off after him, bare-headed, mittenless, unmindful of the risk of breaking a hip on the rocks and roots hidden under the foot of snow in the sheltered woods. She'd had Rupert thirteen years now. He was an old dog with a young dog's courage.

She arrived at the landing site, less than a quarter mile away, to find a glowing red sphere in the middle of a tiny clearing. The tops of at least a dozen spruce trees were burning in a straight line, their sap and needles popping and crackling, and a bunch of spruce and aspen had been pushed down in a circle around the sphere. The thing itself wasn't more than ten feet in diameter and had knobs and lines all over it. It was clearly a made thing but even a hermit like her could tell that it wasn't anything made by human hands.

At least, she didn't think so. Maybe it was a satellite?

For the first time in the ten years she had lived in her little cabin in the Yukon woods, she wished she had a cell phone. And cell service.

At last she spotted Rupert. His thick white coat glowed ruddy in the light. He was maybe fifty feet away from her, and much too close to the sphere. The thing was probably emitting radiation.

"Rupert!" she called, hoping he would hear her above the crackling of the burning tree tops. Rupert was completely focused on the sphere, his upper lip curled away from his teeth in a snarl. It was startling in a face she usually thought of as smiling.

Then a movement at the sphere caught her eye. A dark line in the curve suddenly elongated, then widened into a doorway.

The next few seconds would forever remain a blur in her memory. She had a sense of Rupert launching himself at the opening, of something black and weirdly shaped hurtling out of the sphere, of Rupert's yelp of pain as the thing wrapped itself around her dog.

And then she was yelling and running toward it, in spite of the fact that she had no weapon.

Then the thing straightened and spread its wings wide and she got her first glimpse of it in the fading glow of the sphere and the burning tree tops.

Before she could even register what she was seeing, an atavistic part of her took over and she turned and ran. She didn't stop running until she pounded up the steps of her log cabin and pushed the door closed behind her.

The heat from the wood stove hit her in the face as she grabbed the rifle from where it rested against the wall between the door and the kitchen counter. Then she jerked the nearest drawer open and frantically rummaged through it for the box of shells she kept there. She finally found it and pulled it out only to drop it on the rough-hewn pine floor. Falling to her knees, she plucked shells up and fed them into the rifle as quickly as she could. Then she scrambled back from the door, not caring that her jeans were catching on the planks and barely missing the wood stove.

When her heart finally slowed down and she managed to get oxygen into her lungs, her brain kicked in again.

She had abandoned her dog.

Shame flooded her, replacing the fear.

Oh, God. Rupert. Had he survived, he would have been barking at the door to be let in.

She should have stayed. Should have defended her dog, like he'd defended her all these years.

Then a thought intruded past the shame. Why hadn't the thing followed her?

Was it out there, waiting for her?

All she could picture was that thing wrapping itself around Rupert.

After a long while, she climbed to her feet and blew the kerosene lamp out, setting it back on the kitchen counter. Then she walked over to the window in her tiny living room and tried to peer past the insulating plastic she had placed over the window in the fall. She couldn't see anything.

She would have to go out there to find Rupert.

This time, she pulled on her heavy parka, scarf, hat and mitts before stepping out onto the porch. She stood for long minutes, listening and watching. After a while, she went down the porch steps and past the wood pile, and crept into the woods, silent in her mukluks.

She made her way back to the sphere. The glow had died down and so had the fires. The doorway on the sphere had closed and there was no sign of the thing that had come barreling out of it.

She slowly circled the site, keeping an eye on the sphere, and eventually found Rupert. He was lying on a pile of melted snow that had turned to ice. His beautiful white coat was burned black, revealing blistered and bleeding skin beneath. He was dead.

The creature had torn a great chunk of flesh out of Rupert's neck, leaving him to bleed out.

As she stood staring down at her dog, grief and rage welled up in equal measure. Someone would come, eventually. Someone would have seen the sphere on a radar, or reported a strange light to the police. Someone might be racing toward her right now.

In the meantime, she wasn't letting that thing run around loose.

Naomi's little Nissan coasted to a stop, its tires crunching on the ice-crusted shoulder. She sat staring at the snow-covered road stretching out whitely in the high beams of the head-lights. No streetlights, no house lights. No tire marks in the fresh snow.

Dear God in Heaven, where the hell was she? In the back end of nowhere?

On either side of the road, black spruce and ghostly poplars and aspen hunched over the white ribbon of a road. Who knew what those trees hid? Wolves for sure. Wolverines. Feral dogs. Maybe the odd bear, even though it was the middle of January and they were probably hibernating.

Of course they were all hibernating.

Her gloved hands remained clenched on the steering wheel, her foot still on the brake. Finally she put the car in park and stared at the gas gauge. The needle was firmly, irrevocably, on the big, fat "E."

It had been on "F" when she left Whitehorse less than an hour ago.

She must have punctured her gas tank on one of the numerous hidden potholes she had hit.

She had taken the wrong turn off the highway and now she was lost. Lost and out of gas. She should have turned around the minute she started wondering if she'd gotten the directions wrong. She should have listened to her little voice like she always did.

But there was a boy and a party and written directions to his friend's cabin near Tagish, and her friend Julie's taunts that Naomi was too chickenshit to actually go.

She almost hadn't. She hated driving at night, especially in winter. Julie called her a chickenshit, but really, Naomi saw no reason to expose herself to risk if she didn't need to.

But the boy was cute. Instead of listening to her little voice, she had driven to an unfamiliar, remote location, in winter, at night…just in time to die of exposure.

Julie would be so proud.

Naomi pulled her cell phone out of her purse but there were still no bars.

She glanced in the rear-view mirror and saw nothing but her white-rimmed eyes set in her brown skin. If it wasn't for the full moon, she wouldn't even have seen that.

She had seen nothing along this stretch of road except for a coyote and, once, a pair of gleaming yellow eyes a foot off the ground. She had passed no driveways in the three miles since she'd turned up the road. That alone should have clued her in. This close to Whitehorse, most of the secondary roads held cabins tucked away at the end of narrow driveways. No electricity, no running water. The folks who lived along these roads revelled in chopping wood for their stoves, hauling their water from town, and lighting their log cabins with kerosene lanterns.

And going to the bathroom in outhouses, risking themselves to whatever lurked in the woods every time they needed to pee.

Naomi shuddered.

Before walking three miles back down the dark road to the highway, she might as well walk up the road a bit and hope to find a cabin with someone in it. After all, the road had to go somewhere. Maybe she'd even find *the* cabin, with the boy and everybody else. They would all laugh at her misadventure but congratulate her on her fortitude.

She sighed.

Everything she had ever read told her she should stay with her car, but if she did, her rescuers would find a popsicle. She hadn't passed a single vehicle since she turned off the highway. If she was going to die at the ripe old age of twenty, it would be trying to save herself, not waiting for rescue that would come too late.

Still, it was a long time before she turned the ignition key off. The headlights stayed on another ten seconds, then shut off, leaving her alone in her car in the middle of the woods. It took another minute for her to actually open the door and get out.

As the cold attacked her ears, forehead and nose, she walked to the back of the Nissan, opened the hatch, and pulled out the parka she kept there for emergencies. Then she exchanged her pretty party boots for heavy-duty Sorel snow boots that went up almost to her knees and pulled a scarf around her nose and mouth before pulling the hood over her skimpy hat. Before she pulled her minus-forty-wind-proof mittens on over her gloves, she patted the pockets of her parka. Energy bars, check. Lighter and matches, check. Flashlight, check. Swiss army knife, check. Emergency blanket, check. Duct tape, check.

The damned coat weighed a ton.

All right. She was as ready as she could be. She pushed the hatch down. The sound of its slam echoed against the trees, so eerily high-pitched that she paused and pulled her hood down to listen, but the sound wasn't repeated.

With an uncomfortable chill down her back, she set off down the middle of the road, leaving boot prints behind her in the pristine snow.

Maggie's head snapped up as the sound of a car door slamming travelled on the frigid air. At the same time, the creature emitted a weird, high-pitched noise, halfway between a squeal and a cough.

Its head twisted around, clearly trying to locate the source of the sound that had startled it. So maybe it did have ears.

She held her breath, aware that she had scraped her cheek on the bark of the spruce tree but not daring to reach up and touch her face.

Somebody *had* come, only they didn't know what they were walking into. She had to warn them.

The wind picked up, making Naomi's eyes water and forcing her to keep her head down so that she almost walked right past the entrance to the narrow track. She stopped in the middle of the road when she realized that what she was seeing was faint tire tracks, almost completely covered over by fresh snow.

A driveway. Dear God, it was a driveway.

She figured she'd walked maybe half a mile and had been on the point of turning back when she spotted the tracks. Tire tracks meant a vehicle. A vehicle going somewhere. There hadn't been any traffic on the track since the last snow, which was yesterday.

That didn't necessarily mean no one was at home. They could just be hunkered down.

She pulled out her cell phone again and checked. Still no bars. Glancing behind her, she saw her shadowed footprints in the snow. If rescuers did come looking for her, at least they'd have a trail to follow.

No one was coming. She knew that. They wouldn't know where to start looking.

She was going to have to get out of this herself.

Pulling the hood closer around her face, she set out down the driveway, praying someone would be home and if they weren't, that they had left the door unlocked.

People did that here, apparently. More worried about finding someone frozen to death in front of their locked door than of being robbed.

She didn't know how she felt about that. Risk analysis always came out fifty-fifty.

The wind crept up the bottom of her parka and she pulled it closer to her body. Her feet felt like they weighed fifty pounds each in the heavy snow boots, but at least they were warm.

The farther down the driveway she walked, the darker it became. The spruce trees grew close to the narrow driveway and the only slice of sky visible did not contain the moon. After a few minutes of trudging, she still couldn't see any lights twinkling in the distance to indicate a cabin. Her heart sank a little. Was she going to have to trek back to the car and wrap herself in that stupid emergency blanket?

She got no warning. One moment she was looking up at the sky and the next she was tackled off her feet to land heavily on her back in the snow.

Someone fell on top of her, knocking the breath out of her, and a mitten suddenly covered her mouth and nose.

She couldn't breathe!

Panic took over and she struggled to push the person off.

"Stop it or you'll get us both killed. Calm down. Calm down." The words kept repeating, barely loud enough for her to hear.

Eventually, the calm behind the voice penetrated and Naomi stopped struggling.

"I'm going to take my hand off," whispered the person on top of her. "Don't make a sound or it will find us."

It will find us?

It?

The mitten smelled of tanned moose hide. She took a shallow breath past fur and hide and exhaled. She nodded.

The mitten lifted and Naomi took a quick breath. The mitten hovered above her face, ready to clamp down again if she made the slightest sound, but Naomi remained silent and still.

The dark blob leaned in again. "Get up slowly, as silently as you can. Don't make any noise."

The voice belonged to a woman.

The weight lifted off her as the woman finally got up. Naomi took a deep breath. Nothing broken. She rolled onto her side and struggled to her feet in the deep snow, trying to be quiet. Her hood fell back and she turned to face her assailant.

The woman was looking away from her, standing perfectly still, staring off into the woods.

Slowly, Naomi turned her head to see what the woman was looking at. In the end, it was only when it moved that Naomi's gaze caught it.

Something…

Something big stood among the bare branches of an aspen tree. It was black and shaped like a skinny oblong, and it stood out among the ghostly branches like soot on snow.

It shifted slightly, its shape growing a little wider before returning to its original size. As if it were breathing.

Her own breath caught in her throat as the skin on the back of her neck prickled with alarm.

Whatever it was, it looked like it was waiting.

Out of the corner of her eye, she caught a movement and turned slightly to see the woman slowly raising a rifle to her shoulder. She was aiming at the figure in the tree.

Without thinking, Naomi reached out and knocked the rifle upward just as the woman squeezed the trigger.

The rifle flew through the air and the shot rang out like the voice of doomsday, echoing in the trees and startling an owl that rose from the trees, its shape outlined in black against the night sky.

Then she caught another movement and whirled to see the thing in the tree launch itself toward them.

Jesus H. in a handbasket!

All Maggie had time to do was slap her mittened hand over the woman's mouth again. They both froze in place.

To her credit, the fool didn't struggle. They waited, barely breathing. Finally, Maggie dared to look up.

The thing was standing on the ground no more than ten feet from them.

It seemed to teeter on the snow-covered ground as if it had a poor sense of balance. Or maybe its feet—paws? claws?—were too small to balance on. Maybe it was more comfortable perched in a tree.

It stood partly turned toward them and, for the first time, Maggie noticed that the central part of it was much thicker than the membranous wings. It really did look like someone had stuffed a fat cigar between two sheets of black tinfoil, with just the tips of the cigar sticking out above and below.

The back of the thing wasn't the same as the front. Where the front of the cigar was segmented like an insect and seemed to be covered in glistening fine hairs, the back was covered in diamond-shaped protuberances. Even the back of the membranes seemed to be covered with the protuberances.

It gave off a strange, astringent smell—something between vinegar and bleach. She found herself holding her breath.

The thing spread its membranes again. It shifted, turning slightly toward her, and her heart stuttered in fear. Even through the thick moose hide of her mitten, she could feel the woman next to her tremble.

Surely it would see them. Even under the cover of trees, there was enough moonlight and starlight to show them plainly against the snowy ground.

She was trembling, too. It was all she could do not to bolt. It had wrapped those membranes around Rupert and, seconds later, her dog was dead. She couldn't let that thing touch them.

She glanced down quickly but the rifle was ten feet away. Too far.

The thing just stood there, teetering, its membranes billowing slightly as if they breathed. But its face was featureless except for a wide slash filled with those gleaming teeth.

It had no eyes to see them with. It seemed to depend on hearing only, in spite of the fact that she couldn't see any ears. It couldn't even smell them, as far as she could tell.

At last the creature leaped into a spruce tree and once again landed awkwardly. After ten minutes of watching it thud from tree to tree, it was far enough away that Maggie felt safe in releasing the woman. Only then did she notice how young she was. Couldn't be more than twenty, and those scared, wide eyes made her look even younger.

Great. The Powers That Be had sent someone who turned out to be a baby.

In disgust, she went to retrieve her rifle and begin tracking the creature again.

"Wait," whispered Naomi, grabbing the woman by the sleeve of her parka. "We have to call for help."

The woman turned to her and, for the first time, Naomi realized that the woman was old. At least fifty, maybe sixty. Even in the gloom under the trees, she could see the woman's glare.

"Aren't *you* the help?" demanded the old woman in a fierce whisper.

What?

"I came *looking* for help. My car ran out of gas maybe half a mile from here."

Naomi couldn't read the look the woman gave her.

"You've got shitty timing," the woman said.

Well, that was true.

"What is that thing?" Naomi asked her. "I've never seen anything like it."

The woman finished wiping down her rifle and finally shrugged.

"I don't know. Its ship landed in the woods not far from here and the first thing the creature did was kill my dog."

There was a catch in her voice and Naomi swallowed hard against the sympathy welling up in her. No time for that now.

"Landed?" *Ship?*

And then the woman told her what she had seen and what she had been doing since.

Naomi listened in silence and growing disbelief. What the woman was describing was an alien. In a spaceship.

It was insane. And yet... Even as she tried to deny it, shivers ran up her spine as she thought of the creature she had seen. It wasn't from Earth.

"Why did you stop me?" asked the old woman. "I could have ended this here."

Maybe. But Naomi hadn't known what the woman was shooting at and that was enough to stop her.

She really, really wanted to leave and let somebody else deal with this, but there seemed to be just her and the old woman. And she needed more information to assess the risks.

"I want to see it," she said finally. "The spaceship."

That was where the creature would go, eventually.

"Fine," said the old woman. "But don't let that thing touch you. I think it kills with acid."

It took almost an hour to work their careful way back to the landing site. Maggie would pause every few feet to listen, finally removing her fur hat with its lovely ear flaps so she could hear better.

The girl had identified herself as Naomi Wright from White-horse. Judging by where she had planned to go and where she had ended up, she had no sense of direction. Maggie didn't think the girl would be much help in dealing with that creature. She still hadn't explained why she had stopped Maggie from shooting it, but if Maggie was being honest with herself, she had to admit that she might have done the same thing.

They knew very little about it, about why it was here. Maybe killing Rupert had been an accident. Maybe it was actually here on a peaceful mission.

She almost snorted. If its first reaction to encountering an in-digenous life form was to kill it, she didn't hold out much hope for the whole "we come in peace" thing.

The now-familiar sound of dislodged snow thudding to the ground reassured her that the thing was a distance away. The girl had suggested that the creature was practising, and that made sense to Maggie. Why else would it continuously throw itself at trees only to land so awkwardly? It was as if it was lighter here than it was used to. Maybe the gravity where it came from was greater than Earth's.

But why bother? Why bother practising to get better? Was that why it had landed here, in such a sparsely inhabited place? So it could practise unseen?

For the first time, Maggie regretted her choice. She had squatted on the land ten years ago and the government had never bothered kicking her off. But they didn't supply her with electricity, either, or any other amenities. And the only reason the road beyond her driveway got plowed at all was because it led to a small windmill testing site at the top of Jessup Hill, five miles past her cabin. She loved the solitude, but right now she could use a few more people.

"It doesn't seem to see us," whispered the girl, startling Maggie. She had just about forgotten the girl. Nobody had shown up from the government at all. They were probably unable to pinpoint the exact landing site. Or maybe they thought it was a meteorite and would wait for someone to phone in its landing site. Either way, she and the girl would have to deal with the creature themselves. They couldn't just leave it out there.

"No," Maggie finally replied. "I don't think it has eyes. I think it senses sound. Like waves, maybe. That's why it opens up those... wings, I guess. Like a satellite dish receiving a signal." Or bat ears getting a signal bounce back. She had heard the thing make a sound earlier—was that how it navigated? Not bat ears—hell, she couldn't even *see* its ears. As for why it hadn't heard them yet... maybe they had to be closer for the thing to receive their sound waves. Especially in the trees.

In spite of everything, Maggie found herself grudgingly respecting the girl tromping along behind her. She had to be tired, hauling those heavy boots through a foot of snow for the past hour, but she didn't complain.

That was something, anyway.

"The backs of the wings look different," said the girl. "Like baffles in a sound room."

Maggie had never been in a sound room, so she ignored the comment. They were almost at the landing site. The smell of burnt green wood, spruce boughs, and sap was growing stronger. So was the smell of burnt hair.

She caught sight of her earlier trail and cut across, careful to step lightly. Any sound could carry to that thing's... not ears, maybe, but whatever system it used to hear. She raised a hand to indicate a stop and listened carefully.

Her ears were freezing, but she didn't dare put the hat back on. She needed to hear.

The smell of burnt hair and charred meat was all the warning Naomi got.

She'd been following the woman almost mindlessly, her only concern to be as silent as she could. Despite the heavy parka, she felt chilled. Her eyelashes were crusted with ice from tears and the breath escaping her scarf. The scarf itself felt damp and cold with frost, and the knit cap she wore was definitely not warm enough, especially with her hood down. But she needed to hear that thing's progress through the forest.

Its movements mystified her. It really did seem like it was practising, but to what end? A theory was beginning to form at the edge of her thoughts, but she was so tired she had trouble thinking straight.

Then the smell hit her and she stopped just as Maggie raised a hand.

Naomi followed the woman's gaze. At first she didn't see it, half-buried as it was in the ice and snow. And then she realized she was seeing the shape of a dog with weird-colored hair. Then she blinked and saw that its hair had been burned off, leaving only charred tufts and blackened skin beneath, with red oozing out of cracks.

She couldn't help it. Her gorge rose and she gagged.

At once Maggie whirled on her, clapping a mittened hand over her mouth, which only worsened Naomi's need to vomit.

Then they heard it. The dull thud of snow falling off branches. It was coming closer.

Naomi pulled Maggie's hand off and straightened, taking deep breaths and turning to face the direction of the noise. Maggie raised her rifle, facing the same direction, and Naomi pulled the heavy-duty mitten off her right hand and fished through her pocket for the Swiss Army knife. She had to use her teeth to pry open the largest blade. She didn't know how much good it would be, but it made her feel better.

This time, she wouldn't stop Maggie if she tried to shoot the creature.

Her mouth tasted of bile and she had to fight the urge to throw up. She breathed through her mouth, not wanting to smell the dog's corpse.

She had been frightened of the creature, yes, but really, she had been more fascinated than fearful. It was hard to be too worried about a creature with no face that kept running into trees. But now, seeing what it had done to the dog…

She listened hard, aware that the woman next to her was doing the same thing. The noises no longer seemed to be coming straight at them.

She leaned toward the woman and placed her lips very close to her ear.

"The landing site?"

The woman pointed and Naomi set off, only to be hauled back.

"What are you doing?" whispered the woman.

Naomi pulled her sleeve out of the woman's grasp.

"We have to stop it," she said. "It's heading for its ship."

"Good," said the woman.

"Not good," said Naomi. "What if it's a scout?"

That was what her tired brain had been trying to work out. A scout might well have been sent to a sparsely inhabited area to learn more about the geography, the gravity, the whatever. It would explain why the creature kept jumping from tree to tree—that might be how it moved on its own planet, and now it wanted to figure out how best to move on hers.

If it got away, what information would it bring back? Was there an armada waiting somewhere, hidden?

The thing was dangerous. They couldn't leave it to run around the woods. And they couldn't let it get away, either. Too much risk either way. What if it went elsewhere and killed someone else's dog? Or someone else?

Then another thought struck her and her blood chilled. Were there more scouts? Were they nearby?

Maggie was staring at her, her own thoughts clearly horrifying her. Naomi nodded and set off in the direction the woman had indicated.

Before long, Maggie touched her arm and Naomi's gaze followed the pointing mitten. There, in a scooped out section that was more ice than snow, lay the sphere.

They stopped beyond the flattened trees, examining the area for signs of the creature. The crowns of the spruce trees still smoked, but otherwise the fires were out, leaving behind the faintly trashy smell of forest fire. The sphere looked dark and gleamed dully in the setting moon.

They both stood staring at the thing in silence. After a while, Naomi realized that the forest was too silent. The distant thumping had stopped.

They walked past Rupert's body, not looking at him, and the ball of rage threatened to choke Maggie. She wanted to blast that alien monster back to where it had come from and see what color *its* blood was.

But Naomi was right. If the alien was a scout, that would explain the small ship in which it had arrived. Maybe the ship was too small to be caught on radar. Maybe there was a big mother ship somewhere, waiting for the scout to get back to the sphere and report back.

Had Naomi not stopped her, Maggie would have already dealt with the murdering sonofabitch. Now she wondered if that might have been short-sighted. Maybe they should keep it alive, keep it from leaving, from rejoining its brethren. Of course, maybe the sphere was broken and it *couldn't* leave.

If it left, nobody would ever believe that it had been there, despite the burned trees and Rupert.

No, she and Naomi had to capture it. Turn it over to the authorities.

She was about to lean over and tell Naomi when the girl suddenly grabbed Maggie's arm.

Unprepared, Maggie jerked her arm away and stumbled back. Her heel caught on a root hidden by the snow and she fell flat on her back, dropping her rifle. Even as her body made a muted "thump" in the snow, Maggie had enough presence of mind to swallow her exclamation of surprise.

Only then did she realize how quiet it was. She tilted her head forward, scanning the trees beyond her feet. Nothing. She glanced from side to side but saw nothing but trees and moonlight on snow. Then she slid her gaze over to the girl.

Naomi was looking past Maggie's head. Her mouth was open slightly and her dark eyes were wide with fright.

Slowly, Maggie tilted her head back. Snow crept into the collar of her parka and began melting down her neck. Her own mouth parted in shock.

The creature was less than five feet away from them. It stood on the snow-covered ground, its lower extremities sunken in the snow, its membranes spread wide, and its upper appendages clinging to two trees for balance. Its knob of a head seemed to be angled downward, as if it was looking right at her. But there were no eyes on its head, only the wide, gaping mouth filled with sharp teeth that gleamed in the moonlight.

Its cigar body glistened wetly.

It had to be something like acid, to have burned Rupert like that. Something to incapacitate him before those teeth ripped into her dog.

A movement to the side caught her attention and she shifted her gaze to see Naomi moving slowly away from the creature, already ten feet away. While part of Maggie felt disappointment that the girl was abandoning her, most of her urged the girl onward. One of them should survive to tell people what they had seen tonight.

Meanwhile, Maggie had to find a way to keep the creature from getting back into the sphere and taking off, even if she had to kill it.

Then Naomi slowly changed direction and Maggie realized the girl was trying to outflank the creature. Sweet Jesus, why didn't she just make a run for it?

As Naomi lifted one booted foot and took another careful step, Maggie looked around for her rifle. It was only a few feet away. She glanced back at the creature and, to her alarm, it was turning toward Naomi, its membranes curving as if ready to pounce on her.

Then Naomi's heavy boot landed on a buried branch. The resulting snap was muted, but loud enough for the creature. It launched itself toward Naomi.

"Get down!" shouted Maggie as visions of Rupert's mutilated body filled her mind's eye. She scrambled awkwardly to her feet and turned to find the creature half facing her, half facing Naomi. Despite Maggie's warning, the girl was standing, knife in one hand as if to ward off an attack. Maggie hurriedly pulled off her moose hide mittens, exposing her hands to the cold.

The creature hesitated. Its segmented cigar body was covered in liquid and the smell of vinegar and bleach suddenly increased, searing Maggie's nose.

"Hey, cigar head!" she yelled, drawing the thing's attention. It turned toward her and her heart almost stopped at the sight of that open maw.

Then it gathered itself to leap at her and Maggie dove for her rifle.

Her hand found the rifle just as Naomi shrieked. Maggie scrambled up and turned in time to see the girl land on the creature's back, sending them both tumbling to the snowy ground.

Naomi landed on the creature's back, praying she wouldn't end up like Maggie's dog. The creature fell flat on its belly, unable to break its fall. Naomi spread herself over it, her arms crossed over the back of the thing's head.

"Maggie!" she screamed. "We have to tie it up!"

The thing moved under her, surprisingly strong for something that looked like it was made of pipe cleaners and parchment paper. She pressed down harder, not caring if it choked.

"Maggie?" Had the older woman run off? Naomi risked a glance around and finally saw the older woman standing behind her.

"How do you propose we tie it up?" asked the woman calmly.

Naomi felt a surge of triumph. For once, all her preparations would pay off.

"In my parka pocket," she said. "I have duct tape. And I think I dropped my knife somewhere back there." She nodded in the general direction she had been standing.

"It's in your hand," Maggie pointed out wryly as she fished through Naomi's deep pockets to find the duct tape.

It took a while, but they finally managed to wrap the creature's membranes around its body and tape them tightly shut to keep the acid from escaping. Before they could, however, they taped its mouth closed, to keep it from slashing at them.

When they were finally done, they stood up and stared down at it, breathing heavily. The moon was setting but there was enough light to see that the creature had curled around itself. It looked like a black worm on the snow.

"Now what?" asked Naomi, speaking normally. The back of the thing's membranes quivered at the sound and she wondered if the protuberances were designed to scatter sound, rather than absorb it.

"Now we take it to the Jeep," said Maggie. "And then we drive it into town."

Naomi nodded slowly. "The cops aren't going to know what to do with it," she pointed out.

Maggie laughed. "I don't think anyone's going to know what to do with it, but it'll be someone else's problem."

Naomi nodded again. They had done what they could. Probably the cops would call in the military. Someone would take the creature away. Someone would haul that sphere away.

Naomi wondered if Maggie would get to bury her dog, or if they would haul him away, too.

She spared a thought for the party she wouldn't get to, now. Somehow, it didn't matter if her friend Julie laughed at her for being overcautious. Caution had saved her life tonight and helped her capture a dangerous alien.

Who cared what Julie thought?

In the end, Maggie removed her parka and they carried the creature in it, neither one of them being too anxious to actually pick it up and touch it. Maggie found some rope inside the cabin and lashed the thing tightly to the hooks in the back of the Jeep. She toyed with the idea of tying it to the roof rack, but Naomi pointed out that it might die of exposure.

Maggie didn't really care, but someone would.

As they drove down the road, following Naomi's footprints in the snow, Maggie found herself glancing at the girl seated next to her. She wouldn't have thought so when she first met her, but Naomi might actually be worth getting to know.

Who the hell walked around with duct tape in their pocket?

About the Author

Marcelle Dubé grew up near Montreal. After trying out a number of different provinces—not to mention Belgium—she settled in the Yukon, where people outnumber the carnivores, but not by much.

She writes science fiction, fantasy and mystery stories, and has 12 novels to her name. Her upcoming novel, *Epidemic: An A'lle Chronicles Mystery*, will be released in late 2018. Her short fiction has appeared in a number of magazines and anthologies.

Find out more about Marcelle at:
marcellemdube.com

In the Shade of the Slowboat Man

Dean Wesley Smith

One

I was used to the sweet smell of blood, to the sharp taste of disgust, to the wide-eyed look of lust. But the tight, small room of the nursing home covered me in new sensations like a mad mother covering her sleeping young child tenderly with a blanket before pressing a pillow hard over the face.

I eased the heavy door closed and stood silently for a moment, my clutch purse tight against my chest. One hospital bed, a small metal dresser, and an aluminum walker were all the furniture in the room. The green drapes over the window were slightly open and I silently moved to stand in the beam of silver moonlight cutting the night. I wanted more than anything else to run. But I calmed myself, took a deep breath, and worked to pull in and study my surroundings as I would on any night in any city alley or street.

As with all of the cesspools of humanity, the smell was the most overwhelming detail. The odor of human rot filled the building and the room, not so much different than a dead animal beside the road on a hot summer's day. Death and nature doing its work. But in this building, in this small room, the natural work was disguised by layer after layer of biting poison antiseptic. I suppose it was meant to clean the smell of death away so as not to disturb the sensitive living who visited from the fresh air outside. But instead of clearing, the two smells combined to form a thick aroma that filled my mouth with disgust.

I blocked the smell and focused my attention on the form in the bed.

John, my dear, sweet Slowboat Man, my husband once, lay under the white sheet of the room's only bed. His frame shrunken from the robust, healthy man I remembered from so many short years ago. He smelled of piss and decay. His face, rough with old skin and white whiskers, seemed to fight an enemy unseen on the battleground of this tiny room. He jerked, then moaned softly, his labored breathing working to pull enough air to get to the next breath.

I moved to him, my ex-husband, my Slowboat Man, and lightly brushed his wrinkled forehead to ease his sleep. I used to do that as we lay together in our featherbed. I would need him to sleep so that I could go out and feed on the blood of others. He never awoke while I was gone, not once in the twenty years we were together.

Or at least he never told me he had.

I had never asked.

Two

I was hunting the night we met. The spring of 1946, a time of promise and good cheer around the country. The war was won, the evil vanquished, and the living bathed in the feeling of a wonderful future. I had spent the last thirty years before and during the war in St. Louis, but my friends had aged, as always happened, and it was becoming too hard to continue to answer the questions and the looks. I had moved on many times in the past and I would continue to do so many times in the future. It was my curse for making mortal friends and enjoying the pleasures of the mortal world.

I pleaded to my friends in St. Louis a sick mother in a faraway city, and booked passage under another name on an old-fashioned Mississippi riverboat named *Joe Henry*. I had loved the boats when they were working the river the first time, and now, again, loved them as they came back again for the tourists and gambling.

For the first few days I stayed mostly to my small cabin, sleeping on the small bed during the day and reading at night. But on the third day, hunger finally drove me into the narrow hallways and lighted party rooms of the huge riverboat.

Many soldiers and sailors filled the boat, most still in uniform, and most with women of their own age holding onto their arms and laughing at their every word. The boat literally reeked of health and good cheer and I still remember how that smell drove my hunger.

I supposed events could have turned another way and I might have met Johnny before feeding. But almost immediately upon leaving my cabin, I had gotten lucky and found a young sailor standing alone on the lower deck.

I walked up to the rail and pretended to stare out over the black waters of the river and the lights beyond. The air felt alive, full of humidity and insects, thick air that carried the young sailor's scent clearly to me.

He moved closer and struck up a conversation. After a minute I stroked his arm, building his lust and desire while at the same time blocking his mind of my image. I asked him to help me with a problem with the mattress on my bed in my cabin and even though he kept a straight face the smell of sexual lust almost choked me.

Within two minutes he was asleep on my bed and I was feeding, drinking light to not hurt him, but yet getting enough of his blood to fill my immediate hunger.

After I finished I brushed over the marks on his neck with a lick so that no sign would show, then cleaned up myself while letting him rest. Then I roused him just enough to walk him up a few decks, where I slipped away, happy that I might repeat the same act numbers of times during this voyage. It was an intoxicating time and I felt better than I had ever remembered feeling in years.

I decided that an after-dinner stroll along the moonlit deck would be nice before returning to my cabin. I moved slowly, drinking in the warmth of the night air, listening to the churning of the paddle wheel, feeling the boat slice through the muddy water of the river.

Johnny leaned against the rail about mid-ship, smoking a pipe. Under the silver moon, his Navy officer's white uniform seemed to glow with a light of its own. I started to pass him and realized that I needed to stop, to speak to him, to let him hold me.

He affected me like I imagined I affected my prey when feeding. I was drawn to him with such intensity that resisting didn't seem possible.

I hesitated and he glanced over at me and laughed, a soft laugh as if he could read my every thought, as if he knew that I wanted him with me that instant, without reason, without cause. He just laughed, not at me, but in merriment at the situation, at the delight, at the beauty of the night.

He laughed easily and for the next twenty years I would enjoy that laugh every day.

I turned and he was smiling, a first smile that I will always remember. He had the simple ability to smile and light up the darkest place, he had a smile that I would lose myself in many a night while he told me story after story after story. I never tired of that smile, and that first exposure to it melted my every will. I would be his slave and never care as long as he kept smiling at me.

"Beautiful evening, isn't it?" he said, his voice solid and genuine, like his smile.

"Now it is," I said. I had to catch my breath even after something that simple.

Again he laughed and made a motion that I should join him at the rail gazing out over the river and the trees and farmland beyond.

I did. And for twenty years, except to feed on others while he slept, I never left his side.

Three

The smell of the room pulled me from the past and back to my mission of the evening. I looked at his weathered, time-beaten form on the bed and felt sadness and love. A large part of me regretted missing the aging time of his life, of not sharing that time with him, like I had regretted missing the years before I met him. But on both I had had no choice. Or I had felt I had had no choice. I might have been wrong, but it was the choice I had made.

Since the time I left him I had never found another to be my husband. Actually I never really tried, never really wanted to fill that huge hole in my chest and my very being that leaving him had caused.

But now he was dying and now I also had to move on, change cities and friends again. I had always felt regret with each move, yet the regret was controlled by the certainty that the decision was the only right one, that I would make new friends, find new lovers. But this time it was harder. Much harder.

I sat lightly on the side of his bed and he stirred, moaning softly. I again brushed his forehead easing his pain, giving him a fuller rest, a more peaceful rest. It was the least I could do for him. He deserved so much more.

This time he moaned with contentment and that moan took me back to those lovely nights on the *Joe Henry*, slowly making our way down the river, nestled in each other's arms. We made love three, sometimes four times a day and spent the rest of the time talking and laughing and just being with each other, as if every moment was the most precious moment we had.

During those wonderful talks I had immediately wanted to tell him of my true nature, but didn't. The very desire to tell him surprised me. In all the years it had not happened before. So I only told him of the twenty years in St. Louis, letting him think that was where I had been raised. As the years together went by that lie became as truth between us and he never questioned me on it.

He was born in San Francisco and wanted to return there where his family had property and some wealth. I told him I was alone in the world, as was the true case, just drifting and looking for a new home. He seemed to admire that about me. But he also knew I was free to move where he wanted.

I wanted him to know that.

The day before we were to dock in Vicksburg, I mentioned to him that I wished the boat would slow down so that our time together would last. The days and nights since meeting him had been truly magical, and in my life that was a very rare occurrence.

He had again laughed at my thought, but in a good way. Then he hugged me. "We will be together for a long time," he had said, "but I will return in a moment."

With that he dressed and abruptly left the cabin, leaving me surrounded by his things and his wonderful life-odor. After a short time he returned, smiling, standing over me, casting his shadow across my naked form. "Your wish is granted," he had said. "The boat has slowed."

I didn't know how he had managed it, and never really asked what it had cost him. But somehow he had managed to delay the boat getting into Vicksburg by an extra day. A long wonderful extra day that turned into a wonderful marriage.

From that day forward I called him my Slowboat Man and he never seemed to tire of it.

Four

"Beautiful evening, isn't it?" he said hoarsely from the bed beside me. His words yanked me from the past and back to the smell of death and antiseptic in the small nursing home room. Johnny was smiling up at me, lightly, his sunken eyes still full of the light and the mischief that I had loved so much.

"It is now," I said, stroking him, soothing him.

He started to laugh, but instead coughed and I soothed him with a touch again.

He blinked a few times, focusing on me, staring at me, touching my arm. "You are as beautiful as I remembered," he said, his voice clearing as he used it, gaining more and more power. "I've missed you."

"I've missed you, too," I somehow managed to say. I could feel his week grip on my arm.

He smiled and then his eyes closed.

I touched his forehead and again he was dozing. I sat on the bed beside him and thought back to that last time I had sat beside him on our marriage bed, almost thirty years earlier.

That last night, as with any other night I went out to feed, I had put him to sleep with a few strokes on the forehead and then stayed with him to make sure his sleep was deep. But that last night I had also packed a few things, very few, actually, because I had hoped to take very little of our life together to remind me of him. It had made no difference. I saw his face, his smile, heard his laugh and his voice everywhere I went.

I had known for years that the day of leaving was coming. And many times over the years we were together I thought of telling him about my true nature. But I could never overcome the fear. I feared that if he knew he would hate me, fight me, even try to kill me. I feared that he would find a way to expose those of us like me in the city and around the country. But my biggest fear was that he would never be able to stand my youth as he aged.

I could not have stood the look of his hate and disgust.

At least that was what I told myself. As the years passed since I left him I came to believe that my fear had been a stupid one. But I never overcame that fear, at least not until now.

I know my leaving to him must have felt sudden and without reason. I know he spent vast sums of money looking for me. I know he didn't truly understand.

But for me I had no choice. During the month before I left, comments about my youth were suddenly everywhere; Johnny and our friends had aged, I hadn't. I even caught Johnny staring at me when he thought I wouldn't notice.

Three nights before I left, one waitress asked him, while I was in the ladies room, what his daughter, meaning me, wanted for desert. He had laughed about it, but I could tell he didn't understand and was bothered. As again he should have been.

The night I left, hidden in a pile of magazines recycled from his office, I found a book about vampires. A well-read book.

I could wait no longer and I knew then that I could never talk to him about it. I had to go that night and I did so, leaving only a note to him that I would always love him.

I moved quickly, silently, in an untraceable fashion, to the East coast. But less than a year later, no longer able to even fight the fight of keeping him out of my mind, I returned to San Francisco under a new name and began to watch him from afar.

As with me, he never remarried. Many nights he would walk the streets of the city alone, just smiling, almost content. I paced him, watching him, protecting him from others of my kind and from the mortal criminals. I imagined that he knew I was watching him. Pacing him. Walking with him. Protecting him. I pretended that knowing I was there made him happy. Many nights I even thought of actually showing myself to him, holding him again.

But I never did.

I never had the courage.

Five

He stirred under the nursing home sheet and I watched him as he awoke. He opened his eyes, saw me, and then smiled. "Good. I was hoping you were more than a dream."

"No, Slowboat Man, you aren't dreaming."

He laughed and gripped my hand and I could feel the warmth flowing between us. I leaned down and kissed him on the cheek, his rough skin warm against my face. As I pulled back I could see a single tear in the corner of his right eye. But in both eyes the look was love. I was amazed.

And very glad.

I had feared he would hate me after I had left him without warning. I had feared that when I came to visit tonight he would ask the questions about my youth and how I had stayed so young, questions that I had always been so afraid to answer. I had feared most of all that he would send me away.

But he didn't. And the relief flooded through my every cell. Even after almost thirty years he still loved me. I wanted to shout it to the entire world. But instead I just sat there smiling at him.

In the century I had been alive I had never felt or seen a love so complete and total as his love for me.

It saddened me to think that in the centuries to come I might never find it again.

"I'm glad you decided to come and say good-bye," he said. "I was hoping you would."

I gently touched his arm. "You know I wanted to when—"

He waved me quiet. "Don't. You did what you had to do."

My head was spinning and I wanted to ask him a thousand questions: How he knew? What he knew?

But instead I just sat beside him on the bed and stared at him After a moment he laughed.

"Now say good-bye properly," he said. "Then be on your way. I overheard the Doctor telling one of the nurses that I might not make it through the night and I don't want you here when I leave. Might not be a pretty sight."

I just shook my head at him. I had seen more death than he could ever imagine, but I didn't want to tell him that.

A long spell of coughing caught him and he half sat up in bed with the pain. I stroked his forehead and he calmed and worked to catch his breath. After a moment he said, "I loved it when you used to do that to me. Always thought it was one of your nicer gifts to me, even though I never understood just how or what you did."

Again he laughed lightly at what must have been my shocked look. Even after all these years, even with very little force behind it, his laugh could still gladden my heart, make me smile, ease my worries. Again this time it took only a moment before I smiled and then laughed with him.

"Now be on your way," he said. "The nurse will be here shortly and I have a long journey to make into the next world. I'm ready to go, you know? Actually looking forward to it. You would too if you had an old body like this one."

I nodded and stood. "Good-bye, my Slowboat Man." I leaned down and kissed him solidly on his rough, chapped lips.

"Good-bye, my beautiful wife."

He smiled at me one last time and I smiled back, as I always had.

Then I turned and headed for the door. I knew that I had to leave immediately, because if I didn't I never would. But this time he wanted me to go. I wasn't running away.

As I pulled the handle open to the dimly-lit hallway, he called out to me. "Beautiful?"

I stopped and turned.

"I'm sorry I couldn't slow the boat down this time."

"That's all right," I said, just loud enough for him to hear. "No matter how long or how short the lifetime, sometimes once is enough. Sleep well my Slowboat Man. Sleep well."

And as the door to his final room closed behind me I added to myself. "And thank you."

About the Author

Considered one of the most prolific writers working in modern fiction, *USA Today* bestselling writer, Dean Wesley Smith has published almost two hundred novels in forty years, and hundreds and hundreds of short stories across many genres.

At the moment he produces novels in four major series, including the time travel Thunder Mountain novels set in the old west, the galaxy-spanning Seeders Universe series, the urban fantasy Ghost of a Chance series, and the superhero series starring Poker Boy.

His monthly magazine called *Smith's Monthly*, consisting of only his own fiction, premiered in October 2013 and is at issue #44, with over 70,000 words per issue, including a new and original novel every month.

During his career, Dean also wrote a couple dozen *Star Trek* novels, the only two original *Men in Black* novels, Spider-Man and X-Men novels, plus novels set in gaming and television worlds. Writing with his wife Kristine Kathryn Rusch under the name Kathryn Wesley, they wrote the novel for the NBC miniseries The Tenth Kingdom and other books for *Hallmark Hall of Fame* movies.

He wrote novels under dozens of pen names in the worlds of comic books and movies, including novelizations of almost a dozen films, from *The Final Fantasy* to *Steel* to *Rundown*.

Dean also worked as a fiction editor off and on, starting at Pulphouse Publishing, then at *VB Tech Journal*, then Pocket Books, and now at WMG Publishing where he and Kristine Kathryn Rusch serve as executive editors for the acclaimed *Fiction River* anthology series.

Find out more about Dean at:
deanwesleysmith.com

Neck Bolt Lynch Pin

or Frankenstein Meets the Mounties

Steve Vernon

You can call me Maple, if you like.

Maybe you've read one of my comic books?

Some of them are considered highly collectable.

Or maybe your Granddad might have told you the story of how he waded ashore with me on the blood-stained dirt of Juno Beach on June 6, 1941. He might tell you how I ran straight towards the enemy through a storm of kapocketing machine gun fire and whiz-banging eighty-eight blasts—or how I kicked down the door of a reinforced German bunker and beat a squad of elite Wermacht soldiers into meat paste with a blunt entrenching tool.

Back then I was known as Major Maple—the Canadian Commando. A bit grandiose as labels go, I think—but it made for good copy in the pages of *The Stars and Stripes*.

I made it into sixteen separate issues—until that wanna-be with the shield showed up. His whole stars and bars yankee-boy-blue get-up was a much better match for their market demographics. I didn't really care. Truth to tell I have always preferred the quiet northern sunlight to the gaudy spotlight of Uncle Sam.

You know how the song goes—or if you don't I can hum a few bars and let you fake it on the chorus.

In days of yore, from Britain's shore—Wolfe, the dauntless hero, came...

I was there, you know.

The early mist-filled morning of September 13, 1759.

There I was, coming in off of the long wet artery of the St. Lawrence River, nearly ten thousand soldiers and twenty thousand

English sailors and myself scrambling ashore at the sheltered cove of L'Anse-au-Foulon with General Wolfe and his brigadiers. We clambered up a fifty meter cliff, lugging two six-pounder cannon up a sheer mass of granite and heartbreak considered absolutely unscalable by the French general, Montcalm.

We surprised the French forces on the plateau of the ridge and took the high ground from out of their grasp. From there, we attacked without mercy, meeting Montcalm and his French forces on the Plains of Abraham. It took a mere fifteen minutes, during which General Wolfe was the unhappy recipient of three French musket balls—one in the arm, one in the shoulder and one in the chest.

...and planted firm Britannia's flag—on Canada's fair domain...

Your Great Granddad might tell you how he huddled beside me in the trenches of Ypres, hacking and coughing as the grim green clouds of chlorine gas sank down around us. I wore a pair of heavy ammunition boots with bright red puttees twisted sportily about my calves and a heavy red leather great coat that smelled a little like dead fish. I wore an aviator's helmet and a pair of black-rimmed goggles in place of a mask—but those goggles didn't help me one bit against that goddamn green gas.

I remembered seeing it coming at us across the long, muddy field. First a rolling green cloud and that distinctive reek of pineapple and black pepper. Your head felt as if it were being slowly split open upon a rusty cleaver. Your lungs brittled up and you spat bubbling gobs of grass-stained spit. The doctors described it as drowning on dry land. Your skin yellowed and your eyes bugged out and at the end of it you would kill your own brother for a swallow of tepid pond water—even though you knew that the water would only hasten your ultimate extinction.

...here may it wave, our boast our pride—and, joined in love together...

History teachers and folklorists and bald-faced liars will tell you of the rumors of me standing next to General Isaac Brock himself at the battle of Queenston Heights—wearing a maple leaf emblazoned frock coat and carrying a musket that could thread the eye of a needle wasp five full furlongs away. That was the War of 1812, and I guess the Americans were better shots than the French because they took down Brock with a single shot, directly through his heart.

I might have died at all of these battles—depending on who is telling the story—and men might call me some sort of super hero, only there isn't really all that much super about me at all. The truth to tell is I'm just a big guy with a bit of a grudge bone, a lingering Quixote complex and a shiny red leather mask.

I'm nothing more than a dime store story—but a story, if told well and often enough, in time can grow a life of its own.

...God save the Queen and heaven bless—the Maple Leaf forever!

I can't really explain to you how that happens. It's not like I came into this world with a user's guide. I'm nothing more than a tale that has grown two legs and learned to walk about on its own. Like I said—my name is Maple—and I work for the Spiritual Operations Branch, known to the newspapers as the SOBs—a semi-official paramystical working division of the Canadian Royal Mounted Police.

I take my orders from the ghost of Sam Steele, another story made flesh. We operate from a complex hidden beneath the sub-sub-basement level of the last standing Diefenbunker Complex. According to the budget that Complex has been decommissioned years ago—but the lies of the fabulist and the storyteller are nothing but pale figments of wanton fibbery compared to the skillfully woven fabrications of a duly elected government.

Nowadays I go to work with the likes of Paul Bunyan and the Sasquatch—more stories, grown into meat. I have fought beside the twin tricksters—Raven and Coyote—going toe to toe with the Wendigo, Gougou and the Ca-git of the British Columbian Haida.

I'm not really even sure if the word "hero" needs to come into play. I do try and get the job done when I am asked to—but my ways and means are often suspect, to say the least. I have very little pride or ethic and will stoop to any means to accomplish what I set out to do—which is why certain people call on me whenever something even remotely weird comes up.

Like right now.

I got to the hospital and the police assault team had already been deployed. I am talking wall-to-wall Kevlar and more gunpowder and blue-tinged testosterone than you could swing a dead billyclub at. I could see blue and brass and badges and buckshot, collectively surrounding the Children's Intensive Ward at an upscale Toronto hospital.

Yup, there was nothing weird here, folks.

Right in the middle of this monument to lawful jurisdiction stood the big guy.

You couldn't miss him. He stood there—long and tall and gangly, giving the casual onlooker the distinct impression that someone had stuck a scarecrow of a Harlem Globetrotter mascot on top of a totem pole standing upon a stepladder on a pair of rickety wooden stilts. This guy had more stitches in him than a team full of Canadian hockey enforcers.

That flat slab of a head and those neck bolts were a dead giveaway. Still, in this business you could never be sure.

"Is that you, Frankie?" I asked.

I knew who he was.

I was just being polite, is all.

He usually stayed up North about six hundred miles beyond the frost line. He had built himself what he generally referred to as a Bastion of Seclusion—constructed from glacier bone, Precambrian granite and the occasional fossilized grudge. I had visited him up there more than a couple of times. I liked his company. He had that same way of looking at life through a pair of squinted eyes that I likewise shared. Still, Frankie wasn't much of a social animal. I mean—why else would you build yourself the ultimate man cave unless you really wanted to be alone?

So I mostly stayed away.

Frankie liked it that way—I figured.

Besides, the cable reception that far north absolutely sucked.

"It's him all right," the police captain confirmed, as if he really believed that this nine-foot-tall patchwork dead man could be anything else than the Frankenstein monster himself.

"No kidding," I said. "It's a good thing you've got him outnumbered."

I never was much for restraining my sarcasm.

"Are you kidding me?" the captain asked. "Just as soon as we got word that he'd been sighted here in the hospital we moved in with everything we had."

"Are you sure you couldn't find an army or two?" I asked.

Have I ever told you just how much I hate policemen? It's not anything personal, you understand. Hell, I even work for the ghost of a Mountie—but it's just the way that some of the policemen I have encountered seem to have somehow transplanted an entire manual of bylaws and dysfunction in between their ears in place of a functioning cerebellum.

"My name is Cavender," the captain announced. "Captain Cavender and I'm in charge of this here arrest."

He stepped and leaned closer, intent upon intimidation.

I could smell his cheap aftershave and the sour of his day old sweat. He'd eaten something with garlic for breakfast yesterday and his teeth were roughly the color of last year's lawn clippings.

I'm not saying he was pretty.

"Would you mind standing back a bit?" I asked. "Unless you are figuring on giving me a warm wet kiss upon the lip bone—in which case you ought to at least buy me dinner first."

Cavender spit upon the hospital floor.

Nice.

"I thought you super heroes were supposed to be polite," he said.

"You're thinking of Dudley Do Right," I told him. "Don't you dare believe all of that Canadians-are-born-polite horse-puck propaganda."

Cavender did not care much for that remark.

"I'm in charge here, hero," he reminded me. "You just got called in because some politician believes that the SOB can do a better job than the actual city police force—but that doesn't mean I have to take any kind of guff off you."

"Oh, I'm trembling," I diplomatically replied. "Can I feel your muscle when you flex it?"

He glowered at me.

He did have a pretty good glower. I wondered if he practiced it in the bathroom mirror or if this was just something he'd been born with.

Whatever the case, I was pleased to note that I did not feel a cold surge of terror.

So I turned my back on Cavender and got back to the business at hand.

Namely, Frankie.

He was standing over the bedside of a little girl with more tubes in her than a fifty-year-old television set. As far as I could tell she couldn't have been much more than ten years old. My heart went out to that poor little girl.

I had to do something about it.

"Hey, big fellow," I called out to Frankie. "Why don't you step away from that little girl you are looming over. All of that ominous Germanic shade that you are casting is bound to stunt her growth."

I stepped a little bit closer, still trying to figure out just exactly what my plan was supposed to be.

It would have been awfully nice to have somebody bigger on my side—like maybe Sasquatch or Big Bunyan. But Sam Steele had already informed me that he had dispatched the two of them to British Columbia to deal with a situation involving the lake monster Ogopogo and a camp of lawful clear-cutting lumberjacks.

So I was on my own.

"The shade is good for her," Frankie said. "Too much sun can burn you dry."

I snorted derisively.

"Have you been talking to that Transylvanian, again?" I asked. "You know that you can't count him for anything, don't you?"

"Get back, Maple." Frankie warned.

His voice was as flat as a tumbled tombstone.

My ears wanted my feet to run away fast—but my eyes couldn't turn away from that girl in the hospital bed.

I took one more step forward.

"I'm warning you," Frankie said.

Backwards was not an option.

"This isn't going to end well," I replied. "You know it, don't you?"

"It never does."

"So why are you doing it?"

"It's my nature," Frankie replied. "She called me here. That's how it always starts. Somebody little needs my help."

"Like that little girl at the river?"

I hadn't been there, but I knew the story well.

"That was different," Frankie said.

I knew that too.

Frankie had been just trying to help—no matter what the movies or storybooks say.

"You should have stayed up North," I pointed out. "It's quiet up there. No assault squads."

"I get bored with no one to talk to but my maker's gravesite," Frankie replied. "Victor just doesn't say all that much these days."

"Can you blame him?" I asked. "It's rough work coming back as a haunting. Not even a ghost. He's trapped in that grave for as long as his story lasts."

Frankie shrugged.

"It's not my fault that so many people still call me after his name. Whenever anyone mentions the name Frankenstein it is me they are thinking about. His story-soul has been watered down with every barely remembered collective recollection of a half a thousand mad doctors in a billion B movies, pulp novels and comic books. If he'd only had a better agent maybe things might have gone differently."

I couldn't argue with that.

I thought about all of the many Canadian superheroes that time and poorly-told legend had long ago forgotten. Kip Keene, Black Wolf, Whizz Wallace and the Mysterious Secret Seven. All of those characters had been lost to the slow tidal erosion of time and neglect. I had just been lucky that there had been enough stories told about me, enough legends catalogued by enough doctorate-chasing scholars, and enough comic books reprinted to keep me alive. That and a campy 1960s American television series that had put me in a cape and a Mountie's hat that had fortunately been remade into a really crappy Eddie Murphy movie had bought me just enough cult film notoriety to maintain an existence upon this plane.

"So what are you doing down here anyway?" Frankie asked.

I looked at Frankie.

That's when I knew what I had to do. There was no way that I was going to turn him over to this lot.

"I was called in as a consultant," I said.

"Well, let me consult you," he said. "Did you bring a gun?"

"You know how I feel about guns," I said.

"Let me guess," Frankie replied. "You don't believe in them. You swore a sacred oath upon your father's grave that you would never use one against another human being."

"That's not bad," I said. "Maybe I'll use that someday. But the truth is I believe in guns alright—but I just can't afford to buy one, is all."

"Don't you get paid for what you do?"

"Sure," I replied. "But have you looked into the cost of handgun permits these days?"

"So you don't have one."

"No," I said. "But I know where I can get one."

I looked back over my shoulder.

"Hey, Cavender. Come over here. He wants to surrender peacefully but he tells me he'll only give himself up to the proper authority. That'd be you, wouldn't it?"

Cavender almost tripped over himself stepping towards us. He had his pistol out and was aiming directly at Frankie as he strode manfully towards the two of us. He wasn't even paying attention to me at all. He was living his story—the big, heroic police captain—waving a Desert Eagle that a Freudian scholar would have had a field day with.

I turned suddenly as he passed me and caught the side of his pistol with my right bicep, just hard enough to knock his gun arm off-target. I followed through with a good left hook, catching him on the chin with enough gesundheit behind it to jar him.

I caught hold of the fumbled automatic.

Cavender didn't let go at first.

I twisted hard enough to pull the knuckle of his trigger finger out of joint. I really didn't mean to break the finger, but I heard the snap just the same. I caught better hold of the pistol and jammed its muzzle into his ear—sticking another stiff jab into his chin just because I did not like the man.

"You tell your crew to back off now," I said. "You may think that you are running the show, but I am calling the shots—and the first shot is going straight through this ear and straight out the other if you don't do exactly what I tell you to."

It would have been a good plan if he'd only cooperated—but he didn't.

He tried to fight me, twisting away from my grip.

He almost made it.

"Hold still," I gritted.

Cavender was tough. I'll give him that. He was a little bulldog of a man with the kind of low center of gravity that made hanging on awfully tough.

So I caught hold of his arm and bent it a little further than it was built to go.

There was another snap.

Cavender whimpered a little but mostly maintained his dignity.

Meanwhile, the rest of the assault team kept angling for a shot, but I just kept myself and Cavender posed directly in front of Frankie, who was likewise posed directly in front of the girl.

Hero complexes. What can I tell you? They are as contagious as a bad case of the pox.

"Tell them to back off," I retold Cavender, screwing the muzzle of the big Desert Eagle just a little deeper into the cop's left ear hole.

"Back off," Cavender weakly barked. "Do what he says."

Only one of his men wasn't listening all that well. He had himself fitted up with a big loaded shotgun and he was just dying to use it on one of us.

So I screwed the Desert Eagle just a little deeper into Cavender's ear until I felt the ear wax yielding to gray jelly.

"He's not listening, Cavender," I said. "Tell him a little louder. If that shotgun of his goes off there's no telling who he'll hit or what happens next."

"Put that shotgun down, Watkins," Cavender ordered.

"But he's going to get away," Watkins argued back. "I can take him down."

"You can take him? Do you think you're in a movie? Are you going to wing him with a shotgun blast?"

Watkins opened his mouth.

Closed it.

Nothing fell out of his lips in between that set of actions.

"Now listen," Cavender went on. "I was in charge of this unit when we walked into this hospital. This is a direct order. Back—the- hell—away!"

Watkins started backing.

"He's still got that shotgun," Frankie reminded me.

"That's right," I said. "Get him to drop that shotgun. In fact, I want everyone to drop their weapons."

"Everyone except you," Frankie said.

"DO IT!" Cavender said.

Watkins gently placed his shotgun on the ground.

Then he drew his pistol.

"I can get him in the leg," he said to Cavender. "One good wound will take him down."

Cavender seemed to be listening to that suggestion, so I screwed the muzzle of his pistol a little harder into his ear to sort of jog his memory.

He caught the hint.

"Watkins—if you wound him with one good shot then this masked knucklehead is bound to put a .45 caliber wound in my skullbone. How good of a wound would that be, do you think? Now listen to me bonehead or I'll have you bounced back to beat cop status before you can whistle Boots and Saddles."

Watkins laid down his weapon.

He backed away.

Frankie picked up the little girl.

"Let's go," he said.

"I can't let you take her," a doctor spoke up nervously.

I hadn't seen him come into the ward.

"She's better off here," the doctor added.

I kind of think the man had a point but Frankie only growled in reply—a low rumbling sabretooth sort of sound climbing deep from out of the rusty gearbox of his throat. The doctor's face paled to the color of his bleach-bone white smock—but he still wouldn't back off.

"He might have a point," I remarked. "That girl is hooked up to an awful lot of tubes. Some of them might actually be important."

"I don't care if he has a point," Frankie said. "I don't much care for doctors."

"I don't much care for tactical assault teams either," I replied. "But we're not going to get anywhere with you carrying that girl like you are. So put her down and let's get out of here, okay?"

"Go if you want to."

"Frankie…"

"I'm taking her out of here."

He wasn't going to change his mind.

So we walked out of that hospital with Cavender in the lead, followed by the muzzle of the big Desert Eagle, followed by me, followed by Frankie and the little girl. The assault squad followed as closely as they dared. The whole thing began to feel like some sort of weird slow-motion line dance choreographed by a drunken performance artist in a fit of sullen gunpowder angst.

"You're not going to get away with this," Cavender predicted.

"Fine by me," I replied. "I don't really want to get away with anything but YOU right now."

Cavender shook his head.

"That doesn't matter. Sooner or later somebody is going to think too much or not enough to take a shot at you."

I knew that.

"It's bound to happen," Cavender concluded.

Frankie growled again.

The man had himself an awfully fine growl.

"Anything happens," I said to Cavender. "And I shoot you and feed your remains to Frankie, unless you shut up and let me think for awhile."

I don't really know if Frankie was capable of anything resembling cannibalism—but Cavender shut up, just the same.

We walked to the lobby.

There were more police officers waiting for us.

We just kept on walking.

"We could put her in a wheelchair," I suggested. "Might be easier to push her."

"Might make it easier for them to take a shot too," Frankie said. "I'll settle for carrying her."

We walked out to the parking lot.

"Is that your squad car?" I asked Cavender.

Cavender grunted in assent.

The man clearly wasn't enjoying our company.

"Keys," I said.

He handed them to me.

I climbed inside and fired up the engine.

"Needs tuning," Frankie noted.

"So now we know that this guy isn't much more of a mechanic than he is a cop," I replied. "Let's just get out of here."

I drove with Cavender beside me in handcuffs and Frankie pretzel-folded into the backseat with the little girl.

The back seat of a squad car REALLY isn't built for a guy as big as Frankie, but he was making the best of in. He was singing to the little girl now, in a voice that sounded like something that had been torn from out of the working end of rusty combine. Not quite as bad as Tom Waits, but pretty close.

I would have been happier having the two of them apart from each other. I still wasn't all that certain about Frankie's intentions—but there was no way Frankie would have fit into the front seat—and besides, I wanted Cavender close enough to shoot, if I had to.

I could see in the rear view mirror that we were being followed by about twenty squad cars and one armoured assault vehicle.

"You keep talking on that radio," I warned Cavender. "Tell them not to follow too closely. They make me nervous and my trigger finger might slip."

I wasn't really sure if I was really going to shoot Cavender. He had only been doing his job, I guess—but up to now it had *really* been one bad, bad day.

Cavender had no doubts of my intentions. He kept talking on that handset like a man with a mission to spread the word of the true gospel. They must have been listening to Cavender's sermon because I could see them falling back, just a little bit, in my rear view mirror.

"They're not going to stop," Cavender warned me. "No matter what I tell them."

"I don't want them to stop," I told him. "I just want them to slow down long enough for me to get to where I'm driving to."

"So where are you going?" Frankie chimed in from the backseat.

"It's a surprise," I said.

Meaning I hadn't thought of anything in particular.

Yet.

"How many us four are going to be surprised when we finally get there?" Frankie wondered aloud. "I don't know about you, but I am betting that it's all four of us will be amazed."

"Don't worry," I told him. "I've got a plan."

"Gee," Frankie replied. "I wasn't worried until you told me that."

"Oh ye of little faith."

"I've got plenty of faith," Frankie said. "What I'd like to see is some sort of an escape route."

We turned the corner and I sped up a little, hoping to lose our pursuit.

I was beginning to get the beginnings of an escape plan.

I'm not saying it was a good one.

"Almost there," I said.

And then I pulled up outside of the cathedral, just as close to the front doors as I could possibly get.

"This is it," I said. "The biggest church in town. Stone walls and a solid hardwood door."

"Are you figuring on an Alamo?" Frankie asked.

"I was thinking more of running a Quasimodo on them."

Frankie snorted derisively. "I had a hunch you'd say that. Do you think it'll work?"

"Do you have any better ideas?" I asked him.

We got out of the car and we ran for it. Cavender tried to hold back, hanging onto the car door handle, but a well-reasoned argument with the butt of the big Desert Eagle gently applied to the back of his skull allowed him to see the reasoning of my argument and to settle down into an indisputable state of gently-bludgeoned unconsciousness.

"Sanctuary! Sanctuary!" Frankie and I shouted at the top of our lungs. "We claim sanctuary!"

We were met at the door by a protesting priest who likewise accepted the same argument that had worked on Cavender. There are some folks who might tell you that it is bad luck to pistol-whip a priest in a cathedral—but I left him lying facedown in the entranceway like a holy doormat.

"See if you can find us a bottle of communion wine," I told Frankie. "All of this fleeing from the forces of the law is mighty thirsty work."

"Sacrilege," the priest muttered from the floor tiles.

I took pity on the man, and picked him back up and leaned him in a pew.

"It's communal wine, isn't it?" I asked him. "The last time I checked, communal meant share and share alike—and I sure hope that you like to share, padre, because you haven't seen any-one guzzle wine like a twelve-foot dead man."

I pointed at Frankie when I said that, just in case the priest got confused over who I was talking about. After all, I had hit him pretty hard. He still looked a little cross-eyed, which, come to think of it, might have actually been his natural state.

"Is it working?" I asked. "Are they honoring sanctuary?"

Frankie took a quick peek out of the closes clear window—which was just high enough for him to reach without needing to stand on tip-toe. The sun was beginning to sink and the dusky light made pretty pictures in the stained glass altar windows of the church.

"They've parked their cars and holstered their pistols," Frankie said. "Mostly they seem to be standing there and scratching their heads. Some of them are scratching other places, but that's just a little too vulgar for me to mention here in church."

That picture sounded pretty good to me.

The last thing I wanted was a firefight in a house full of this many windows.

"There must be a lot of good Catholics out there," I decided. "How about that wine?"

"He can probably find it faster than I could," Frankie said, pointing at the priest, who had just begun to find his own feet.

"Sacrilege," the priest muttered again.

I guess he liked that word a lot, but he stopped using it after I re-cocked the Desert Eagle significantly. Of course I really wasn't going to actually shoot a full-grown priest. I had some pride and sense of ethics—and besides, bullets were far too useful to waste on the likes of him.

He saw the light eventually and brought us two full bottles.

He put the bottles at my feet and backed away. Then he found himself a quiet corner that must have looked safe enough to him. He knelt down and began to pray.

"No need to say grace," I told him. "We'll drink this straight up. Words only spoil the bouquet of a good bottle of bug juice."

I pulled the cork and took a swallow. It was bitter and felt as if somebody might have baptized the proofing down with a dose of holy water.

"There is nothing worse than a cheapskate high-collared bartender," I observed, taking another good swallow.

Booze was booze, watered down or not.

"So what were you doing in that hospital anyway?" I asked Frankie.

"Just what I told you," Frankie replied. "She called me in her dreams. When a child gets that close to the shadows she'll call out to them, just like you might call out in a dark room and ask if anybody was there or not. She called out and I answered her."

He was rocking her in a cradle of long bony arms and stitched flesh shot through with electricity and wine-purple rays. He was humming a lullaby that was one part dirge and one part death rattle. I could see her breath, thin and wispy in the cold of the cathedral, like tiny ghosts circling about her slowly bluing lips.

"What's the matter with her?" I asked.

"She's got AIDS," he said. "They have been pumping her with chemicals and cure-alls, but all they really did was to buy her a little unwanted time—and right now I'd say that her credit is all run out."

I looked at her laying there in his arms. He looked a little like the world's ugliest nanny—but she seemed more than happy.

"How'd she get that?" I asked. "Did somebody infected rape her?"

"She was born with it, moron," Frankie said. "Maybe her mother slept with the wrong fellow. Maybe her daddy shared needles with someone he shouldn't have. There are an awful lot of ways for a person to catch death."

I shook my head in disbelief.

I had seen far too many young boys shot down in the heart of battle. Sights like that had embittered me to the point of no return—but seeing a child born with death in her veins left a taste far too bitter to ever swallow down.

"She's so damn young," I said.

"Age doesn't mean a thing," Frankie said. "Just look at the numbers. In 2008 over two million people in the world had this disease, and one out of every seven of them happened to be children just like her."

"You've got a head for statistics," I said.

"I think Victor put a calculator in there when he was piecing me together," Frankie said. "Either that or I have the spleen of a mathematician."

"But you've looked into it some," I pointed out.

"It looks into me," he told me. "Being made out of death like I am, I spend a great deal of life living in the shadow world of the Grim Reaper. Me and the boogeyman and the closet monster and the under-the-bed-creaker are generally called upon by those people who are living with one foot in the shadow and one in the sun—and it's mostly the children who call on me."

"Why just kids?"

"I don't really know why," Frankie admitted. "Maybe they think I am big enough and ugly enough and scary enough to chase off Death himself. Maybe they just think that I'll introduce them to him—maybe get on his good side. Maybe they just see me as some sort of a stitched-together lynch pin keeping the flywheels of life and death from binding up against each other. Who knows? It's one of those unfathomable mysteries—like the way that people who are mostly dying think a whole lot differently than the people who are mostly living."

I waited a moment.

Let that all sink in.

"Was that how it was for the girl by the river?" I asked.

Frankie looked away.

"She was different," he said. "Her Daddy was doing things he ought not to be doing to her. She went down to the water with one thing on her mind. I just helped her to get there, was all. Afterwards I helped her Daddy, too—only not nearly as gently."

"Couldn't you have done that first?" I asked. "Couldn't you have killed him first and then let her live?"

"You'd think that, wouldn't you?" Frankie replied.

He heaved a long heavy sigh—an autumn wind whispering through a rusty-stringed harp.

"Some scars don't heal," he whispered softly. "I was doing her a favor, whether you believe it or not."

I chewed that over.

I kind of envied the little girl, sliding down in that deep cold good-bye water. I envied the notion that she wasn't going to have keep coming back like I was. That there wouldn't ever be enough stories told about her to pass her from the state of merely mortal into the cold undying realm of urban mythology.

Of course, if enough people talked and Twittered and Face-booked and YouTubed about what was going on today, then maybe she would come back. Maybe her ghost would haunt this cathedral forever.

I shivered a little.

It might have been the cold.

"At least it's in a church," I said. "That makes it holy, doesn't it?"

Frankie looked around at the dead statues and yellowed prayer books and the big brass crucifixes that hung on every wall.

"I don't much like the look of all of those crosses," he said. "It looks a little too much like a windmill to me."

I looked up at the dead stone man hanging up there on that cross of his.

"Me too," I said.

"Sacrilege," the priest whispered again.

"Shut up and bring us another couple of bottles," I said.

The priest scurried off obediently.

"So how long do you figure?" I asked.

Frankie looked at the little shadow in his arms, fading away. "Soon," he said.

I shook my head gently. "I mean, how long do you think that they will wait before they come in and get us?"

Frankie looked away for a minute.

I watched his eyes slide.

I had seen far too many men wearing that cold, thousand-yard stare—men who had looked into the laughter of battlefield death and had seen it swallow them whole. Right now Frankie was wearing a look that was yearning past light-years—like he had looked somewhere far down in the darkness, farther and deeper than any mortal man ought to look into—like he had been that far and had himself a long lifetime conversation with something down there that told him what grew in the shadows, and what ought to best be forgotten.

"They'll come when the sun rises," he told me. "They'll come and they will drag me away with crosses and torches and shotguns and clubs. They will cut me into pieces and they will burn me with acid and maybe they will shoot me and crush the burned shot-up pieces between rocks, and then beat on those rocks with hammers made out of blessed silver."

He stood up.

Looking at him standing there beside that man on a cross, I kind of found it hard to tell the difference between the two of them.

"They will kill me in as many ways as is humanly and inhumanly possible," Frankie went on. "Just the same as they have been doing to me for the last four hundred years."

He looked down at the little girl.

She was still now, and the ghosts of good-bye had stopped whispering at her thin blue lips. A few careless strands of soft blonde hair lay across her closed eyes like someone's forgotten angel wings.

"They will kill me, and I will pass back into the shadow until some damned Tokyo grindhouse studio makes another movie, and the Halloween factories pump out another hundred thousand masks, and the dreams and nightmares of a billion sleeping children will rouse me from my shadows, and I will come to their rescue and repeat this whole damned cycle one more time."

He was right.

There always had to be a sequel.

"Isn't there anything we can do?" I asked.

Frankie just shook his head.

"It is the way that things must go," he said. "Night must follow day, and death must follow life, and they are going to do just exactly what they would have done to me in the hospital."

"So I've wasted my time?"

"No, it wasn't a waste," Frankie said. "Your rescue attempt bought this little dead girl a few moments of peace to die alone and tubeless in the quiet of this church. That and a couple of bottles of watered-down wine. That's what your sacrifice has bought for me."

He raised the bottle to his lips.

"Thanks for that, at least," he said.

And then he tipped the bottle back for one long last swallow.

I watched the wine jiggle down his throat, those two neck bolts stuck out like a pair of sullen tombstones.

There was nothing left to say.

We sat there together—a monster and a hero—emptying wine in the shadow of a church, waiting for the biplanes of sun-up to arrive.

About the Author

Steve is a writer and an oral tradition storyteller; he learned the storytelling tradition from his grandfather, and regularly tells stories to in-person audiences ranging from 5 to 5,000 spectators. He writes horror, paranormal, dark fantasy, and ghost stories, and specializes in the fine old art of booga-booga.

Think of Steve as that old dude at the campfire spinning out ghost stories and weird adventures and the grand epic saga of how Thud the Second stepped out of his cave with nothing more than a rock in his fist and slew the saber-tooth tiger.

Find out more about Steve at:
stevevernonstoryteller.wordpress.com

The Bitch

P. D. Cacek

"Oh, God."

Karin had heard Ross say those two words in a number of ways for a number of situations. It would be an explosive murmur while making love, a groan after she told a bad joke, or an epithet when he discovered a new oil spot on the driveway—but the way he said it this time sent a chill racing through her, freezing her hand halfway to her wineglass.

"Russ?"

His eyes moved slowly from some point over her right shoulder to her eyes, then down to his plate, his mouth set in a firm, bloodless line. Suddenly the restaurant's ambient sounds—the quiet conversations from the other tables, the soft click and clatter of flatware against plates, the sweet, seductive music that hung in the air…all of it became a distraction as Karin leaned forward. "Russ, what *is* it?"

He looked up and said one word: "Lily." The chill deepened.

"Shit."

"Yeah."

For the six months they'd been dating, Lily—the ex who wouldn't go away—had been a constant, determined, and, up until that night, discreet rival for Russ's affections…even though he'd made it clear to Karin that he no longer felt anything for the woman.

Karin believed him.

Lily, apparently, did not.

They'd be at a movie and—surprise—Lily would be sitting two rows back. They'd be at a party and Lily would be standing across the room, glaring at Karin until Russ turned around, at which point tears would magically form in her pale gray eyes and she'd leave in a flurry of weeping and garnered sympathy. For six months Lily would show up, accidentally, wherever they were. Karin should have expected it, but somehow, she thought tonight would be different.

"Ah, Jesus…"

Karin didn't have to look, she knew when the air, suddenly scented with lilacs and musk, moved between them and the candle flame shuddered as a shadow fell across the table.

Russ shook his head. "Karin, this is Lily."

Karin's hand finally reached her wineglass as she looked up. They hadn't officially met until that moment. *Fragile* was a term she'd heard most from people, including Russ, used to describe Lily. *Broken* was another, but from where she sat, looking up at the pale woman with thick black hair and blood-red lips, Karin couldn't see it.

Except for the tears glistening in her eyes, and the flowing, über-feminine dress the color of ash, Lily seemed as hard—and invulnerable—as marble.

Smiling politely, Karin cleared her throat and nodded. "Hi."

The sadness in Lily's eyes crystallized momentarily when she glanced at Karin, before melting back into twin pools of dejection as she looked down at the table.

"Oh," she whispered, voice hoarse with emotion, "I see you're having dinner."

It was a flat statement that made Karin feel as if she'd done something horribly wrong…or simply *was* something horribly wrong. She lifted the wineglass and took a quick sip to wash the taste out of her mouth.

"Yes," she said after swallowing. "The food's very good here."

Lily brushed at her coal-black hair, dismissing Karin and her comment, before turning her full and undivided attention back to Russ.

"I always thought so; it was one of our favorite places."

Russ made a sound that was halfway between a cough and groan. "We never ate here, Lily."

"Oh?" Confusion deepened the slight—very slight—wrinkle between the woman's eyes. "That's strange...I thought we had. Well, we ate at so many good restaurants I guess I got..." She sighed and Karin fought the urge to applaud. "Anyway, I was just driving by and saw your car in the parking lot and thought I'd stop in. To say 'hi.'"

Karin's stomach tightened uncomfortably around the portion of the night's meal that she'd already eaten. "How nice."

Lily gave her a small, weak smile before utterly dismissing her. Again.

"You look good, Russell."

"Thanks."

"And you've put on some weight. *She* must be a good cook."

The color deepened along Russ's cheeks as the *she* in question finished off the wine in her glass and toyed with the idea of *accidentally* spilling the rest of the bottle down the front of Lily's dress.

Russ grinned but pushed his plate away. "Is there something you need—"

"I saw Ben and Dee the other night," Lily interrupted with the precision of a surgeon removing a tumor. "They said you seemed happy. *Are* you happy, Russell?"

Russ smiled at Karin and winked. "I'm working at it."

"Oh, dear. That's rather an evasive answer, isn't it? You're either happy or you're not. You shouldn't have to *work* at it, Russell."

Despite the obvious chill that had descended, Karin felt a slow burn creep up along her throat, but managed—somehow—to keep her voice light. "Oh, I think Russ is doing okay in that department."

"Really?" Lily said, then reached down and helped herself to the piece of roast beef on Russ's fork.

He shook his head when Karin started to say something. Holding herself still, she watched the woman's lips slowly part to reveal a set of strong white teeth that closed over the meat with a kind of predatory finality.

"Well." Lily handed Russ back the empty fork and leaned over, kissing his cheek. "If you're not going to invite me to join you... It *was* good seeing you again, Russell."

Turning, she gave Karin one last withering *dry-eyed* glare before walking away. Karin watched the rest of the performance—Lily wiped at her eyes a number of times between their table and the door—before she could force herself to look away. Russ was busy looking at nothing in particular.

"Join us?"

Russ was toying with his wineglass but never picked it up. "Sorry about that. Sorry."

"Did she *seriously* think we were going to ask her to join us?"

"I don't know, yeah...maybe. That's just Lily being Lily."

Karin poured another glass of wine and finished it in one long, continuous swallow.

He reached across the table to take her hand when she started to refill the glass. "Don't. She was just trying to rattle you."

"Well, it worked. How could she see your car? We parked in the back."

"I don't know...she has a way of doing things like that."

"She's...barged in on your other dates?" Karin did a quick mental rundown on the things Russ *had* told her about Lily and couldn't remember that particular point of interest.

"What? Oh...no, no, but for the first couple of months after we broke up I'd go somewhere—to the market or hardware store or even a fast-food drive-thru—and I'd see her. We wouldn't talk or anything, but she'd be there. And when I'd get home, there'd be a message on my answering machine or a text message on my cell... We never actually spoke but she wanted me to know she was there...that she'll always be there."

Russ let go of her hand and finished the wine.

"And, in case you're wondering why this happened tonight...I suspect it's because I've been with you longer than any other..."

Karin took pity on him and nodded. "Six whole months, going on seven."

"And that bothers the hell out of her...because this is real."

Karin couldn't say anything and it was probably just as well when, instead of letting the moment continue, he added:

"We started dating a few months after her husband died and that was a mistake. She was so devastated by his death, so helpless..." He shrugged. "I don't know, but she *needed* me and, I guess, I liked the feeling, so I stayed even after I knew the relationship wasn't what I wanted. A couple of years into it and I'd really had enough and tried to break it off..."

Karin leaned forward but didn't say anything. This was the first time she'd heard about that.

"She threatened to kill herself if I left. And...I believed her."

"So you stayed."

"For another eighteen months, and then... Christ, I couldn't take it. She thought she had me so she felt she could do or say anything to belittle me and I'd take it. We were at an office party and my boss's wife—who was a bit drunk and flirty at that point—was complimenting me on my suit when Lily walked up. 'Oh yes, the poor man knew nothing about fashion or... much of any of the social skills until *I* showed him. He's so helpless without me.'"

"Yikes."

Russ nodded. "Yeah, and Lily made sure everyone in the room heard it. When I took her home...back to *her* home, that is, I told her how I felt and she laughed and said it was only a joke and that she felt sorry for me if I didn't know that. I walked her to her door, then turned around and left."

"Wow."

"I didn't answer the phone for three days, and on the fourth, she showed up at my office in hysterics...making me the bully, of course. Then—Christ, I don't want to talk about this anymore, okay?"

Karin nodded. She could get the rest of the story from friends. "Sure."

They ate the rest of their meal making careful small talk about safe subjects and were laughing and holding each other as they walked to his car. But later that night, when they made love, Karin had the distinct impression that there was another person in bed with them.

A woman with long dark hair and sad gray eyes and sharp white teeth: a bitch in flowing sheep's clothing.

"So...you met Lily?"

Karin could hear the pity in her friend's voice and almost wished she hadn't called. But what's the use of having a girlfriend, especially a girlfriend who knows all the players and doesn't have to be brought up to speed?

"Yes," Karin said. "Yes, I did."

"And?"

"Scary lady."

"You think so?" Karin was a bit surprised by the comment. "I just think she's sad. And, yeah, okay, maybe a little…pathetic. I mean, it *has* been three years. I keep telling her it's time to move on."

"You still talk to her?"

"Oh, sure. Ben and Russ work together, so I knew Lily from the start and…" Her friend's sigh echoed softly in Karin's ear. "Well, she still calls sometimes to ask about Russ. Last night she was in tears, sobbing her heart out because she saw the two of you together and wondering how he could go to *their* restaurant with another woman and—"

"It *wasn't* their restaurant. Russ said—"

"—do that to her because he knew she still cared so much. Yadda, yadda, yadda. Same song, different verse. Don't let it get to you."

Karin heard a faint snap and looked down at the broken mechanical pencil in her hand. "Uh-huh."

"C'mon. It's just her way of trying to get sympathy. I know she probably hoped I'd call Russ and tell him, but I told her to knock it off instead. She got real quiet and then hung up."

"Why does the word 'manipulation' come to mind?"

"Yeah, but she's just running scared. Ben and I haven't seen Russ this happy in…a long time, and I'm sure Lily notices it, too."

The mailbox icon flashed in the upper corner of her computer screen and Karin smiled. Russ liked to send her jokes or cartoons or just "Hi, miss you" messages to brighten her workday.

Setting the broken pencil down, she clicked open the e-mail...
and stopped smiling.

"Oh, joy."

"I know." Dee sighed. "But don't let her get to you. It's hard
when someone won't let go, but she's really only hurting herself."

"I know...and I can remember how Lily doesn't want to give up.
Russ is a wonderful man and I don't intend to simply walk away."

"It may get rough."

Karin nodded and reread the message on her screen:

*I simply don't understand why you're with him. You're average
at best and Russell requires a woman who is much more than that.
I'm saying this only as a friend, but if you continue to burden him
with your presence, you'll only bring him down to your level, and
one day he'll notice that and leave you. Show me I'm wrong. Leave
him now and gain my respect—Lily*

"Oh," Karin said into the phone and she pressed the *delete* key,
"there's no doubt about it."

"Excuse me?"

Russ smiled weakly. "She wants all of us to be *friends*."

"And you know this because..."

"She called me at work this afternoon...weeping and asking
me to forgive her for last night. She said she'd be happy and be
able to get on with her life if we could be friends. All of us."

Karin took a deep breath and pretended to think about it without adding any comment about aeronautically gifted swine. She
also didn't mention Lily's e-mails—five in total, all along the
same "you're not good enough for him, leave now, you pitiful excuse for a woman" line—or the phone message on her answering
machine:

"I don't think Russell will ever know just how much he meant to me...but he was my world and I—I—" (sound of weeping) *"—I hope you both know that I only want him to be happy. If not with you, then... I hope you can make him happy but I worry because he should have said that last night. If a man is happy, he wants to tell the world. Has he ever told you? He told me so many times how happy I made him...but he must have lied. He must still be lying—to himself. Please, Karin, call me and let's talk. There are so many things you apparently don't know about him...that only I can tell you. We need to talk. Please call. My number is—"*

She'd erased the message and, just for the annoyance factor, turned off the machine before heading over to Russ's for the night. The woman was obviously nuts...or not.

"The lady does get around..."

Russ stopped tearing lettuce apart and looked at her. "Excuse me?"

Karin shook her head and stole a grape tomato out of the bowl. "Nothing. So she wants to be friends, huh? What did you tell her?"

He looked down so quickly Karin thought she heard his neck pop. "I...told her I'd ask you—but that I didn't think it was a good idea."

"Uh-huh."

Russ finished dismembering the lettuce and picked up a home-made cheese crouton and held it out to her...an offering she couldn't refuse.

One of the many things Karin loved about Russ was his skill in the kitchen. The man could cook, and while she managed well enough to keep from starving, her meals tended to be of the simple boil-in-the-bag variety. Russ, on the other hand, prepared *real* food, from scratch, using recipes that required more than "place in pot" and "turn on heat."

If ever a man knew the way to a girl's heart…

Karin sighed—a bad mistake, considering the mouthwatering aromas that filled the kitchen. She took the crouton and crushed it between her back teeth. "It's not going to happen you know…the friends bit, I mean."

"I know."

"Then why didn't you tell her?"

He shrugged. "I don't want to hurt her any more than I already have. Lily may seem strong, but she's not, Karin…not like you."

Karin concentrated on chewing and swallowing and not destroying his obvious delusion about his *fragile, broken, weak* ex. "Yeah, well…I guess she'll figure it out eventually."

"Here's hoping." He leaned across the island counter and planted a kiss on her nose. "Now, how'd you like to do me a favor?"

Russ generally didn't need any help when it came to cooking, so Karin had already toed off her croc sandals and made herself comfortable on one of the counter's tall bistro-styled chairs—where she could filch the occasional nibble while he worked. She was already looking for a glass when he picked up a wine bottle and upended it. A lone drop, the color of rip plums, landed on top of the lettuce.

"I thought I had another bottle of Cabernet when I made the dressing. How do you feel about running out and getting some wine? Do you mind?"

Karin snagged her purse off the back of the chair and slid her feet into the plastic shoes. "I can do that. Need anything else?"

"Not a thing. Thanks. Now scoot."

She left him wreathed in a cloud of steam and paused only a moment to listen to the utterly domestic sounds coming from the kitchen. They were good sounds, echoes of hearth and home and refuge—sounds that she had missed and hadn't even realized until that moment.

"I don't hear the door closing," he shouted, and it made her smile.

"Yes, sir. Right away, sir. At once, sir." Karin stepped out into the bright late-summer evening and made sure the door banged behind her. Smiling, she walked past her car and continued down the drive to the sidewalk. It was too pleasant a night to drive the quarter mile to the wine-and-spirit shop.

One of the benefits, if there were any, of living in a "covenant-controlled planned community," aka "acre-o-condos," was that there was *always* a strip mall within walking distance.

Not the many of the community-dwellers seemed to take advantage of it, as was evident by the number of cars that filled the parking lot. Their loss, she thought, and waved the right-of-way to a harried-looking woman in an SUV that could have housed a family of six, plus pets. Given the choice, Karin preferred feeling the ground beneath her feet.

He called her cell just as she'd finished signing the credit card receipt.

"You walked, didn't you?"

"Can't put anything over on you." Mouthing her thanks to the salesclerk, Karin picked up the bagged wine and began weaving her way through the crowd to the door. "I won't be five minutes…start dishing out the salad."

Russ *humphed* through the phone. "Okay, but the wine's supposed to breathe before it's served, you know."

"I'll jog and we can give it CPR when I get there."

Karin snapped the cell phone shut and dropped it back into her purse. She had no intention of jogging, even though the sky had grown considerably darker while she'd been perusing the wine aisles. Night didn't bother her. And even if the city planners had attempted to keep the original "country feel" of the area by leaving the sidewalks tree lined and avoiding the overuse of streetlights, it was still upper-middle-class suburbia, for God's sake.

Once she left the strip mall, with its ring of sodium security lights, Karin had only the full moon to guide her way, and that was fine. What could happen to her?

She'd only gone two blocks when she heard a soft scuff on the sidewalk behind her. It could have been a dog or cat or a deer or a—

When a second, then third, then fourth scuff condensed into steps, Karin felt the hairs stand up on the back of her neck. Someone was following her, and that someone was getting closer.

Tightening her grip on the wine, Karin forced herself to look straight ahead and continue with the same easy, unhurried stride, as if she hadn't heard a thing. Every college self-defense lecture she'd ever heard came thundering back to her, along with each possible reaction's chance of actually working:

Run—50%, if you were faster than your assailant.

Scream "fire"—75%, but only if you were near a building.

Scream "rape" or "murder"—0%.

Fall down and play dead—minus 5.3 billion%.

Fight—100%, but a bad idea for a number of reasons.

The breeze shifted and carried the scent of lilacs and musk…and a low, trembling growl that slowly, very slowly formed into words.

"He's…mine."

Before Karin could react, something cold and hard and sharp raked down her back, shredding her shirt and the skin beneath.

Karin spun to the left, only partially aware of the squeal of brakes and a blaring car horn as she darted out of the tree shadows and into the street.

—

Russ was setting the table when she walked in.

"A couple of minutes? I was about to send out the... *Jesus,* what happened to you?"

Setting the bottle down on the table, she glanced over her shoulder at the tattered remains of her T-shirt and gave him a sheepish grin. "You won't laugh?"

There was only concern in his eyes. "Of course not."

"I...slipped and fell into some bushes...rose bushes. Never said I was overly coordinated."

"God, apparently not." Turning her, Russ gently examined her back. "You're lucky you only got scratched. They don't look very deep, skin's hardly broken, but you'd better let me put some antiseptic on them just in case."

"After dinner?"

"Now."

While Russ went to fetch the disinfectant and cotton swabs, Karin opened the wine and poured herself a glass.

She didn't give it so much as a moment to catch its breath.

Lily was in the phone book, too. She answered after the third ring.

"Hello?"

"Hello, Lily. You're right, we need to talk."

"Who is this?"

"You know very well who this—"

"Oh, *Karin,* of course." The laughter was condescending. "Yes, I suppose we should talk if you want to. Frankly, I thought you'd have already gotten my message. But if you insist..."

"I do."

"All right then." She yawned. "Where and when?"

"Now's good for me. Open your front door."

Lily wasn't dressed for company—cutoffs and a shapeless tank top, no makeup, hair in a tangle—but the look on her face, although she was trying hard to suppress the shock as she opened the door, made Karin wished she'd brought a camera. It was one of those precious moments she'd want to remember.

For a long time.

"There's a law against stalking, you know."

Karin closed her cell phone. "Funny *you* should mention that."

Pushing past the startled woman, Karin walked into the living room and sat on the edge of an overstuffed white sofa. The room was all cream and beige and lace and soft pillows; silk lilies in china vases and scrollwork furniture; knickknacks and framed pastels. There were no hard edges in the room, nothing sharp or prickly or that in any way reflected the true nature of its owner.

Karin found that interesting and wondered if Russ ever noticed.

"Oh," she said when her hostess finally arrived, "and before you say anything, I know there's also a law breaking and entering… and even if I didn't have an uncle on the police force, I could always say you invited me in. But don't worry…I haven't said anything to my uncle *or* Russ. This is between you and me."

Lily stood like a queen—head held high, movements sure, her eyes as hard as slate and just as brittle. Karin couldn't help but admire that.

"But where are my manners?" Lily asked, hand dramatically placed at her chest…undoubtedly to reinforce the fact that she wasn't wearing a bra. Karin refused to look down at her own size 34Bs, knowing the comparison wouldn't be in her favor. "Please forgive me. May I offer you something to drink?"

"No. Thanks."

"Well, since you've already made yourself at home…"

Silence—profound and heavy—filled the moments until Lily had settled herself in the chair directly opposite Karin.

"So you wanted to talk." Lily crossed one leg over the other. "Go on, then. What did you want to talk about?"

Karin sat a little straighter. "Let's cut the bullshit, shall we? I want you to stop bothering Russ."

Lily smiled. "I've never bothered Russell. We're friends."

"No." Karin smiled back. "You're ex-lovers—emphasis on *ex*—and that's all you are. Now, I know sometimes people can remain friends after a relationship, but, lady, I am positively certain you're not one of those people."

Lily's pantomime smile faded, and before she could control herself, Karin saw the hardness beneath her skin. It was impressive.

"You don't know how right you are. However, you should be very careful about saying things like that. It could be dangerous."

"Oh?"

"I'm not like other women. I can't be intimidated or shoved aside. When I want something, I get it…and when I have it, I keep it—until *I'm* tired of it."

"So what you're saying is that Russ hurt your pride when *he* ended it and you're going to try and get him back just so you can…what, return the favor? Do you think I'd let you do that?"

"You don't have a choice."

Lily's voice deepened until it was a growl more menacing than the one Karin had heard the night before.

"Russell belongs to me. I decided that the first moment I saw him. I never expected to find anyone after my husband died, but Russell…managed to fill the void very nicely. We were good together, he's just forgotten that."

"But he still left you."

"No, he ran because he realized what I am."

"And what, pray tell, is that?"

"Dangerous. Poor Russell, but I forgive him for his weakness and will continue to do so until he finally comes to his senses."

Lily smiled and ran a hand languidly through her hair while Karin dug her nails into the palms of both hands.

"Meaning," she translated, "when he comes back to you?"

"It's only a matter of time."

"And until then, you'll continue to harass us."

Lily laughed, tossing her head like a schoolgirl. "I won't dignify that with an answer."

"Okay, then," Karin said, "how about this—from this moment on, you will leave Russ and me alone."

Lily smoothed down her hair. "No."

"He doesn't want you."

"He doesn't know what he wants."

"I'm warning you, Lily—get out of his life."

And suddenly the hardness was gone and the woman blinked her sad, sad gray eyes. "Oh, I can't wait to tell Russell. I knew I'd find your weak spot. You're just like all the others. I only want to be friends and you…and you come into my house and threaten me." —sniff— "He'll be so disappointed when I tell him."

If Lily hadn't started laughing, things might have gone…differently.

Karin opened her hands and watched the blood that had filled the small crescent-shaped cuts in her palms reverse direction as the flesh regenerated. "You know, I had a strange feeling you were going to say something like that."

She leaned back against the white sofa cushion and Lily gasped. "Don't!"

"It's okay, I'm house-trained. Oh…wait, you're worried about what you did to my back, all that bloody seepage and stuff like that, right? Well, you don't have to be."

Karin stood up, lifting the back of her shirt as she turned around…and wished she could have seen the look on the woman's face. There wasn't a scratch, or a scar, or the faintest hint of the four jagged wounds that had cut her to the bone. Nothing but solid, healthy, unmarked flesh.

"We heal quickly. It's part of some inherited survival trait, I guess. *People* were always trying to kill us." Turning, Karin tucked her shirt back into her jeans but remained standing. "What did you use? My guess is a cultivator…right? And I have to say, I admire the restraint you showed, although it would have done some pretty serious damage if I were human."

"Hu-hu—"

"Me, yes, but we're talking about *you* right now. I hate to say it, even though it's already been established that you're not a wholly rational, understanding woman, but I can't leave a body. The thing is that Russ will think he was responsible for you killing yourself."

Karin extended her jaw, sighing with pleasure as the canines elongated to their full and deadly length. They made her lisp a little, but there was nothing she could do about it.

"He would blame himself until the day he died, and frankly, lady, you've already hurt him enough."

Lily's mouth kept opening and closing, but fortunately for both of them, she didn't say anything.

"So, you see, I really have no choice. Hope you understand."

Karin didn't have to do it—it was an absolute, unadulterated and selfish indulgence on her part and she knew it. Over the generations, her kind had learned it was easier, and much *safer*, to transform after the prey animal was dead...but she'd wanted Lily to see what a *real* Alpha Bitch looked like.

Right before Karin snapped her neck and dragged her body into the downstairs' bathroom.

Tile was much easier to clean than carpet...especially white carpet.

While Russ turned the steaks on the firepit's grill, Karin used the sizzling flames to reread the words that she'd so carefully scripted in Lily's beautiful forward-slanted handwriting. It had taken her a bit more practice than she was used to, but once she'd found a sample, she had to admit she'd done a pretty good job.

Russell...and I hope you noticed I didn't add "dear" or "dearest" or "my beloved"...because I'm finally tired of this. It's over. Foolish me, but I thought you were a different sort of man. I need a man who is my equal, and, let's face it, Russell, you are hardly that. Still, I can't bear the thought of seeing you with...her, so you'll be pleased to know, I'm sure, that I won't be around to witness the charade any longer. There's a wide world out there, and perhaps, if I'm lucky enough, I'll find someone truly worthy of me. The best to you and what's-her-name—

Karin handed him back the note, the scent of Lily's perfume— lilacs and musk—that she had liberally dabbed onto the paper competing with the aroma of roasting meat.

"Ouch."

Russ shook his head and, laughing, fed the note to the fire. "Yep, a real bitch to the end."

Karin smiled. "Well, I know it's selfish of me...but I'm glad it's over."

"Amen, sister." Russ poked at one of the steaks with a long-handled fork and got quiet for a minute. "Tell me you're not the... possessive type, are you?"

She thought about telling him that werewolves, like their *lupine* cousins, mate only once and for life...but it was still too early in their relationship to get into all that family stuff, so she just gave him an "are you kidding" look and sniffed the air.

"Mmmmm...steaks smell done to me."

"Only if you like 'em red and runny."

"My favorite."

"Okay then." He slid the thicker of the two steaks onto her plate and grimaced. "Christ, I've seen cows hurt worse than that get better."

"Oh, ha-ha."

"Yes, well, just remember—you are what you eat."

Karin belched softly and smiled. "Not necessarily."

About the Author

P. D. Cacek originally aspired to be an actress, but her dreams were dashed when, while playing Dinosaur Number 1 in her high school's production of *By the Skin of Our Teeth*, she inadvertently crawled off the stage and landed in the orchestra pit. Dinosaur Number 1 died that night, but the experience put her on the significantly less perilous path of writing horror.

P. D. is the author of over 200 short stories, and has won both a World Fantasy Award and a Bram Stoker Award for her short fiction. She's written five novels: *Night Prayers*, *Canyons*, *Night Players*, *The Wind Caller*, and *The Selkie*.

"Horror is an emotion, something that reaches past all the barriers and finds the one dark corner of our self-image that has not grown up. Horror doesn't have to include dismemberments or gushing wounds or ancient demons dredged up by a new housing development. Anything, even a simple evening's walk, can be horrific if you look at it the right way…and I do."

Cacek's novel *Second Lives* will be coming out from Flame Tree Publishing, April 2019.

Find out more about P. D. Cacek at:
wikipedia.org/wiki/P._D._Cacek

Rites of Passage

Annie Reed

The creep sat crouched in the far corner of the abandoned processing plant smoking a cigarette. The tip flickered orange in the hulking dark, one small spot of smoldering warmth in the damp cold of a waterfront night.

Finn had given up cigarettes decades ago, but the old longing stole over him like it always did.

One more smoke for old time's sake, what could it hurt? He wanted the comfort of a lit cigarette held loosely between his index and middle fingers. The taste as the smoke rolled across his tongue. Wanted to feel the kind of heat that would fill his lungs over and over again until it killed him. Eventually.

The creep would give Finn a cigarette if he asked.

Creeps would give him anything if they thought Finn would let them live.

To his left, a wharf rat the size of an alley cat scuttled along the base of the plant's rust-stained concrete wall. The rat disappeared beneath a drift of trash, and insistent squeaks erupted from the garbage.

Finn could barely hear the rat's babies over the passing thrum of a heavy bass beat. A car sped past the front of the processing plant, fleeing a neighborhood no one should be driving through at this time of night.

The creep ignored the wharf rat. It sat on its scaly haunches, wings tucked in behind its back, blowing smoke out through its nostrils and making a show of ignoring Finn.

So that's the way the creep wanted to play it. Fine. Finn could play along.

For now.

He took a few more steps inside the processing plant, peering into the darkness for the first hints of eerie green light that would signal where the creep planned to bring its master into this world.

On another long-ago night, Finn had tracked a different creep to this building. Back then the processing plant had still been in operation. During the daylight hours, trucks loaded down with fish from the docks disgorged their cargo near where Finn now stood. Conveyor belts had carried the fish down the processing line where they were gutted and beheaded before they were processed for sale.

But once the sun set, the workers had gone home to their families. The few people left walking the street shivered when they passed the plant's battered exterior, no doubt imagining that the darkened windows along its sides were malevolent eyes that watched them hungrily.

They weren't far from wrong.

That night Finn had spotted a faint green light from outside the building. The creep had made no effort to hide what it was doing inside.

Finn had been much younger then. Maybe the creep had thought he would turn tail and run.

That was something Finn would never do. He knew what was at stake.

The creeps didn't belong to this world. They had been sent here to prepare the way for the invasion of Finn's world by their masters, massive monsters who would devour everything and everyone in their path.

The creeps had only one job—create a portal in this world, an anchor for one end of the passageway their masters used to invade new worlds.

Finn's job, and the job of others like him, was to stop them.

The only way to stop them was to kill them. Killing them interrupted the flow of dark magic the creeps used to fuel the portal.

And the only way to kill them was to cut off their heads.

The green light Finn had seen from outside the building signaled a location where the border between worlds was the thinnest, but the green light was only visible once a creep had started working on the portal. Even then, only a select few could see it.

Finn could. It was the first reason Finn had been chosen for this job.

But it was only one reason.

The creep that night had been crafty and more powerful than any creep Finn had encountered before. Instead of starting one portal, it was creating dozens.

Dozens of possible entry points, each one nearly complete.

Dozens of possible places where a monster could enter Finn's world.

The tactic had nearly worked.

Distracted by the sheer number of portals, Finn hadn't seen the creep dive at him from the pipework over his head.

The creeps had the shape of men, but that was where the resemblance ended. Their thick bodies were covered with scales the color of bilge water. Their arms were heavily muscled, their fingers tipped in razor-sharp talons. Their leathery wings were tipped with barbs. Except for their angry yellow eyes, they were nearly impossible to see in the dark.

The attack had come so fast, Finn had no chance to draw his blade. He had to dodge away from the dive-bombing nightmare instead.

He didn't quite make it.

The creep's talons missed his neck but ripped into his right arm instead.

Finn went sprawling on the dirty concrete floor. Pain shot down his arm and raced along his spine, hot white and urgent.

Before the creep could attack him again, Finn struggled to his feet and drew his katana in as smooth a move as his injured arm would allow. The damn creeps weren't stupid. They always got his blade arm first.

The creep propelled itself back to the ceiling, its heavy wings churning up a windstorm inside the plant. It taunted Finn with curses and promises of a long and painful death, but Finn focused on the creep's movements, not its words.

They had fought that night among the machines and the belts. Over the piles of entrails and fish heads, sending the scavenging wharf rats scurrying for safer ground.

Finn had ignored the way his own blood fell in thick splatters every time he swung his blade.

Ignored the bone-rattling thrumming coming from the dozens of portals.

Ignored the rumbling, grating laughter as the creep's master shoved its bulk through a passageway that had no right to exist.

Finn's injury had sapped his strength, but at last his blade found its mark. He'd put every spare ounce of strength he had left into the swing of his katana, and the creep's mottled head had separated cleanly from its shoulders.

When the creep died, the portals faded from existence—each and every one—as if they'd never existed at all.

Finn had allowed himself a grim smile when the creep's master screamed, the sound of its fury fading to a distant echo.

Stuck in the passageway with no place to go.

"Take that, monster," Finn had said, his voice little more than a hoarse whisper.

The scars on his shoulder from that long-ago encounter had faded. He had new ones to replace them, and when those faded, more would take their place.

He was a Guardian. Scars came with the job.

Ever since that night, Finn had checked the processing plant just in case another creep decided to try creating a portal there. Tonight was the first time he'd seen another creep inside.

The belts and machines and shipping crates that had cluttered the floor of the processing plant were gone now. The place was nothing more than a deserted building in a long row of deserted buildings in a part of town the city fathers didn't like to acknowledge existed. It still smelled of fish guts and seaweed and the oily murk that dripped off the overhead pipes.

Street gangs had claimed this place as their own. Graffiti marking their territory covered the walls. Only, in this part of town—the rough part of town—the goblins ran the gangs. Finn had recognized the runes they'd mixed in with the graffiti. Simple threshold wards, most of them.

Thresholds wards didn't work on someone like him. He'd broken through just by stepping inside.

Enough faint streetlight filtered through the filthy windows that Finn could see the creep still crouched in the corner. Its mottled, brackish face was surrounded by a thick cloud of cigarette smoke, but Finn caught no hint of green light.

The creep hadn't started a portal yet.

"Nice place you got here," Finn said. "Love what you've done with the décor."

The cigarette flared brighter, then the creep chuckled, a deep, throaty sound. "Only for you, asshole."

"I'm flattered."

The creep nodded its head. If it had been wearing a hat, it might have tipped it in Finn's direction.

In all his years as a Guardian—more years than Finn wanted to think about—creeps had never acted so nonchalant, not around him.

Another car drove by, its bass-heavy music rattling the windows. Different song, same beat. Finn preferred classic rock.

He moved closer, his katana a comforting weight in the sheath against his back.

"Got one of those for me?" he asked, pantomiming taking a drag off a cigarette.

The creep studied him for a moment before it shrugged and reached down beside itself toward the floor.

Finn tensed. He didn't draw his blade, not yet, but he had a feeling the creep had noticed his reaction.

He also had a feeling the creep was enjoying this.

Instead of drawing a weapon, the creep merely tossed a pack of cigarettes in Finn's direction. "Knock yourself out," it said.

The cigarettes landed on the floor a few inches in front of Finn. He didn't bend to pick them up, just arched an eyebrow at the creep.

"That's not very hospitable."

"My aim sucks," the creep said. "So sue me."

Finn ignored the cigarettes. He still didn't see any hint of green light, not even in the windows. Eyes might be the windows to the soul, as the old saying went, but real windows made for easy places to frame a portal to another world.

Or dozens of portals.

This whole thing was downright weird.

"So what's the deal?" Finn asked. "You're just hanging out, having a smoke?"

"No law against it," the creep said.

That wasn't quite true. While no laws prevented this world's magic folk from moving freely about the city—provided they didn't practice magic without the proper licenses and permits—the creeps weren't from this world.

The creeps were basically illegal aliens, and hostile ones at that. Finn was within his rights to kill them. He even had a license to prove it.

Take that, 007.

"No law against me taking your head," Finn said.

The creep went very still, the cigarette still in its mouth. Smoke swirled around its head. "You see a portal here?" it asked.

"You're here. That's all I need."

"Not very sporting of you. Guardian."

Outside another car drove past the plant. More window-rattling music. Finn was starting to yearn for a good Aerosmith song to break up the monotony.

He'd had enough of the creep, too. It was sparring with him. It might not have opened a portal yet, but it would. Finn had never met a creep who lived for anything else.

"Who said this was a sport?" Finn asked.

He started to draw his katana from its sheath when something popped behind him, and an unseen fist slammed into his left shoulder.

The impact nearly knocked him to his knees.

"We do, asshole."

The new voice came from a broken window in the back of the plant. The voice was grating and guttural and unmistakable.

A goblin.

Not only a goblin. A goblin with a gun.

How was that even possible?

The creep laughed as more guttural voices took up the words and turned them into a chant: "We do, asshole!"

Another pop.

Finn felt more than heard the bullet speed past his head.

He dove toward the closest wall, trying to make himself as small a target as possible. His injured shoulder was on fire.

In an instant he'd gone from hunter to hunted and being shot at by goblins with guns, his katana his only weapon.

Goblins who could see better in the dark than he could.

Goblins who knew as well as he did that in this empty shell of a building, he had nowhere to hide.

Sweat dripped down Finn's face. The garage didn't have air conditioning, just practice mats and an old-fashioned boom box currently belting out a song that must have been popular about a half century ago.

"I still don't know why we can't just shoot them," Finn said.

He'd been practicing with a katana for hours. The weapon was elegant and the blade incredibly sharp, but it seemed like such an old-fashioned, dangerous way to kill anything. With a katana, he had to get up close. A bullet could kill from a distance. The creeps weren't fairies, so why couldn't he shoot them?

Finn's master gave him an indulgent look. "You telling me your lily-white ass is too good to learn the blade?"

Movies always portrayed martial arts masters as tiny, wizened old Asian men. Finn's master was a powerful black man who'd been born in the Deep South. He was well over six feet tall. His shoulders were massive, his legs heavily muscled, and his tattooed skin deeply scarred from surviving battles with the things Finn was still training to kill.

"I'm saying there's got to be a better way to do it," Finn said.

His master laughed. "Maybe someday you'll find it. You live long enough, that is."

He made a circular movement with one hand.

Finn had seen the gesture often enough. Keep going.

His shoulders ached, but he went back to practicing the latest kata his master had given him. At least it wasn't "wax on, wax off."

Before he'd met the real-life version of Mr. Miyagi, Finn used to spend his time doing things normal seventeen-year-olds did. Hanging out with friends at the mall. Going to movies. Convincing some girl to let him feel her up in the back seat of a friend's car. Finn had especially liked that one.

Now he spent all his free time learning how to kill monsters.

With a katana.

Sometimes life was just surreal.

His life had turned into a never-ending episode of *The Twilight Zone* the moment he'd seen his master kill one of those monsters.

He'd been out past curfew with one of his buddies. They'd been drinking beer and lost track of time. His buddy's car had the kind of muffler you could hear a mile away. The last thing Finn had wanted was to get caught coming home late with beer on his breath, so his buddy had dropped Finn off on the other side of the field behind his neighborhood.

A twenty minute walk and Finn would be able to climb through his bedroom window with his parents none the wiser.

He'd done it before. He had no doubt he'd be doing it again before he got out of high school and left his parents and this boring-ass neighborhood behind.

The field was empty except for a few cows and a weathered old lean-to that had definitely seen better days. A quarter moon hung high overhead in the cloudless midnight sky. Finn could see just well enough to avoid stepping in cow shit, another thing he needed to avoid in order to successfully sneak into his own room.

The lean-to sat almost precisely in the center of the field. Walled in on three sides, it had to be at least twice as big as the garage at home and nearly two stories tall. Finn had no idea what it had been built for. Whenever he cut through the field, the lean-to was always empty. It sure made a good landmark, though. His street dead-ended almost directly behind the lean-to's back wall.

Finn always thought the lean-to might be a good place to hang out with his buddies when they wanted someplace private to drink since it was always empty.

Except that night the lean-to wasn't empty.

An unearthly glow filled it. The glow wasn't bright like neon signs, but more like what the glow-in-the-dark stars he had on the ceiling of his bedroom looked like once he turned out the lights at night.

And, bathed by that eerie light, a tall black man was fighting a creature that looked like it had crawled out of someone's nightmare.

The creature was shaped like a man, but it was taller than any man Finn had ever seen. It had huge leathery wings and rough-looking skin, and the fingers on its hands were long and came to sharp points.

The man's only weapon against this thing was a sword. An honest-to-God sword!

Finn was fascinated. Maybe he was just drunk enough to forget that this wasn't a movie, or maybe something else drew him in, but he didn't run away.

Instead, he moved toward the battle.

Everyone knew magical creatures existed in the world. How magical beings finally integrated with the human world after centuries of remaining deliberately hidden was a part of both his history and government classes.

It was a whole different thing to actually see one.

Finn had never seen a magical creature. None of the fairies or elves or gnomes he read about lived in Finn's neighborhood. None went to his school. He'd never even seen one at the mall. One of his buddies said his dad worked for an elf, but that was it.

Finn and his buddies and everyone else he knew was human. Plain old regular people without an ounce of magical ability.

Not like the man fighting the monster.

This guy jumped higher and faster than Finn thought a regular person could. Each sweep of his sword looked effortless. He did the kind of martial arts moves Finn had only seen in the movies. He wouldn't have even seemed human except for the sheen of sweat on his bald head.

The creature didn't sweat. Instead it puffed out huge clouds of breath in the chill night air. It didn't look like a dragon exactly, even though Finn was pretty sure what he'd thought was rough skin was really scales, but those steamy breaths reminded him of smoke.

Could this creature breathe fire?

If it could, how cool was that!

Finn forgot all about how he needed to get home before his parents noticed he wasn't there. He forgot about his buddies. He even forgot about the girl he'd been thinking about asking out.

He felt like his entire world—the real world, not the world of movies or textbooks or things that happened to someone else's dad—had just gotten bigger.

It was the most exciting thing Finn had ever felt.

Which was why, he told himself later, he didn't think twice about jumping into the middle of the fight when the creature knocked the man flat on his back and his sword went flying.

And landed right at Finn's feet.

The goblins could have killed Finn several times over by now. He had no defense against bullets. The fact that he was still alive meant they were playing with him.

Like cats playing with a mouse.

Finn didn't like being a mouse, but at the moment he didn't have much of a choice.

The goblins had pinned him down against the front wall, where he was in clear view from the goblins' position at the back of the processing plant. Bullets struck the concrete floor in front of him every time he tried to move. His shoulder throbbed where he'd been shot. His arm on that side—thankfully not his sword arm—was useless, and his head felt wobbly.

He'd never been shot before, but he'd been hurt enough over the years to know his body was going into shock. Even if he could get away from the wall, he wouldn't be able to run very fast, if at all.

Add to that the fact that the interior of the plant offered exactly zero places to hide, and Finn knew he was in the worst position he'd ever been in since he'd become a Guardian.

He could very well die here tonight, and all because he hadn't simply killed the creep the moment he'd walked into the processing plant and been done with it.

He closed his eyes for a moment. Thinking about what-ifs really would get him killed.

He had to center his mind on the here and now.

Had to get the job done.

Somehow.

At least he didn't have to be quiet. The goblins knew exactly where he was.

"You invited your friends to the party?" Finn asked the creep.

"Happy coincidence," the creep said.

Finn didn't believe it. The creep had been counting on the goblins to show up. That's why it had been biding its time.

He'd been stupid, all right.

His master had been stupid, too, the night he died.

The creep stood up and crushed the remains of its last cigarette beneath one massive foot. It lumbered to the nearest window and began to etch a circle in the filthy glass with its claws.

The sound grated on Finn's nerves. Worse than fingernails on a chalkboard because he knew exactly what the creep was doing.

It was creating a portal for its master.

Finn had to figure out a way to stop it.

The sound of a heavy body smacking against concrete drew his attention away from the creep.

The goblins were coming through the windows at the rear of the plant.

Finn had never liked goblins. Their greenish-gray skin looked diseased. Their feet and hands were too big for their bodies. Their over-sized, pointed ears stuck out like bat wings from either side of elongated skulls complete with heavy brow ridges and stunted, malformed noses that looked like a human's nose, half rotted away.

Maybe those noses were the reason goblins didn't mind the stench from their unwashed clothes. Or maybe it was the things they ate. Goblins also didn't care how long the things they ate had been dead.

From where he sat, Finn could make out the strips of colored cloth wrapped around their wrists.

Great. Just great.

Not only were his attackers goblins, they were gang members.

The processing plant must be their territory.

And he was smack in the middle of it without their permission.

Finn wondered what the creep had given the gang in return for allowing it to use their turf to create its portal. Maybe the creep had promised that its master would grant the gang favors once it arrived.

If so, the gang was about to be deeply disappointed.

The Elder Gods did not keep promises made by their minions to vermin that inhabited a world the Gods intended to conquer.

Finn didn't know for sure that the monsters the creeps served were the Elder Gods of myth. But the more he'd studied the creeps—and the more he learned from the ones who'd begged for their lives before he killed them—he believed their masters were the massive, terrible creatures men mistook as Gods in ancient myths and stories handed down through the ages.

He also believed that at least one of them had made its way through a portal to this world, and found it a tasty treat indeed.

Otherwise why would the monsters keep trying to come back?

The goblins congregated at the far end of the building as if they couldn't decide what to do. Finn counted nine of them.

On a good day he could handle nine goblins. Even on a bad day he could hold his own against that many with only a few minor injuries and maybe a broken bone or two to show for it.

But never, even on his worst day, had he ever gone up against nine goblins armed with guns.

Steel was poison to fairies and goblins and their kin. Just picking up a gun should have caused the goblins incapacitating pain, much less holding one long enough to fire it with any precision.

And at least one of these goblins was a precision shooter.

The shots that had kept Finn pinned down had been placed in exactly the right spots to prevent him from running for a window or back toward the open bay door he'd used to enter the plant. But none of the shots had come close enough to actually hit him.

Which meant that the gunshot to his shoulder hadn't been an accident. The shooter had wanted to wound him—to incapacitate him—but not kill him.

The goblins probably wanted him alive so they could present him to the creep's master.

But then why not shoot him in his sword arm?

He'd gone for his katana right before he'd been shot. The shooter should have known which arm to take out of commission.

Just like the guns, this made no sense.

An eerie green light started to emanate from the circle the creep had etched in the windowpane. It threw a ghoulish aura over the interior of the plant.

"I've always wanted to kill a master," Finn said to the creep.

The only response Finn got was a grunt. Apparently the time for distracting the creep by insulting it or its master was long past.

Too bad. Finn had some good insults lined up.

He watched the creep slice open its wrist. Blood that looked black in the greenish light seeped out of the wound.

The creep dipped a claw from its other hand into the blood and began to draw symbols on the glass.

The goblins hooted and screeched with glee. They must have felt the same energy in the air that Finn did.

The use of dark magic always gave Finn chills, but the goblins apparently enjoyed it. They scrabbled toward the window, all but two of them walking with their backs hunched forward, as if invisible weights were tied around their necks.

The other two had to be the leaders of this particular gang. They stood with their backs straight and looked down their stubby, misshapen noses at where Finn sat leaning against the wall. Both had stringy hair that hung nearly to their waists. Finn was surprised to see that one of them was female.

Both of them held what looked like white plastic toy guns in their hands. Only, Finn knew they weren't toys.

The female goblin gestured at Finn. "Stand up," she said. "You're in the presence of Ooveth."

He didn't move. "You say that like I'm supposed to be impressed."

She shot a chunk of concrete out of the wall two inches to the left of Finn's temple.

"I won't tell you twice," she said.

Finn stood.

He'd just found out what he needed to know.

Ooveth and the female goblin were the only ones with guns, but she was the one assigned to keep the prisoner in line. That made her the precision shooter.

The other gang members carried weapons that were more in line with what Finn was used to. Knives with thick wooden handles to keep the steel blades away from their skin. Chunks of concrete fastened to wooden handles, the modern version of an old-fashioned stone club. Spears with obsidian points, the tips no doubt dipped in poison.

If Finn could draw the katana strapped to his back, he could take them all out.

If he hadn't been wounded, that was.

The female goblin gestured at Finn again, this time with her gun. She wanted him to stand in front of the male goblin.

Finn obliged. No point in getting shot again for no good reason.

The gang's leader had the kind of face that not even a mother could love. His teeth were too big for his mouth, twisting his lips into a permanent sneer. Chunks of flesh had been ripped from the ear on the right side of his head. Together with his flat skull and dull, yellow eyes, the damaged ear made him look like an alley cat who'd lost one too many fights.

A not-very-bright alley cat.

"Ooveth, I presume," Finn said.

Ooveth hit him across the face. The goblin's hand was as big as Finn's head, and the blow hurt like hell.

This night just kept getting better and better.

"You're in my territory," Ooveth said. "You will show me respect."

"You want me to kneel?"

Another blow rocked Finn's head in the other direction.

Ooveth had anger management issues. Finn might be able to use that if the goblin didn't knock his head off first.

A deep thrumming filled the building, a sound like a subterranean jet airplane getting ready for takeoff. Finn felt the vibrations in his bones.

An instant later the greenish flight from the window turned bright, hot white.

Instead of filthy glass, the window now framed a rip in reality. Light so bright it hurt Finn to look at poured through the rip.

Something moved inside that light, making it ripple and writhe like a living thing.

The creep had managed to finish the portal. Its master was in the passageway, mere steps from breaking into this world.

Finn was out of time.

"We're all going to die here," he said to Ooveth. "I don't know what kind of deal you made, but the thing coming through that portal won't care."

Ooveth wasn't paying attention to Finn anymore. The goblin was staring into the light. He looked like he was experiencing the rapture.

Instead of responding to what Finn said, Ooveth waved his massive hand at his female lieutenant. "Take care of this annoyance," he said.

She tilted her head. The intense light had washed out the greenish-gray color of her skin. Except for her prominent brow and misshapen nub of a nose, she almost looked human.

She raised her white plastic gun and pointed it at Finn.

"Duck," she said.

From the moment Finn passed his driver's test, his dad had told him, over and over again, that drunk driving would get him killed.

"And don't you let any of your buddies drive you when they're drunk," his dad always said. "I used to be a teenager once too, you know."

At this point in the tirade Finn's dad would point a finger at him, and Finn would sigh. He knew what was coming.

"You're just lucky I survived my teenage years," his dad would say. "Otherwise you wouldn't be around to look at me like I'm crazy."

Finn didn't think his dad was crazy. He also didn't like thinking about what his parents had done to bring him into existence. He didn't know any teenager who did.

He always got out of the conversation by assuring his dad he wouldn't drive drunk.

Too bad his dad never warned him about drunken sword fighting.

When the creature had knocked the long, curved blade out of the man's hand, Finn hadn't thought twice about picking it up.

He'd never held a sword before, but this one felt like a natural extension of his arm.

But more than that, it felt like it belonged in his hand.

Whether it was the sword or the beer, Finn suddenly felt like he could defeat anything.

Even the winged creature charging at him.

"Future Guardian," it said, its gleeful voice raspy but clearly understandable. "Tonight I kill two. What a present for my master."

Finn had been about to swing for the fences when he hesitated.

What in the world was a future guardian?

That hesitation could have cost him his life if the man hadn't knocked him out of the way.

"Get the fuck out of here, kid!" he yelled. "And give me back my blade!"

The creature's claws slashed at the air where Finn had stood a moment ago.

Finn handed over the sword and tried to get out of the way. His feet didn't seem to want to work right, like he'd lost any coordination he might have once had along with the sword. He fell in a disjoined heap on the dirt floor of the lean-to.

Right next to the raging battle.

Up close, the creature smelled like a combination of cigarettes and the rotten stench of sulfur. The claws on its feet and hands were tipped with razor-sharp talons. Scales that glistened wetly in the eerie light covered its body instead of clothes. It had yellow eyes in a face that looked entirely too human for comfort, like someone had crossed a lizard with a man.

The man could have been a badass fighter in a *Shaft* movie. He wore a black leather jacket and black jeans and heavy black boots. The backs of his hands were covered with scars, and a long scar ran down one side of his face from his ear to the corner of his mouth. The edge of a tattoo was visible on one side of his neck.

And he knew more martial arts moves than Bruce Lee.

One of those moves brought the sword straight down at—and through—the creature's arm at the wrist.

Its severed hand hit the ground next to Finn. He scrabbled backwards away from the hand just in case that thing could come at him on its own. It would be about as logical as anything else that had happened to him that night.

The creature bellowed as blood poured from the stump where its hand had been. It lunged at the man, but he slid to the ground beneath it, the sword held up in front of him.

The creature couldn't stop in time. Even though its leathery wings flapped in what Finn thought was an attempt to put on the brakes, the creature impaled itself on the sword.

The man used the creature's weight to flip it over his head. It landed in a boneless heap on the far side of the lean-to.

Finn let out the breath he hadn't realized he was holding. He scrambled to his feet, ready to congratulate the man, when he noticed the creature was getting to its feet as well.

"Not good enough, Guardian," it said.

The man rolled to his feet. He didn't look surprised.

The creature lumbered toward him as blood the color of midnight gushed from its wounded chest.

The man didn't wait for the creature to reach him. He ran toward it, swinging the sword in a graceful, deadly arc.

This time the creature's head hit the ground next to Finn.

He yelped and jumped away.

The eerie glow in the lean-to winked out of existence, plunging the field into sudden darkness.

Finn stood rock still as he waited for his eyes to adjust. He figured by the time he could see again, he'd be alone in the lean-to wondering if what he'd just seen was a very vivid drunken dream. If that was the case, he might never drink another beer again.

To his surprise, once he could see well enough to get his bearings, the man and the decapitated creature were still there. The quarter moon gave off just enough light to let Finn see the carnage.

"That," Finn said, his voice a mere ghost of its usual self, "was messy."

The man nodded. "Cut off the head. Only way to kill these suckers." He pointed at Finn with his index finger in an eerie but unmistakable impersonation of Finn's dad. "That's lesson number one."

Finn blinked. "Lesson?" he said.

"You saw the green light, right?" the man asked. "Before you decided to go all Dirty Harry on me?"

Finn nodded, even though Dirty Harry used a gun—a big one—not a sword.

"Most people don't," the man said. "Or even if they do, they tell themselves they don't so they don't have to get involved. You? You waded right on in."

He took a rag from an inside pocket of his jacket and began to wipe down his sword. Finn heard a cow grunt as it settled down for the night, and one of the neighborhood dogs started barking its fool head off, as his dad would say.

A dose of normal with the weird. Yeah, this night was real Twilight Zone material.

"We got a lot to talk about," the man said, his attention on the blade. "If you decide to do what you were born to do, that is."

"You mean, kill those things?"

According to his dad, all Finn had been born to do was be a pain in the ass.

"They're called 'creeps,' and yes, I mean kill them." The man shrugged, still not looking at him. "Takes years of training until you're good enough. You up for it?"

Finn remembered how natural the sword had felt in his hand, like a part of him that he hadn't known was missing.

"Will I get my own sword?"

The question earned him a snort and the ghost of a grin. "It's called a 'katana,' and yes. Once you earn it."

Finn thought about it. Could he kill something? Kill more than one somethings? He'd never gone hunting in his life, and he hadn't liked it the one time his dad had taken him fly fishing.

Then again, the fish had never tried to disembowel him.

"Those things," Finn said. "The creeps. They're bad, aren't they?"

"So are the things that sent them here. The worst." The man finally looked up from the clean katana and stared at Finn, all traces of humor gone from his expression. "It's a hard life. A lonely life, but I like to think that everybody's lives are worth defending at any cost. That's what's at stake here."

A chill ran down Finn's spine. Everybody's lives. His parents. His buddies. The girl he wanted to ask to the movies.

And he could make a difference?

He could save them from a threat they didn't even know about?

And probably wouldn't believe if he tried to tell them.

How could he live with himself if he didn't at least try?

He felt more grown up than he ever had before, even the first time that he got behind the wheel of his parents' car for the first time, brand new license in his wallet, without his dad in the car to supervise.

"Okay," Finn said. "Count me in."

The man held out his hand and Finn took it.

"Welcome to the Guardians," Finn's new master said.

Finn's years of training as a Guardian had been long and hard. He'd built muscles he hadn't known he had. Learned martial arts kicks that threatened to split his groin in two. Developed calluses on calluses until his feet looked like old shoe leather, and he didn't even get a nifty uniform out of the deal.

But the most important thing he'd learned, especially when he was still an apprentice, was to follow commands without question.

One of those commands was "duck!"

When the female goblin told Finn to duck, he didn't hesitate.

He dropped to the dirty floor of the abandoned processing plant at her feet, and she shot Ooveth right between his stupid yellow eyes.

The gang leader hit the floor like a bag of rotten meat. Thick black blood bubbled up from the wound in his forehead, hissing and spitting like his brain inside was boiling.

"What the hell?" Finn said.

Lead bullets, no matter how they were jacketed, didn't kill goblins any more than they did fairies.

Or creeps, for that matter.

Finn should know. He'd tried more than once over the years. The best he'd done was blow a creep's arm off with a .50 caliber handgun. He'd still had to cut off the creep's head with his blade to prevent it from completing its portal.

Even a shot to the head shouldn't have killed Ooveth, but he was clearly dead.

"Special bullets," the female goblin said.

The remaining gang members turned on her. She took out four of them before her gun clicked on empty.

"I could use a little help here," she said to Finn.

He lunged to his feet and drew his katana in a move that wasn't quite as smooth as it should have been.

He ignored the floaty feeling in his head. Yes, he'd lost a lot of blood, but he wasn't finished yet.

He'd taken out two of the three remaining goblins by the time the female goblin had retrieved Ooveth's gun. She shot the last goblin in the back of its head as it ran away from her.

The floor trembled beneath Finn's feet.

The creep had fallen to its knees, its head pressed to the garbage-strewn concrete.

It was in prayer, Finn realized. A supplicant praying to its master.

Finn squinted at the portal.

Something was coming through. Something massive.

A monster from Finn's worst nightmare was pulling itself through the portal on thick, muscular appendages. Finn refused to think of them as tentacles. They were more than that. They were almost alive on their own.

The appendages seemed to scent the air. The window frame surrounding the portal. The filthy floor. They left wet, slimy trails wherever they went, and the trails hissed like acid.

Finn realized he'd been standing like he was rooted to the spot.

Watching one of the Elder Gods being born into this world instead of trying to stop it.

That was his second mistake of the night. One mistake was all it had taken to kill his old master.

But Finn could still stop this. All he had to do to was cut off the creep's head.

He tried to run toward the creep, but he'd lost too much blood. The fight with the goblins, as brief as it had been, had taken too much out of him. The most he could manage was a staggering walk.

He wouldn't reach the creep in time.

The female goblin was on her way toward the back of the building. Finn didn't trust her, but he had no other choice.

"Could use a little help here!" Finn shouted after her.

She turned around. He could see the indecision on her face.

"If we don't stop this, we're all going to die," Finn said.

He had no idea if she'd heard him. His voice was losing strength too.

She raised the plastic gun. It made a ridiculously small popping noise when she pulled the trigger.

A hole the size of a dime appeared in the side of the creep's head.

The creep's body stiffened as the blood dripping from the hole in its head bubbled and hissed just like Ooveth's had. Its feet hammered at the floor as its wings flapped uselessly, and then it was still.

She'd actually killed the thing.

Finn had to get himself one of those guns.

The creep's master bellowed in rage. The appendages that weren't tentacles writhed as the brilliant white light started to dim.

But the portal didn't wink out of existence.

The monster was still coming through.

Finn summoned strength he didn't have to spare. He staggered up to the dead creep and decapitated it where it lay.

His katana rang as it hit the concrete beneath the creep. The cut was straight and true, but the portal still didn't close.

One of the master's appendages reached Finn.

The monster struck Finn square across his body. He felt a rib break, and then he was sailing through the air.

Something else broke when he landed.

He hoped it wasn't his back.

One of the master's eyes was visible now. As big as Finn's entire body, the eye glared at him from inside the portal with a triumphant, vicious insanity.

Finn had lost.

All of his years of training had been for nothing.

His parents would die. His friends would die. All of the women he'd longed for but never had time to meet would die.

All because he had lost.

He dimly heard the female goblin empty her gun into the monster, but the shots had no effect.

"Give me your blade," she said.

She was standing next to him. When had that happened?

He looked down at his good hand. He was still gripping his katana.

"You wanted my help," she said, her voice a near growl. "Give me the damn blade!"

He handed it over.

He thought she'd handle the katana carefully. The sharp steel could kill her just by touching her skin. But she grabbed the long handle with the kind of ease that made her look like she'd been wielding his sword her entire life.

Goblins were naturally stronger and faster than humans. Finn had always thought they were also far less graceful.

Watching the female goblin fight the monster, he realized he'd been wrong.

She fought as well, if not better, than his old master. She sprinted around the edges of the portal, deftly avoiding the grasping appendages and the slime trails on the floor. She hooted and yelled at the monster in a language Finn didn't understand, and he realized it was her battle cry.

Whenever she had an opening, she attacked an appendage with the blade.

Each slice made the master roar. When she finally managed to sever an appendage completely, the entire building shook with the volume of the master's bellow.

The monster's anger only seemed to spur her on.

Finn lost track of her individual moves. She was a blur against the fading light of the portal, a busy stinging hornet who knew she had her prey on the run.

She cut and sliced and sprinted away, laughing and chattering at her foe.

She was magnificent, a warrior like none Finn had ever seen.

And when she thrust the katana deep into the monster's mad eye, he knew she'd done something he'd never had.

She'd defeated an Elder God.

She yanked his blade out of the mess of blood and ichor that had been the monster's eye just as it pulled back into the portal, drawing its wounded appendages after itself.

The brilliant light turned sickly green, and then it was gone, leaving only a filthy, cracked window behind.

The goblin trotted across the floor to lay the katana at his side. She wasn't even breathing hard.

"You should keep it," Finn said. "You earned it."

She shook her head. "Pretty poison is still poison, but thanks for letting me try it."

He got the feeling she liked to try all sorts of things.

She picked up the empty plastic gun he'd dropped at his feet.

"What are those things?" he asked.

"Haven't you heard?" She gave him a wicked grin as she slipped the gun through a loop on her leather belt. "Human technology. You creatures can print almost anything these days, given the right incentive."

Finn thought he understood. "And the bullets?"

Her grin got wider. "My little secret."

One of those secret bullets had taken out a creep. That was impressive.

He'd always wanted to kill a creep with a gun. Maybe someday she'd let him use one of hers.

The thought made Finn pause.

He was getting up there in years. He'd made mistakes tonight. Those mistakes would have been fatal if he hadn't stumbled into the middle of a goblin gangland coup d'état.

Or had he stumbled into it?

What if fate had sent the female goblin into this building tonight, just as it had sent him to walk through a field on the night he was destined to meet his own master?

He'd never taken an apprentice before. He hadn't had the stomach for it after his own master died. It was time. Hell, it was long past time.

She turned away from him. The gun on her hip made her look like a parody of the cowboys in the old Westerns his dad had liked so much.

"More of those things are out there," Finn said to her back. "You could learn how to fight them."

"Learn?" Her voice had an edge as sharp as his katana. "I kicked its slimy ass, human." She turned to glare at him. "Better than what you did."

"You had just shot me," Finn said. "You weren't exactly seeing me at my best."

She stared at him for a long moment. Finn could see her working things through in her mind. She'd killed the rest of her gang. That might buy her respect among the other goblin gangs, but that respect would be short-lived.

"What's your name?" he asked.

"Keesa." She bit the word off like she hated it. "Why?"

He tried to smile, but he was pretty sure it came out a grimace. Every part of his body hurt. Guardians weren't super human. He was going to need medical attention, and soon.

"I'm Finn."

"Finn," she said. "Stupid human name."

"It's what I've got." He held up a hand. "Think you can give me an assist?"

She started to reach for him but stopped a split-second before their fingers touched. "You even think about calling yourself my master, you can forget about the whole thing. I've seen those movies."

He didn't let himself laugh. It wasn't easy.

"How about partner instead?"

She pulled him to his feet. He gritted his teeth against the pain, but it all seemed to come from his ribs, not his back.

She let go of his hand like it burned her. "You assume a hell of a lot, you know that?"

Finn's old master had assumed a hell of a lot, too. Not that he'd been wrong.

Finn didn't think he was wrong about Keesa. She had all the energy and passion he'd lost during the years he'd spent killing more creeps than he could count.

His master had been right. The life of a Guardian was a hard life. A lonely life, especially the way he'd lived it, but maybe it didn't have to be. Apprentices eventually left their masters behind. Partners didn't have to say goodbye to each other.

"You'll learn to love that about me," he told his new apprentice.

She snorted. "Arrogant, too. Have I told you that I hate humans?"

She hadn't, but Finn didn't mind. She could hate him all she wanted. He didn't like goblins much either.

Great partnerships had started with far less.

About the Author

A frequent contributor to the Fiction River anthologies and *Pulp-house Fiction Magazine*, Annie Reed's recent work includes the urban fantasy mystery novels *Unbroken Familiar* and *Iris & Ivy*, and the near-future science fiction short novel *In Dreams*. Annie's also one of the founding members of the innovative Uncollected Anthology, a series of themed urban fantasy stories published three times a year written by some of the best writers working today.

Annie's full-length novels include the Abby Maxon private investigator novels *Pretty Little Horses* and *Paper Bullets*, the Jill Jordan mystery *A Death in Cumberland*, and the suspense novel *Shadow Life*, written under the name Kris Sparks, as well as numerous other projects she can't wait to get to.

Find out more about Annie at:
annie-reed.com

Beach Comber

Sèphera Girón

Ten-year-old Isidora walked along the beach, the early morning dawn spilling across the sand and the fallen branches strewn from the previous night's storm. The sounds of the stormy night still haunted her as she picked her way through sea-weed and other debris. The howl of the wind had been worse than ever that night, or perhaps she had just been awake for more of it than usual. However, it was nothing compared to Hurricane Maria, which had hit Puerto Rico in 2017. But perhaps it was because of that earlier, devastating hurricane that any storm was upsetting.

There was more of the ocean on the beach than in the ocean itself, this low tide. She hummed away the last of the creepy night terrors, hoping that her mama might find some clams or oysters to eat, and that she could find something cool to sell to Diago who ran the beach-comber trading post.

Many of the other islanders had the same idea as they bustled to the bare mud of the exposed undersea with pails and shovels.

You never knew what was glittering in the sand until you pulled it out and brought it home, her daddy used to say, back before the hurricane had swept him away. Life before the hurricane had hit Puerto Rico had been hard, but her daddy had provided for the family. Now it was up to Isidora to help Mama and her little brothers.

Isidora went far from the others, knowing that she would be of little help to her family in the race for what few edibles the sea had coughed up. She was looking for something different.

She swung her basket and climbed over several rocks. There was a pocket in the rocks. She'd had good luck in this crevice before. She couldn't always get to it, as the tides were fickle and sometimes didn't go down far or long enough during her allotted treasure-hunting time.

She climbed along the sharp edges of the rock, barnacles cutting her hands, seaweed causing her to slip and slide several times.

She found crevices where she'd had good luck before in finding washed-up jewelry, fish, and other useful items. Her sneakers sloshed in the swill of the muddy sand. It was her bowl. Her own personal treasure chest.

What do you have hidden in here for me today?

She put down her basket and took out the pail inside. It held a small rake and tiny shovel. She learned long ago not to dig in the mud with her bare hands. There were too many sharp, broken clam shells that sliced up her fingers. The same went with her feet. Many things were buried in the sand and most of them weren't good.

The sand fleas had already found her and begun their vampiric breakfast. She swatted with one hand and lightly scraped the rake along the sludge with the other.

The rake hit something firm. Something not sand. Isidora smiled. She put her finger in the rake tracks to touch the object, making sure it wasn't just a hard clump of mud. She dug her finger around a bit. The object had a long, smooth shape. Very long. Longer than her hand, nearly halfway up her forearm.

She carefully and slowly ran the rake along the sand around the object. Sweat dripped down her face. Salt from her self and the air stung her eyes.

She wiggled the object from either side with both hands. She rocked it back and forth and finally pulled out a long, smooth grey rock. She rolled it in the seawater pooled in another bowl among the rocks. The rock had strange patterns on it. The weight was odd in her hands. It was heavier on one end than the other.

Was it an egg?

It was far too big for the pail. She carefully placed it into the basket. The egg was large, much larger than her hands, larger than both her hands put together. What kind of egg was it? It was much too large to belong to any bird she'd ever seen. It didn't look like any of the snake eggs she'd seen in her life. Too big for caiman. Gators weren't likely to lay eggs in the ocean. And these were far too big and the wrong shape for tortoises.

Isidora poked around the mud some more and dug up another huge egg.

She lined the knapsack and the basket with seaweed so that the eggs wouldn't bounce around too much as she made her way back across the rocks and past the beach combers.

The air was so thick, so hot; a damp, humid heat that rose from fallen brush and muddy trail and beamed down from the sky.

Isidora reached the trading post just as Diago returned from his lunch. He opened the door with his key and then propped it open to entice customers. Isidora went over to the counter. Diago was about to step behind it. Then he stopped.

"What do you have today, dear Isi?" he asked as she put her heavy basket on the ground.

She opened the lid and pulled back the seaweed. "I found this egg. It's a magic egg. Maybe a fossil egg from a pterodactyl."

Diago peered down. "An egg? That big? No, it's likely a rock."

"No, Diago. Touch it. Hold it. It's not a rock."

Diago bent down and touched the egg. He stroked it gently with his finger. "Huh." He picked it up. He held it up to the light. "It's an egg all right. Not sure what kind. Might make a good dinner."

"Dinner?"

"You eat eggs, don't you?"

"Well, yeah, but..."

"An egg's an egg," Diago sighed. "This one is one."

"I was hoping you'd buy it, sell it..."

"No. I have no use for eggs. Is that all you have for me today?" Diago fussed with some small statues on a shelf.

"I...I...Good-bye, Diago," Isidora whispered as she covered up the egg in its seaweed blanket

Isidora slowly walked home, disappointed that she hadn't been able to trade her findings. The waves rolled around her, a steady, unending crash and pull. Above the sound of the waves was a distant screeching noise. Isidora looked back to see what it was but saw nothing. A shadow swept across her face, the beach, but when she looked up, she only saw distant birds circling. And then the distant screeching noise once more.

Her mother was sitting in the only good chair in the living room when Isidora got home. The little hut was still a disaster. The bamboo walls were slanted, the roof still leaked despite thatch and palm leaves constantly being woven into it. Rebuilding from the hurricane had been slow. Most of the island was in a similarly bad state.

"Mama! Look what I found!" Isidora said as she dragged in the basket, pushing away the seaweed.

Mama looked sleepily up from her chair. "What is it, my child?"

"Eggs! I found eggs for us for dinner."

Mama fanned herself as she stood. She stretched, then sighed, as if she were carrying far more weight on her shoulders than merely her own self. "You and your treasures. What do we have here today?"

"No treasures, mama. Food. We're having food." Isidora triumphantly held up one of the eggs.

"Oh, my goodness. Where did you find such a huge egg? I don't think I've ever seen such a thing."

"Me neither, Mama. But I have two, ready to eat. Dinner or breakfast." Isidora pulled the other egg out of her knapsack.

"But are they fresh? Are they good to eat? Where did you find them?"

"They were in the rocks at low tide. Maybe a tortoise or something?"

"Maybe." Mama took a giant bowl down from one of the kitchen shelves and picked up one of the eggs. "Heavy. But not heavy like a rock. You might be right that these are eggs."

"Diago said they are eggs."

"He wouldn't buy them?"

"No. He didn't want them."

"Hmmm," Mama said as she carried the egg out the door.

"Where are you going, mama?"

"I'm going to open the egg outside. Just in case."

"In case of what?"

"In case it's rotten. There's no way to get rid of the smell if it's rotten."

Isidora followed her mother outside and down the short path to the spot where they slaughtered chickens so that they would be some ways from the house when they died. Mama cracked the egg into the bowl while Isidora stood by and watched. As the contents of the egg hit the bowl with an audible slosh and splat, Mama wrinkled her forehead.

"What is it, Mama?" Isidora asked.

"Something strange about this egg."

"I don't smell anything, Mama. At least, nothing different than the usual smells."

"No, it isn't rotten, I don't think, but I don't know what it is." Mama stared into the bowl.

There was no egg yolk, just a bunch of slimy goo with a little snake or maybe it was a lizard inside. An embryo.

"Is it a caiman?" Isidora asked.

The creature made no movement in the ooze.

"No." Mama poked it with a stick. "It's dead, whatever it was. I'm sure the other is the same."

"We can't cook it?"

"I don't think so. I'm not going to risk it. Not with the nearest hospital still without power. If we get food poisoning, we're on our own."

"What should I do with it? Or the other egg?"

"You can throw them away or put that other egg back."

Isidora thought about putting the other egg back where it still might be able to hatch, but the sun was high in the sky now. The heat of the day was upon them. It was time to do indoor chores, as they used less energy than working out in the sun. Maybe she'd put it back the next morning. She hauled the unbroken egg into her room. She went back and took the bowl with the dead embryo into her room as well. She wasn't sure why she wanted to look at it anymore. But she didn't want it cooking out in the heat of the sun, either.

Isidora helped Mama sweep the dirt floor as much as she could. She remembered a time when the floor had been white, and Mama had proudly scrubbed it with lemon water nearly every day. But the storm had spilled the island's outside into their inside and no amount of lemon water would make it clean.

As night fell, Isidora went to her room and fussed with her egg. If they still had Hydro for electricity, she could put it under a light to keep it warm like its mama would have done but there had been no Hydro in months. The glow of the full moon filled her room.

Isidora wrapped the egg in a blanket and put it into a basket in her closet.

She looked at the bowl with the dead embryo in it. She poked it a bit with a stick and it swirled around the bowl. It seemed to twitch. She even thought its eye blinked. She knew she'd have to throw it out eventually, but for now it was kind of cool to look at.

But the thing would never get to live. Because they had opened the egg. Tears welled up in her eyes. "I'm sorry, egg-thing. I didn't mean to kill you."

Mama would have a fit if she knew Isadora had brought the bowl with the dead egg back into the house, so she covered it up and slid it into the closet.

"Good night, egg and egg-thing!" she whispered as she slid the door shut and hopped into bed. She turned off the flashlight. The moon was very full and very bright.

She was dreaming about a place she had once seen on TV before the power went out. Her daddy used to tell her about it. It wasn't far, he had said, as he pointed to it on the large spinning globe in the living room. The happiest place on Earth.

She was in a roller coaster. She was happy, Mama was happy, her little brothers, Pedro and Jose, were happy. Daddy waved to her as the cart climbed the track, higher and higher into the sky, into the sun.

The wheels on the tracks clicked and clacked as the car rose. And screeched. Screeched as if they needed to be oiled.

Click.

Click.

Click.

Clack.

Clack.

Then there was a mighty roar. Isidora laughed as she waited for the car to dip but it didn't. Screams filled her ears. She was hot, so hot, and when she opened her eyes she knew she was still dreaming. Her bed was high in the sky but she wasn't on a track. She was in the claws of some sort of dark demon who stared at her with red flashing eyes that glowed in the bright light of the full moon. The smell of the ocean and rot was thick and horrible. The monster breathed heavily, each outward breath another garbage-fuelled stench.

Isidora opened her mouth to scream as the monster tipped her bed. She was about to tumble right into its wide-open mouth.

She stared down at long, sharp teeth and a long rolling tongue.

The monster roared, the sound horrifically deafening.

"No!" cried Isidora. Her racing heart and the foul smell of the monster shook the last remnants of the dream away.

She dived off the bed just as her pillows fell into the monster's gaping jaws.

"Isidora! Isidora!" Mama cried out as she banged a pan with a metal spoon.

The monster roared again and tore away what remained of the roof.

As Isidora rolled across the floor, she saw her brothers huddled in a corner. "Stay there!"

The monster had a long, snakelike neck and long arms with huge claws. Its leathery wings flapped for a moment in the moonlight and folded up again. It stank like seaweed at low tide, only a thousand times worse.

Isidora heard another sound. A high-pitched screeching was coming from her closet.

Claws tore apart the room, the monster peering into the house, picking through it as a child would a toy box. Every now and again, it cocked its head, listening.

The screeching continued.

The beast picked up the TV that hadn't worked since the hurricane and held it up to its face, then flung it out into the jungle. There was a crash as the screen shattered.

The monster's red eyes glowed. It flung bookcases around. The large talons wrapped around the spinning globe in the living room, the globe that Papa used to spin. The monster roared and flung the globe. It split in half as it hit the wall.

Isidora watched from under a blanket on the floor.

The monster's gaze landed on the young boys still hiding in the corner.

It picked up Pedro with one of it claws.

He screamed and flailed, pounding at the grip of the beast. "Let me go! Let me go!"

Mama screamed and ran to grab Pedro's legs. The beast lifted them both from the floor.

Pedro cried, "Mama! Mama! Help me!"

Mama lost her grip and fell. She scrambled across the floor. "No!"

The beast flung Pedro into the yard. He was gone.

Jose screamed and ran. The beast easily caught him in its claws.

It lifted him up, examining him with red eyes. It sniffed deeply of the boy, then roared.

Jose, too, was thrown into the yard.

The beast roared, its long red tongue flicking into the sky like a giant lizard. It flicked its tongue several times. Isidora watched it, trying to remember what she might have learned in her fairy tales about dragons and sea monsters. The monster was looking away from her. Mama waved her to come to her, on the other side of the room.

Isidora scrambled across the floor.

The beast saw her.

She froze in her tracks.

Mama shouted and banged on a pot, trying to get the monster's attention. "Run, Isidora, run away from the beast!"

Then gunfire echoed across the ruined house. Puffs of smoke appeared around the monster.

"Are you okay, Isidora?"

Diago crawled through the door, aiming his shotgun at the monster and shooting once more. The bullets bounced off the slippery scales. "It wants those eggs, Isidora. You have to give them back."

Diago shot again. The gun clicked. "Oh, for God's sake."

The monster scooped Diago up in its claws.

"Put me down," Diago screamed. "Put me down."

He struggled in the grip of the monster, then pulled a long hunting knife out of his boot. He stabbed the knife into one of the claws, but the monster didn't even seem to feel it. The monster sniffed Diago. It snorted, a puff of smoke billowing out its nostrils. Diago coughed and yelled. The monster dangled Diago above its face, holding him by his shirt.

The monster threw Diago. There was a loud smack and Isidora heard him scream. Then he was silent.

The monster roared so loudly that Isidora thought she might go deaf.

The monster tore away the wall of the hut. All the pots and pans flew. The beast ripped the door from the closet. The high-pitched screeches grew louder. Large, sharp claws wrapped around the covered bowl with the dead embryo. The beast lifted the bowl to its face and sniffed. The monster's wings expanded once more. Huge gusts of wind flew through the house, dirt and mud flying everywhere. Isidora coughed as she watched the monster inspect the bowl, so tiny in its claw.

The monster poked the bowl with the other claw. There was a tiny squeak from the bowl. The monster roared again, snapping its head around as it held the bowl. There was more squawking from the bowl. The monster turned and its wings flapped, this time with purpose. The monster flew up into the air, cradling the bowl.

Isidora watched in amazement as the creature flew towards the beach where she had found the eggs. In the moonlight, the monster was even more frightening, and much larger than she had realized. Its body was long and snakelike yet had front legs and hind legs and a huge tail. It clung tightly to the bowl as it flew.

"Maybe it's gone now," Mama said.

"Maybe..." Isidora said. Her heart was beating loudly in her chest.

Then the beast was back, empty-handed and angrier than before.

"We have to give it the other egg!" Isidora screamed as the monster tore down another wall of the hut.

Mama resumed banging on the pots and pans. By now, some neighbours had arrived, many with shotguns.

"It just wants the other egg!" Isidora cried. "I have to give it the other egg."

No one listened to Isidora or Mama and the guns continued to fire. Someone even threw a lit torch into the rubble. As the flames caught hold of the curtains, Isidora watched as fire spread along the tumbled furniture and strewn books. The broken globe burned. Isidora gulped back tears as she saw the fire spreading towards the closet.

Isidora crawled through the burning rubble of the house, toward the closet. Around her bullets flew, and smoke burned her eyes. She pushed away the broken closet door and tumbled down clothes, then pulled at the basket that contained the remaining egg.

The beast roared and picked up the nearest man with a shotgun. He was flung out of the way as it clawed through more of the debris in the house.

Isidora dragged the basket out into the room, staring up at the monster that continued to battle the gunfire. Tears ran down the child's face as she pushed the basket into the room.

"Here's your egg!" she screamed. "Come and get it!"

Isidora pulled away the blanket and seaweed so that the egg was exposed.

The creature paused, another villager clutched in its claws. It turned its head and sniffed. Its red eyes stared at the basket. Distracted, she dropped the villager who fell to the ground with a howl and thump. The villager lay still on the ground.

"It's your egg!" Isidora screamed. "Go get your egg! I'm sorry, I didn't know…"

The beast roared, its tongue flicking in the air. More guns went off, more bullets bounced off the slippery scales.

The beast swung its tail at the men. They screamed and fell into each other. The beast swung its tail again, taking down more of the house.

Mama left her pots and pans as she took Isidora by the arm. "Run, Isidora!"

Isidora stood transfixed.

The beast picked up the basket in its claw.

The last wall of the house heaved and moaned. The creaking was loud as it slowly lurched over.

"Stand back, Isidora!" Mama cried as the wall shuddered. The beast swung its tail, knocking the teetering wall. Mama pulled at Isidora as she ran from the falling wall but Isidora stood strong, hypnotized by the sight of the monster and the egg. Mama stumbled, weeping, as she ducked out of the way of a large piece of bamboo. One of the village men dove for Isidora, attempting to sweep her away from the tumbling debris. Isidora dodged him, stepping closer to the monster, making her voice as loud as she could.

"Go away now, monster, go!" Isidora waved at it.

The beast roared one more time and flapped its mighty wings, the wind blowing final pieces of the wall over. It rose into the moonlight, carrying the basket.

Isidora looked up at the monster as a large piece of wood fell onto her head and knocked her over. She fell under the weight of the lumber and more pieces landed on her as the house completely collapsed around her, flames and dust rising, as bamboo and wood fell. Mama screamed.

Several men and women rushed to the wall to lift the pieces of wood from Isidora. Her mama cried, pushing everyone out of her way as she rushed to her daughter. "My baby, my baby!" she cried as she found Isidora's little hand and held it.

"Mama!" Isidora whispered.

"The monster is gone. It'll be okay," Mama said. "Isi!"

More people pulled debris from her, exclaiming as they saw what had happened to her when the wall had fallen.

They heard Isidora sigh as she stared at the sky where the beast had flown. They heard her say, "It's okay, Mama. I'm going to see Daddy now. We're going to ride the roller coaster."

While the island struggled to rebuild from the storms and now from the monster, the beach-combers all made an oath not to disturb any eggs that weren't identifiable. Now and again, shrieks of an unusual animal could be heard in the distance, but no one ever ventured out to see what made them. They knew.

And if they didn't, all they had to do was ask Mama, who took over the beach-combing trading store after Diago died. She'd tell them the legend of Isidora and the Monster.

About the Author

Sèphera Girón is the award-winning author of over twenty published horror novels and dozens of short stories. She has stories in *Dark Rainbow, Group Hex 1, Group Hex 2, Abandon, Amazing Monster Tales No. 1, Creatures in Canada - A Darkling Around the World Anthology, The Pulp Horror Book of Phobias* and more. She is working on the next book in her *Witch Upon a Star* erotic horror series from Riverdale Avenue Books. Sèphera is also the in-house astrologer for Romance Daily News and writes the weekly horoscope column. When Sèphera isn't writing, she loves to act and can be spotted as a background performer in over twenty television shows and movies. Sèphera has roles in the horror movies, *Killer Rack* and *Slime City Massacre*.

Find out more about Sèphera at:
sepheragiron.ca

Bargain Hunter

Rebecca M. Senese

Mariella loved to roam the thrift stores in the east end of town. She always dressed for the occasion: flat, slip-on shoes on her pudgy, arthritic feet (better for walking and removing), elastic-waisted skirt, t-shirt, all designed for quick removal, sometimes even in the aisles if the store didn't have a change room, or a change room that was available. For great bargains, Mariella wouldn't be too proud.

Her favourite stores were east along King. Older stores with windows filmed with dirt kicked up by the streetcars. Macie's (trying for a play on the New York store but coming nowhere near), always looked especially grungy with the yellowish brick made faded and dull from countless rainstorms and age. The Thrift Palace across the street faired a little better, although its windows were tinier and the interior darker so it was harder to see inside without entering the store. The red brick of that building looked a little cleaner, like they maybe actually washed it once in a while.

But probably not.

Mariella reigned supreme here, the best of the bargain hunters. Sure, there were other contenders, the occasional yuppie mother slumming it for bargains, but none could hold a candle to her. She could take one glance at a crowded fifty cent table and pick out the one item that should be going for five dollars or ten dollars. She could take a budget of five dollars and come away with enough items to mix and match for three occasions.

No one beat Mariella.

And all the folks in the stores loved her.

Even grouchy old man Carmichael at Thrift 'N Go.

So it was quite a surprise when Mariella was escorted out of the new thrift store, the Bargain Kingdom, at the corner of King and Ballard, during their grand opening.

She hadn't been doing anything wrong, just her usual bargain hunting tactics, checking for flaws, dents, or scratches. Asking for a better price or the tax off. Suddenly, a tall clerk in a sparkling white smock stood at her side.

"Can I help you, ma'm?" he said.

"No, I'm fine," Mariella said. "Is that a scratch on the side of this lemon dicer?"

"We don't have any items with scratches on them," the clerk said. He seemed to barely move his thin lips. "I'm sorry I'm going to have to ask you to leave. You're disrupting the other customers."

And before Mariella could say another word, the clerk took her elbow and propelled her toward the new, sparkling, sliding glass door.

Then she was out on the street, a cloud of exhaust filling her nostrils as a truck rumbled by. Mariella clutched her straw purse and stared back at the new thrift store.

Kicked out.

She'd been kicked out!

And they wouldn't let her back in. She could see the clerk standing just inside the glass doors. He pretended to be greeting customers as they wandered in, but Mariella could tell he was watching her to make sure she didn't try to sneak back.

Like she would really spend any of her money there now.

Her thin fingers tightened on her purse. She pulled back her normally stooped shoulders (stooped from all that bending over tables, searching for bargains), and straightened up to her full height of five feet one inch.

"I will take my dollars elsewhere," she said, making sure to time her speech just as the door slid open, disgorging a shopper.

The clerk didn't even blink.

Mariella turned and walked away, holding her head up high.

This was their loss.

Mariella didn't try the Bargain Kingdom the next day, or even the day after. She didn`t even walk on the same side of the street, but stayed on the north side of King, passing the Thrift 'N Go, waving at old man Carmichael through the big main window.

Two days later, on the Thursday, she spotted Sondra marching out, a white bag with the emblazed logo for Bargain Kingdom bumping against her scrawny left calf. As Sondra cut across King, Mariella hurried after, her shoes swishing on the cracked sidewalk.

"Sondra, wait up!"

Sondra turned her head on her impossibly long and thin neck. Her little pink mouth made an "o" in surprise.

"Mar'ella, watcha doin'?" she said.

Mariella caught up. Her heart pounded in her chest and she had to take measured breaths so she didn't wheeze.

"Goin' for a coffee. Come on and show me your shopping."

She closed her thick hand around Sondra's bony elbow and steered her into the Coffee 'N Cake. They found an empty booth at the back, just before the washroom. The odour of burnt coffee just covered the odour from the washrooms.

After fetching two coffees and a couple of crullers, they sat down. The orange vinyl bench seat crinkled under Mariella as she sat. She leaned on the table. To her surprise, the table top felt clean, not at all sticky.

Sondra peeled the lid off her coffee and dunked a piece of cruller into it. Before it could drip, she shoved it into her mouth, chewing, her thin lips open just a little.

Mariella took a sip of her coffee, grimaced at the taste and added a sugar before setting it back down. Had to be nonchalant about this. Didn't want to spook Sondra.

"So how was your shopping?" she said.

"Oh just great," Sondra said. "I got the best stuff."

She dragged the bag up onto the table.

"Got these hangers, six for a dollar. Got these clay potters, two for a dollar."

She started pulling items out onto the table, hangers, pots, plastic food containers, all the way raving about the prices.

But the prices didn't seem all that different from any of the other thrift stores around.

Seemed exactly the same, actually.

Mariella rubbed a silky blue and purple scarf Sondra had pulled out. Four dollars, according to Sondra. Not that great a deal.

"Prices seem okay," Mariella said.

"Okay? They're fantastic," Sondra said. "Best in the neighbourhood. I'm doin' all my shopping there from now on. Not goin' nowhere's else."

She gave a quick nod with her head, so sharp Mariella feared her neck would snap and her head would roll around the table.

Fortunately, it didn't.

"Well, I'll have to check out this store," Mariella said. "Especially if it's got such great bargains."

"You'll love it," Sondra said. "You'll never want to leave."

"Hmm." Mariella took a sip of her coffee.

That sounded like a challenge.

She didn't quite make it to the store the next day. Instead, she found herself chatting with more ladies in the neighbourhood. She met most of them on the street, clutching white bags with the Bargain Kingdom logo on it. All raved about the prices, the wonderful selection. As they talked, Mariella noticed the faraway looks in their eyes. They even seemed to use the same words.

Were they being hypnotised or something?

She'd heard of some weird advertising stuff, subliminal whatever, ways they tried to make the shopper do something by influencing their minds. Had the Bargain Kingdom done this? Why hadn't they tried it on her?

She pondered these questions as she walked along the street. Something bumped into her hip. Ouch, a new sandwich board. She rubbed her hip. Big blowout sale at the Thrift 'N Go. Hmm, that looked promising.

She headed inside.

Old man Carmichael stood hunched behind the cash register. He brightened as she walked in the door. Gosh, she'd never seen him smile so wide before. Who knew he had such white teeth? Had to be fake. Wait until she told Sondra.

"Good morning," he called. "Half off the list price on everything."

Half off! That was a record for Carmichael. She could definitely get some good stuff in here.

And as she turned to look at the rest of the store, she realized something.

All the aisles stood empty.

Not one other person stood in the store.

No one near the large square front tables, filled with various knick knacks and books. No one in the women's clothing to the left or the men's shoes to the right. Nobody checking out the jewellery or spritzing the cheap perfume knockoffs into the air, strong enough to make a body choke. Not even a kid in the toys down the centre.

Now Carmichael's smile didn't look so much wide as desperate.

Gosh, it was so weird being in a store with no other customers. Even during the middle of the day there was usually a few other people wandering about the aisles. Mariella went through housewares and picked up a set of salt and pepper shakers for three dollars. A set of burgundy cloth napkins still in the new wrapping listed for two.

She wanted to get more, but the stillness made her shoulders creep up toward her ears. Even with the Muzak playing, it was quiet, too quiet.

Set her teeth on edge.

She carried her items to the cash.

"Where is everyone?" she said.

Carmichael's lips thinned. "Dunno."

"This is a great sale," she said.

He brightened a little at that. He pulled out three pieces of tissue paper to wrap the salt and pepper shakers.

"Tell your friends," he said.

"I will."

"Really?"

His eyes looked more watery than normal. He blinked several times, then shoved her purchases into a plastic bag.

"Is it the new place?" she said.

"I don't know what's going on." His voice burst out of him like he'd been holding it in and he couldn't no more. "Nobody comes in anymore. I've never had it like this. Not even when the Bargain Bin opened two years ago. I've always had my regulars, always a trickle crowd, but now no one comes in. No one." His hand shook, rattling the plastic. "You're the first person I've seen this week."

Before he could start blubbering, Mariella shoved a ten across the counter and picked up her bag. She hurried out the door, the tinkling of the bell echoing in her ears as she rushed down the street.

She didn't even wait for her change.

Something was going on. Something bad. She knew it.

She clutched the bag to her narrow chest. Her heart pounded inside. She sucked in air from the exertion, tasting the usual exhaust and stale dust in the air, and yes, she had to admit it, from the fright. Because now that she was walking along King Street, she could see into a few of the other thrift stores.

And they were empty.

All empty!

New homemade signs stuck in the glass, advertising specials, half off, three quarters off. Clerks stood behind the counters or just inside the doorways, desperation kneading their brows and dipping their mouths down. Several raised their hands as if to beseech her to come in.

Come in and shop.

Where was everyone?

But she didn't really have to guess.

The Bargain Kingdom.

She crossed the street and headed back toward Ballard. Two blocks away, she spotted the crowd.

They lined up along the sidewalk in bunches of twos and threes. All clutching the same white bags with the Bargain Kingdom logo on the side, but the bags were empty.

Waiting to be filled.

The line stretched beyond the end of the store and past the furniture store to end just at the bench outside the sandwich shop.

As Mariella drew closer to the end of the line, she spotted Sondra just four people ahead.

"Hey, Sondra!" She waved.

Sondra's head tilted up, chin wagging from side to side, looking like a scrawny bird. She gave a smile when she spotted Mariella and waved her forward.

As Mariella passed the others, she heard angry grumbling. Geez, it was a line up to get into a thrift shop, not to see Elvis.

Sondra grabbed her arm and pulled her close. "Good thing you got here now," she said. "They're having a big sale."

"Really?" Mariella leaned away from Sondra. Funny, she looked like she was wearing the same clothes as a few days ago. They even smelled a few days overdue, with the heady odour of sweat.

"Yes, they have the best prices."

"All the other places are having big sales too," Mariella said.

Sondra waved a hand. "Oh they aren't as good as Bargain Kingdom."

"Bargain Kingdom. Bargain Kingdom."

The words rippled up and down the line around them. People nodded in agreement. Faces stared back with blank expressions, eyes wide. They looked like some kind of cult people. Mariella leaned over to point it out to Sondra then noticed the same expression on her friend's face.

What the hell was going on here?

Before she could say anything, the line started moving. People shuffled forward, faster and faster. Gaining speed. Even Sondra was hurrying, the bag rustling in her hand, bashing against the side of her leg. The people behind them were breathing down Mariella's neck, she felt the hot breath of the man on her skin. She flung her arm back, swatting him with her straw purse.

"Back off!"

He whined but stopped trying to run her over.

They reached the sliding door, now wide open to accommodate the flood of people. As they entered, Mariella kept her eye open for that one clerk who had kicked her out the first day but caught no sign. Good. She wanted a chance to really look around today.

Customers filled the aisles. Over their almost reverential murmurs, Mariella could hear the same old Muzak tinkling in the air. To her right was a line of five cashiers, manned by smiling young teenage girls. With those wide, vacant eyes, Mariella wondered if they had a full thought between the five of them.

Tables with special bargains lined the front of the store, leading to the sections. Ladies on the left, men on the right, kids down the centre. Almost the exact same layout as every other thrift store in the neighbourhood.

Mariella wandered into the ladies section, letting her hand trail over the fabric. All the same stuff, cheap wool blends. Polyester knockoffs of pretend silk. She checked various prices.

Normal. Nothing special.

In fact, some of them were a bit overpriced to her mind.

Yet when she dropped the sleeve of a brightly coloured orange and yellow blouse, another woman snapped it up, practically drooling over the price tag.

"Fifteen dollars!"

Fifteen? In a place like this, that used blouse should have been five.

But the woman clutched it to her oversized breast and scurried away.

In every department, the same repeated over and over. Mariella noticed some item, more often than not, overpriced. As soon as she set it down, someone else scooped it up, swooning over the price and hurrying away.

Now Mariella loved to shop but this was ridiculous.

As she left housewares, she noticed a flare of white out of the corner of her eye. A clerk!

Not the same one, a different one, but he was definitely looking at her. His thick brows drew together. A slight frown showed on his face.

Mariella turned her back to him and picked up a perfume bottle. One of those cheap knockoffs. She spritzed her wrist. The chemically floral scent burned her nostrils and coated the back of her throat, almost making her gag. She turned the gag into a satisfied hum.

"Lovely scent," she said. "And what a bargain."

She ogled the smooth, shiny bottle.

After a few moments, the clerk moved on.

Boy, that was close.

To avoid suspicion, she picked up a spaghetti strainer. She needed a new one anyway and this wasn't too much more at any of the other stores.

And carrying an item that she would buy seemed to hold the clerks at bay.

But all around her, the other customers went on a buying orgy, as if they would never be allowed into a store ever again.

Despite her best shopping tendencies, even Mariella found the sight disturbing.

She finally found Sondra in the men's department, practically in tears over a blue striped tie.

"Sondra, what's the matter?"

"Oh, I was just wishin' Stan worked back in the office again, then I could get 'em this tie," Sondra said.

"Forget the tie," Mariella said. "Get 'em some socks."

Sondra dropped the tie back into the bin. Her face lit up, eyes almost popping out of her head.

"Oh, that's a great idea!"

Socks were a great idea?

Sondra was already hurrying away. Mariella pushed after her, her flat shoes swishing on the tile. She used her basket with the long spaghetti strainer inside to force people out of her way.

Finally she caught up to Sondra. She grabbed hold of the woman's bony elbow. Funny, it seemed even bonier than usual. All of Sondra did actually, all skin stretched over her skull and bones, and dark circles under her eyes.

"I'm heading out," Mariella said. "Why don't you come with me? Coffee on me. Then we can check out…one of the other places."

She dropped her voice low, checking around to make sure no one else heard her.

Sondra shook her head. "What are you talking about? There ain't any other place worth going to."

"Well, sure there are, Sondra. Lots of 'em. Big sales over at Thrift 'N Go and at the Bargain Jeannie."

Sondra yanked her arm out of Mariella's grasp. "I can't believe you can say that. 'nd I was gonna invite you to the blow out."

"Blow out? What blow out?"

"Never you mind. It's not for you, not for ordinary shoppers." Sondra practically spit the word at her.

"I'm sorry, Sondra. I really wanna understand. See, I found this terrific spaghetti strainer and I even tried on some perfume."

She lifted the basket. Sondra's pursed lips softened. She wrinkled her nose, smelling the wafting current of chemical flowers that still lingered on Mariella's wrist.

"Well," Sondra said. "Okay. You can buy me a coffee. But we don't even have to leave for that!"

Sure enough, they didn't. Sondra led Mariella to a tiny coffee shop in the far corner. They perched on plastic chairs and sipped watery coffee. Sondra swooned over it but Mariella had to dump twice the normal amount of sugar into it.

But still she smiled at Sondra and proclaimed it delish.

She was gonna figure out what the hell was going on if it killed her.

It turned out the "blow out" was a big after hours sale by invitation only.

Sondra had been angling for an invite from day one but only twenty lucky shoppers got chosen every week. According to Sondra, Marg Hempman went the week before and got spectacular bargains.

Funny, Mariella couldn't remember seeing Marg around the street over the last week and her blonde hair, teased to gravity defying heights, was difficult to miss.

So Mariella decided it was time to check out this "blow out."

Except Sondra no longer invited her.

"I said I was sorry," Mariella repeated after they left the store. Her own white plastic bag with Bargain Kingdom on it bumped against her leg.

Sondra shook her head. "I can't bring you. I checked 'n they won't let me bring anybody." She snaked her skinny arm around Mariella's shoulder and squeezed. "Next time, I promise."

Sure. If there was a next time.

If somehow Sondra wasn't disappeared like Marg was after.

As they reached the corner, Sondra gave her big kiss on the cheek, leaving a smear of pale pink lipstick and the lingering odour of Noxema face cream.

"I'll tell ya all about my deals tomorrow."

Sondra waved and hurried around the corner, heading toward her apartment building two blocks down.

Mariella headed north, shuffling her flats on the cracked sidewalk. She didn't like the sound of this, not one bit. Had everyone but her lost their minds? Could no one else see there was something horribly wrong with the Bargain Kingdom?

In the tiny kitchen of her apartment, she pulled out the plastic spaghetti strainer and looked at it. Half the holes weren't properly cut out. Damn thing couldn't strain for nothing but at the store it had looked all right.

Even better than all right.

She tightened her hand around the handle of it until the edges bit into her palm.

Something damned wrong.

And she was gonna find out what.

Oh yes she was.

Midnight Madness Blow Out read the sign that stretched across the two front doors of the Bargain Kingdom. Faint light from inside spilled out around the sign. On the other two sides of the building, the window displays had been shuttered with long black panels, shut so tight no light showed at all.

In the doorway of the coffee shop kittie korner to the Bargain Kingdom, Mariella folded her arms against the late night chill. It made goosebumps on her skin even with this cotton sweater.

She ain't never seen anything like those shutters, not on any store, even at midnight. She bet they didn't only block the light but sound too.

Just what was going on in there?

Time to find out.

It had taken all her contacts to find another person with a ticket for tonight's blow out and a full three hundred dollars in cash to scoop up the ticket. But she couldn't just be traipsing in there like herself. Sondra would spot her in an instant, along with several of the other regulars.

So Mariella came in disguise.

She couldn't do nothing about her general body shape, but a curling caramel coloured wig hide her own brown hair. Wide glasses with tinted lenses made her face look wider. Some careful makeup heightened the impression.

Next a few inches of heel changed her height and her walk. Instead of her usual elastic-waisted skirt, she wore hip hugging capris (damn, having to shave her legs), and a matching scoop neck top. The cotton black sweater rounded out the outfit, along with a matching black handbag.

She missed her straw purse.

But when she tottered over to join the short line that waited outside the doors, no one looked at her twice.

Not even Sondra who stood third from the front, only ten people in front of Mariella.

Perfect!

At the chime of midnight, the doors opened and shoppers hustled inside. The clerks at the doors scrutinized each invitation, looking back and forth from the slick postcard to the face. Mariella swallowed as she handed over the postcard. Damn, if it wasn't that first clerk who'd kicked out that very first day.

Would he recognize her?

No, of course not, how could he? He musta seen tons of people since then, especially since how busy this place at been. Just breathe slow. Relax. She could still feel her heart pounding in her chest and her underarms dampened with sweat. Considering she still had goose bumps on her arms, it was a weird feeling.

The clerk studied the card then looked up at her. His eyes narrowed. The urge to look away was strong but she forced herself to keep looking back. Her body felt rigid like a brick. Her fingers squeezed the purse strap. Her lungs felt empty.

He gave a nod, waved sharp and hard with the card.

Mariella blinked. She could move! Air rushed into her lungs as she took a breath. It was all she could do not to stumble away in these damned two inch heels.

Her legs trembled under her as she entered the store. All the overhead lights were off, leaving spotlights shining down on various tables and sections. It created pools of darkness and light throughout the store. A little moody for a thrift shop but probably one of the so-called perks of being part of this "blow out" sale.

She glanced at the closest table, piles of tea towels, four to a bundle. Hey, the price hadn't even been changed and it wasn't that good. Five dollars for four. Mediocre. She ran her fingers over the top of several sets. Scratchy and rough, not even very soft. And they felt thin, like they would wear and tear pretty fast.

Not much of a bargain.

A squeal to her right caught her attention. One of the other shoppers held up a flimsy looking sweater. Green was not her colour and the flopping price tag on the sleeve still looked white, no special red sale sticker or anything, but the woman's face was flushed with pleasure. She bounced up and down with glee.

Some people were so easy to please.

Mariella headed deeper into the store.

The intermittent spotlights created a sort of twilight in the store. Rows of clothing on racks took on a strange, otherworldly feel. As she moved deeper into men's wear, her heels clicked on the cheap linoleum flooring, sounding muffled and strange in the dark. She could almost feel something in the shadows, watching her, stalking her. The air held only the usual slightly musky scent of clothing.

Still her heart kept pounding and her mouth felt dry, tasting the gummy, sourness of anxiety.

Maybe her body knew something she didn't.

Focus. What could she do? Shop, that's what. She was the queen of the bargain hunters. She couldn't let a little darkness and taut nerves get to her.

She started checking out the price tags. In the shadows, it was a little hard to make out. Still none of the prices looked any different. She still heard the occasional squeal of delight, sounding farther and farther away as she moved deeper into the store. It sounded like most of the shoppers were staying near the front. She caught one glimpse of Sondra heading for house-wares in the corner. For a moment, she considered following but Sondra might just recognize her, even with the disguise and the shadows.

Better not take the chance. Sondra might not be too pleased, especially since Mariella wasn't as enamoured with this place as she was.

She reached men's shoes and was checking out the boy's dress shoes, thinking about a pair for her nephew, when she realized she hadn't heard a delight squeal in a while.

Had they all realized the prices weren't that great?

Mariella glanced up, blinking in the shadows.

Strange, she couldn't see anyone nearby. Sure, there was only twenty or so of them and they had the whole store to themselves but she should at least see one of them.

Shouldn't she?

She put the boy's patent leather shoe back on the shelf. It teetered for a moment and then fell to the floor, clattering. Mariella jumped. She scooped it up and shoved it back on the shelf.

Then looked around.

Nothing.

No one.

Not even one of the white clad clerks.

Just darkening shadows among the looming racks of clothes and shelves of cheap merchandise. Darkening? Yes, it was getting darker. The spotlights were growing dim.

And from the back of the store, she heard a deep, low growl begin.

She ran for the front door.

Her heart pounded in her chest. Her arms pumped. She tottered in the heels then finally kicked the damned things away. The left one tumbled off her foot and the right one went soaring into the darkness ahead. She watched it tumbling. Five dollars! And it was gone.

The growl rose in volume. Turned into a raging snarl.

She felt a blast of heat on her back. Smelled sour, stinky breath, like someone who hadn't brushed their teeth or used mouthwash in months. Or years.

Or ever.

She dodged around a rack of ladies' shorts. From here, it was a straight shot to the front door. She pumped her arms, gaining speed.

The roar sounded again behind her. Closer…closer…

Almost to the front door.

A clerk stepped out of the shadows by one of the tables. A hand clamped on her upper arm, dragging her to a stop. Mariella turned her head and felt the wig slip as if it hadn't quite caught up to her movement.

It was that first clerk. A smarmy smirk twisted his thin lips. His fingers tightened on her arm, digging into her flesh.

"I thought it was you," he said. "I wasn't quite sure but I knew you'd never be chosen for one of our blow outs." His grin widened. "That's okay. Good thing you're here. You'll find out just how much of a bargain we are."

He dragged her back, away from the door. She looked back out the front glass door. So close. She'd almost made it.

The roar sounded again.

She wasn't going to look back. She wasn't.

The clerk dragged her past the first set of tables, angling back toward the men's department near the back. As they passed the last set of tables, she saw it was a souvenirs display, full of Canadiana and Toronto souvenirs. In the centre, sat a whole row of CN Tower replicas in plastic.

Mariella grabbed it and swung.

The point stabbed the clerk in the back of his hand. He shrieked and let go. The CN Tower stayed stuck, upside down in his hand as he grabbed his wrist.

Mariella didn't wait around.

Her feet pounded the tile again and she ran for the front door. This time she kept an eye on the shadows.

There on the left, she saw one shift. She ducked around a rack of dresses as another clerk darted forward.

He smashed into it.

Mariella kept going.

A crash sounded behind her, like the table of souvenirs being knocked over. Another roar came, followed the stench of fetid breath.

Right behind her!

She reached the sliding glass doors. But they didn't slide open. She stuck her fingers into the gap between them and shoved. The doors started to part, grinding slowly back on their tracks. Too slow.

She heard the scrape of claws on the linoleum behind her.

She wasn't going to look back. She wasn't.

She pushed harder. Sweat poured down her back, sticking the black sweater to her torso. Her feet slipped a little. Thank god, she'd kicked off those shoes but she sure missed her flats with the rubber soles.

The doors slid open another inch.

A roar trumpeted again. Inches away!

She shoved her left arm through the opening. Then her leg.

Something grabbed hold of the long, caramel hair.

Mariella tilted her head to the right as she shoved her body left through the gap. For a moment, she felt the bobby pins holding the wig to her real hair hold, tugging on her hair, yanking on the roots. Then the bobby pins gave. The wig flew off her head.

The roar of triumph turned to a wail of anger.

Mariella squeezed the rest of her body through the gap and jumped away.

The two glass doors slid shut.

Out of the darkness, a gigantic paw slapped the glass. She saw the glint of claws. Something wet smeared against the inside of the doors.

She stumbled back, her feet barely able to carry her as she hurried away.

She couldn't be sure, but she thought the wet smear looked red.

She turned and ran.

Mariella sat at her green Formica kitchen table, hands wrapped about a scalding mug of tea. She'd wrapped herself in the dark green flannel bathrobe she'd bought last year at the Thrift 'N Go, and when that didn't seem to be enough, she'd draped a leopard spotted throw from the Bargain Bin over her shoulders.

But she still couldn't seem to get warm.

And this tea certainly wasn't doing it.

She retrieved a bottle of whiskey from the cupboard and poured a dollop in. Then a second one. For a moment, she considered returning the bottle to cupboard. Oh, to hell with it. She left it on the table and sat back down.

There was a monster in the Bargain Kingdom.

A monster.

And it was eating all the best shoppers.

Including her friend Sondra.

And all she'd done was run.

Mariella took a swig of the doctored tea. The Pekoe orange softened the bite of the whiskey just a little. A second swallow spread warmth down her throat and through her chest. But still her shoulders shook a little, as if she could still hear the roar thundering behind her.

All she'd done was run.

But what else could she do? She just a regular fifty-four year old woman. Nothing special. All she could was shop and bargain. She couldn't fight a monster. She wasn't strong or brave.

She was scared.

Her shoulders hunched. She leaned over the table, over her tea mug. More whiskey? Her hand shook as she reached for the bottle. Gosh, her mug was only half full of tea and she'd already added two hardy helpings. Any more and she'd be on the floor.

Maybe it would help her forget.

Right, help her forget that she'd just run out on her friend. That she'd run out on all those other shoppers.

Hot tears stung her eyes. She breathed in the scent of the tea, the orange tickling her nostrils. It reminded her of all the times sitting in a coffee shop with Sondra, reviewing their purchases, plotting their next trip to the thrift stores. Sondra used to ooh and ahh over Mariella's ability to get the best deal, always called her the queen of the bargain hunters.

Some queen.

Queen of running away.

Queen of abandoning her friends.

She drained the tea in one long swallow and set the mug down on the table top.

It was a Daffy Duck mug, one of her favourites. She remembered buying it at the Bargain Bin years ago. They'd wanted five dollars, she talked him down to two. Stood toe to toe with the owner, fat Darryl, his juggling chin jutting out, lips pursed and frowning, cheap cologne enveloping her in a cloud, but Mariella stood her ground. Demanded the best price or she would walk. Take her business elsewhere, and make sure everyone in the neighbourhood knew it.

And they would listen to her, because she knew how to get a bargain. Knew how to help other people get it too.

And finally Darryl had hrumphed, dropping his gaze, and given her the mug for two dollars.

Queen of the bargain hunters.

And she'd backed down.

She'd let her friends down.

She'd let her neighbours down.

They'd all trusted her judgement on bargains, and here this store'd come into her neighbourhood, touting itself as the "Bargain Kingdom" and it weren't no bargain. They'd brought a monster in to eat the shoppers.

And she'd run.

Mariella stood up, slamming the Daffy Duck mug down on the green Formica table table. The leopard throw fell off her shoulders and tumbled to the white tile floor.

Not any more.

Now it was war.

Time to go shopping.

She dressed in her usual shopping attire: flat shoes, elastic-waisted skirt, t-shirt. This time she took her big straw purse. After brushing her hair, she stopped in the kitchen and contemplated the knives. Would something like that work on a monster? She didn't think so. There seemed to be something else at work here, something mental. She knew it from the way the other shoppers acted, the way the clerks acted.

It affected them all.

But not her.

Knives weren't the way to go. She was going to have to play on the monster's level.

Show it who the real queen of the bargains was.

She turned away from the knife block and stormed out of the apartment.

At five in the morning, even the earliest of early birds wasn't traveling around quite yet. Traffic, both by car and foot, was almost non-existent. Mariella made it back to the Bargain Kingdom in record time.

Her heart started pounding as soon as she spotted it. The black shutters still covered the windows. They wouldn't go up until seven at the earliest.

Even in the cool morning air, she felt sweat begin to trickle down her back. She clutched the straw purse to her chest. The silence in the street had a weird, unearthly quality and she wished some crazed cab driver would just roar down the street. But none did.

There was only the shuffling sound of her flat shoes on the sidewalk.

She stopped in front of the double glass doors.

This was it. Last chance to turn away.

And leave them all in there to face a monster.

Her hands tightened on her purse until she could feel the ends of the straw poking her palms.

Just do it!

She sucked in a deep breath, wishing she'd brought some gum or a lozenge, anything to take away the sour taste of dread.

She marched up to the doors, ready to peel them apart again like she had only a few hours ago.

But they swished open at her approach.

The darkness beckoned.

Mariella straightened her shoulders and jutted out her chin.

Time to go shopping.

She stepped inside.

Even before the doors slid shut, she realized it wasn't as completely dark as she'd thought. The spotlight still illuminated several sections of the store, but now she could see debris from knocked over racks, spilling clothing on the floor. Or tables shoved aside, half the contents lying shattered or in piles.

Might be some extra bargains on some of those damages items.

As she moved deeper into the store, she heard the shuffling footsteps of someone approaching from her right. She looked over and from the shadows, a figure in white moved. A clerk.

Not just any clerk. Her clerk.

He glared at her, his face animated with dislike, but he didn't seem to be able to move too well. He bumped into a table, then shifted and stumbled forward to bump into another table.

"Get out," he said.

Mariella shook her head. "I'm here to shop. I had a pass and I was let in. I'm here for bargains."

"We don't want you here," the clerk said.

"I don't care," Mariella said. "I've got money and I'm here to shop." She tilted her head. "Would you like me to report this store to the Better Business Bureau?"

The clerk scowled.

"We don't have anything for you to buy," he said.

"Oh, I don't think that's the case," she said. "You haven't even heard what I'm willing to pay."

The scowl thinned out as the clerk's brow twisted in confusion. He tilted his head as if listening to something that Mariella couldn't hear, like he was a dog. Then a slow smile crept across his face.

"How can I help you, ma'm?" he said.

He spread his arms out in a mockery of gentility. Mariella felt all the hairs on her arms stand up. She hadn't realized before just how much of a puppet face he had, the way his lips twisted upward, but didn't quite look natural.

As if someone made him look that way.

Or some thing.

Walk away. She could just walk away right now and never come back.

But that would mean leaving Sondra and the others. And turning a blind eye to whatever else this thing did in the future.

Could she live with that?

A part of her wished she could, but she was too cowardly for that. She forced her shoulders back even as her hand tightened around her purse.

"You can sure help me," she said. "I'm here to shop and I want bargains."

His smile widened. "We've got the best bargains in the city. We are the Bargain Kingdom."

He gave her a little bow and began to lead her deeper into the store.

"We have a special on in men's ware," he called out. "Jeans for thirty dollars."

"That's no bargain," Mariella said. "I can get 'em for fifteen."

The clerk stumbled. He cast a glare at Mariella over his shoulder.

"I'm sure the quality isn't as good as we have here," he said.

"I'm sure they are," Mariella said. "They was Levis' brand, after all. I took a look in your men's department. Seems to me they was mostly no name brand."

She smiled as the clerk glanced back at her again. Was that a shadow of a frown on his face? Maybe some sweat on his brow?

They couldn't fool her with merely claiming to have the best bargains.

Gonna have to do better.

As they moved deeper into the store, the spotlights became dimmer and spaced farther apart. The pools of darkness between became thicker, heavier. The air felt cooler on her skin, tinged with dampness, and she started to catch the faintest whiff of something dank and putrid.

The skin on her legs and arms tightened from the chill. With every step, her heart seemed to beat a little faster. Steady, steady. She took deep breaths to try to slow it down.

She had to keep her wits about her.

Remember: she was shopping.

And she was gonna get a bargain.

"We have a special on our mugs in housewares," the clerk said. "Two for ten dollars."

"That ain't so special," Mariella said. "I got a one of a kind Daffy Duck mug for two dollars."

The clerk stumbled again. His hip knocked against a table. The display of sweaters shuddered. Mariella grabbed a pile before it fell to the floor. In the dimness, she could barely make out the price tag.

"What's this?" she said. "Eighteen ninety-nine? This should only be around four dollars. Why are you selling them so high? I thought this was the Bargain Kingdom? I don't see any bargains here."

Now, even in the darkness, she could see the sweat gleaming on the clerk's forehead, plastering his brown hair to his scalp. His mouth gaped open like a startled goldfish but before he could speak, a deep rumble sounded from the back of the store.

Maybe she'd caught the attention of the manager.

Mariella clenched her straw purse tight. Time to get some price matching.

"I'd like to speak to your manager," she said. She raised her voice. "Can I talk to someone about the prices here?"

The clerk's eyes widened. He stumbled toward her, hands out in supplication.

"Please, I can beat any price you've seen by ten percent," he said. "Just show me an ad and I can beat it." His voice cracked.

"I don't have to show you anything," Mariella said. "I want to speak to the manager!"

She called the last word out, raising her voice. The clerk looked back behind him as the rumble sounded again.

Closer.

"Please," he said. Now he sounded like he was whining.

"The manager," Mariella said.

He opened his mouth to speak again then did that head tilty thing. He glanced over his shoulder. His hands shook.

The puppet master weren't too pleased with him.

He backed away into the darkness. His hands reached out to her, almost pleading. She wanted to reach out to him. Sure he'd been a jerk to her but who knew what his boss was gonna do to him? She couldn't move though, not and risk the others.

His pale fingertips were the last to disappear into the inky black. Mariella peered harder into the darkness but she couldn't see anything. She clenched her straw purse closer to her side.

A moment later, a roar burst from the darkness. A scream followed and was then cut off. She heard a crunch sound. Then silence.

Her legs wobbled under her. She felt that tea pressing in her bladder. Never shoulda had a cup of it this late. Never shoulda come back here at all, what was she thinking?

A shuffling sounded from in front of her. Something moved closer in the darkness.

Mariella pressed her legs together. Why had she come back? What the heck was she doing here?

Shopping. She was shopping. Had to show this place for the rip-off it was. Had to help her friends.

Right. She had to keep focused on that. The racing of her heart slowed a little.

She knew her bargains. Had to remember that.

The shuffling paused at the edge of the darkness. She sensed something beyond but couldn't make it out. The lighting was just too dim here.

She swallowed. Her mouth felt too dry and tasted of stale tea.

"Hello?" she said.

"You wished to speak to a manager."

The voice had a gliding, smooth quality with a deep timbre. The 'r' lasted a little longer as if the speaker drew it out.

"Yes," Mariella said. "I want to register a complaint about your pricing."

"Our prices are the best in the city."

The voice almost seemed to come from all around her. Calm,

soothing, convincing. All she had to do was listen. All she had to do was relax. All she had to do was buy something and give in.

But she wasn't convinced.

"Yours ain't even the best prices on this block, never mind the city," she said.

A low rumbled started around her. Something sharp scraped against the floor in front of her. She felt warm air move across her skin, carrying a thick, putrid odour. Her stomach clenched. Bile burned her throat and her tongue. She swallowed, forcing it down, but her heart started to pound.

"We have the best prices!"

The last word roared at her with a great rush of air. She squinted against it but didn't turn her head away. Couldn't turn her head away. If she showed weakness it would get her.

She knew it.

"Oh yeah?" she said. "What's this two mugs for ten dollars? That's not a bargain. And these bedsheets for fifty dollars? That's no deal, that's regular price. And I seen a better price on kid's running shoes at Breakers' Shoes and they're not even a thrift store. You ain't got the best prices. In fact, some of your prices are the worst!"

Sweat poured down her back, making her t-shirt stick to her skin. She could feel the wet tendrils of her hair sticking to her neck. But it didn't matter. None of it mattered. She was on a roll now.

The rumbling around her built, twisted into growls.

"You ain't no Bargain Kingdom," she said. "Your prices are crappy, your selection is boring, and your return policy is horrible!"

The growl turned into a roar.

But behind the roar, she heard voices. Other voices. People calling out. And someone yelled out, "Mariella!"

She knew that twangy voice.

Sondra!

Still alive! Maybe they were all still alive. Maybe this thing hadn't had a chance to eat them or whatever it wanted to do to them yet.

Something slammed down on the tile in front of her. She caught a glimpse of yellowish nail. Huge, maybe six inches across.

The hand those things belonged to could crush her.

But it hadn't. Maybe it couldn't. Maybe it couldn't without convincing her, cajoling her, the way it had the others.

Maybe she had to buy what it was selling.

And she weren't buyin'.

She pulled her shoulders back, felt a crack snap in her back as the muscles shifted. She lifted her chin.

"You gonna match the prices I see or what?" she said.

Snarls and growls sounded but she couldn't make out any actual words. Was it trying to talk but had gotten itself too pissed off? Already the putrid odour was starting to fade. She caught a whiff of one of those toilet cleaners that you drop into the bowl. Boy, those things could stink.

"This is all a con," she said. "You ain't no Bargain Kingdom and I'm gonna complain about this. Just you wait and see. People listen to me when I shop. I know a good bargain. I got a Daffy Duck mug for two dollars, not a chip, not a scratch. Still had the original sticker on the bottom. That mug originally sold for over twenty and I got it for two. Can you match that?"

The growl sputtered into a cough, then a voice finally spoke again, "Knock off."

Mariella shook her head. "You think I don't know merchandise?" she said. "It had the trademark symbol on the bottom. Two dollars. That's a bargain. And you can't match it."

The voices were louder now. She could hear Sondra calling out. Chanting.

"Go, Mariella, go!"

Soon, the other voices took up the chant. "Go, Mariella, go!"

She felt heat flush her face. Tears filled her eyes and she had to blink fast to stop them from falling.

Working. It was working.

"What are you willing to pay?" said the voice.

The flush of victory drained away. Weren't gonna be as easy as she'd thought. Bargaining always was a two way enterprise.

"Depends on what you've got for sale," Mariella said. "I been a bargain hunter all my life. I'm one of the best you'll ever see. You're gonna have to show me something well worth buying."

The rumble pulled away. Above her, small pot lights in the ceiling began to brighten, leading toward the back of the store.

Time to check out the merchandise.

Her flats made a shush shush sound on the tile. Around her, she caught glimpses of racks and tables, laden with stuff, but everything was so dark she couldn't get a good look at it.

That wasn't what she was shopping for anyway, and she was sure this so-called "manager" knew it.

By the time she reached the last table, the air around her had turned chilly. She shivered in just a t-shirt and her thin skirt. Weird, if this was the devil or something, she'da thought it would need burning heat but already she could almost see her breath hanging in the air as she exhaled.

Just to the right on the back wall, she spotted a pair of double doors. "Authorized Personnel Only." The door on the right shimmied back and forth, as if someone had just gone back through.

Leading her on.

She took a step forward. Then her feet wouldn't work any more.

Still time to leave. Still time to back out of the store.

Then what? How could she face anyone in this neighbourhood if she quit now? Sure, they wouldn't know, but she would. She'd know how far she got.

Quit belly aching and get on with it. Time for shopping.

Her feet started working again.

But her hands still shook a bit when she reached the door and pushed through. Just a bit though.

A darkened hallway led the way forward. It was double wide, probably for fitting big boxes of merchandise. Now she shuffled across concrete. The air smelled of saw dust and something underneath, that putrid, oozing smell again.

It led forward, through another set of double doors at the far end. Probably into the warehouse.

Why not? She'd always loved warehouse sales. Even bigger bargains.

This time she didn't hesitate, just kept right on through those double doors that squeaked as she pushed her way through them, the faint hint of oil on their hinges wafting past her nose, adding a layer of texture under the rising stench of decay.

The warehouse stretched out ahead of her, shrouded in darkness. To her left, she caught a suggestion of looming shapes. Boxes? But to the right…

Movement. Figures behind bars. Hands reaching out toward her. She caught a glimpse of bony limbs, all elbows and knees.

Sondra!

She took a step toward them.

"Bargain now."

The voice boomed out from in front of her. Heard the scrap of claw on the concrete, high-pitched and shrieking, like nails on a blackboard.

Mariella stopped and turned to face the "manager."

She couldn't see him fully in the darkness, just the suggestion of a huge looming figure. She caught a glimpse of yellow claws digging into the concrete, saw the huge gouges in the floor. The stench of the thing's breath grew strong and thick, the oily, rotting smell almost seeming to slide down her throat. She definitely felt it coating the roof of her mouth. It didn't matter if she breathed through her nose or mouth. There was no escaping that smell, that fetid taste.

She shivered, from the cold and the stench. The door was just a few steps behind her. She could still leave.

No, she couldn't.

"So what are you selling?" she said.

She felt a suggestion of movement, a swoosh of something gesturing toward the caged shoppers to her right.

"Them," the voice said.

"And?" Mariella said.

"That is all."

Mariella shook her head. "Oh no, that's not a bargain. I told you, I'm a bargain hunter. You're gonna have to do better than that."

A growl rumbled out from in front of her, shaking the air, the room, the boxes around her, the walls. The shoppers to her right cried out. Hands grabbed hold of the bars. Sondra's voice rose above the others, yelping.

"You bring me here to really bargain or what?" Mariella said. "Don't waste my time!"

The growl faded to a low grumble. Sounding almost…yes, sounding almost like pouting.

This thing didn't like her talking back.

Mariella straightened her shoulders. Okay, time to get down to the meat of it.

"Here's the deal," she said. "I take all of them." She gestured at the shoppers to her right. "You close the store and clear out of here. Find some other place for your "Bargain Kingdom" and make sure it's far away from here, like some other planet or something."

"And you?" The voice purred loudly. A rush of air billowed toward her, carrying the stench of death and decay. "What do you pay?"

Mariella's heart pounded. The sickly flavour soured in her mouth. She felt her body quiver, all the way through, as if her internal organs were vibrating.

What would she pay?

She wanted to curl up away from that creature, hide her face, so it wouldn't pay attention to her. Why did she have to do this? Why?

Because she was the queen of the bargain hunters.

Right.

She tensed her shoulders and jutted out her chin.

"I won't rat you out to the papers or the Better Business Bureau. I'll let you close up shop nice and quiet, with no fuss. You can even hold a going out of business sale to dump this merchandise, but it's gotta be a real sale, and no funny business."

She wagged her finger at the darkness.

A rumbling started and after a moment she realized it was laughter.

"You think that is an offer of payment?" the voice said. "I could crush you where you stand."

It could, she knew it could. She'd seen the size of those claws.

But it hadn't, and she had a distinct feeling it really couldn't.

"You could," she said. "But you won't. I'm guessing you can't for some reason. Maybe cuz I'm not listening to you." She sucked in a fast breath and didn't care about the stink of it.

"That's it, isn't it? You can't control me so you can't hurt me."

The laughing rumbling died off into silence. Nails scraped on the concrete.

Now Mariella laughed.

"Now I think you'd better get down to business," she said. "Let's settle this deal."

And they did settle, just like she wanted. The Bargain Kingdom went out of business two days later with a big twenty-four hour blow out sale. Although tempted, Mariella didn't go shopping that day. Instead, she sat in the coffee shop, reading the paper and enjoying a mug of tea.

Almost as nice as with her Daffy mug at home, but there she didn't get to keep an eye out on the Bargain Kingdom.

Sondra showed up, laden with bags in her scrawny arms. She almost dropped them before she made it across the coffee shop to Mariella's table. Mariella had to hurry over when her friend staggered through the door. Between the two of them, they carried the bags to the table and almost buried it.

"What the heck did you get?" Mariella said.

"Oh Mariella, you shoulda been there," Sondra said "It was the best sale I've ever seen! I got this set of four tea towels for seventy-five cents, and this deluxe curling iron for five dollars."

She chattered on and on, recounting all the bargains she'd bought and how she'd talked the clerks down.

Mariella sat across from her sipping on her tea as Sondra's arms waved in the air.

"I tell ya, Mariella, I was on fire in there. Ain't no one got better deals than me." She puffed up her narrow chest. "I bet they'll be calling me queen of the bargain hunters now."

Mariella smiled and didn't say a word.

She knew who'd gotten the better deal.

The best deal of her life.

About the Author

Based in Toronto, Canada, Rebecca M. Senese survives the frigid blasts of winter and boiling steams of summer by weaving words of horror, mystery, science fiction and contemporary fantasy.

Garnering an Honorable Mention in "The Year's Best Science Fiction" and nominated for numerous Aurora Awards, her work has appeared in *Fiction River: Superpowers*, *Fiction River: Visions of the Apocalypse*, *Fiction River: Sparks*, *Fiction River: Recycled Pulp*, *Tesseracts 16: Parnassus Unbound*, *Imaginarium 2012*, *Tesseracts 15: A Case of Quite Curious Tales*, *TransVersions*, *Future Syndicate*, and *Storyteller*, amongst others.

Find out more about Rebecca at:
rebeccasenese.com

The Grave-Diggers

DeAnna Knippling

The night air was chill and misty after about a week of heavy rain, the kind of night that crept underneath your clothes and lay cool on your skin. It was about as appealing as an earthworm's tender caress. But under the top inch or so of surface, the soil was heavy, wet, and a little loose. Perfect weather, that was, for grave digging.

I'm not above digging up some dirt for cash. As a private detective, it's basically part of my job description. So as I sat underneath the shadow of an old oak tree on the other side of the cemetery wall, I wasn't judging the two men with shovels and a hooded lantern out in the oldest part of the cemetery. I was mostly just grateful not to have to do the dirty work myself.

Nevertheless I couldn't help be irritated by the amateurism they brought to the job. They'd brought shovels and that was it. That's fine if you're digging up a fresh grave. The hard work has already been done for you.

But this wasn't a fresh grave.

It was over a hundred years old. Plenty of time for the tree roots to take over, lacing themselves over and around and even *through* the dead, which were only buried in pine coffins back then. A spade is a spade is not going to hack through a hundred-year-old tree root, and I had thought that those two men had more sense than that.

I had already taken at least a dozen good camera shots with a telephoto lens and a long exposure time of the two men straining and chopping in the dirt, and I was starting to get bored.

I fantasized about walking back to my Buick Super to get my mattock, which is basically an axe you can dig with. Perfect for tree roots.

Hello, boys. Remember me? It's old Dick Delaney, haven't seen either of you for years. But don't mind me! I just happened to drive by and think, well, it's gonna take those two chuckleheads a while to dig all the way down into that old grave, and I thought I'd keep you company. Help you dig?

Don't mind if I do.

The two men, I'd known them since they were in diapers. They were twin brothers from a wealthy family nearby, Arnold and James Ormiston. Or, I should say, a formerly wealthy family. The father had, as fathers sometimes do, lost most of the family money on the stock market all the way back in '29. The family had slogged it out until the second World War, when things started to take a turn for the better for them, as Papa Ormiston did some shady deals with war profiteering over oats, of all things. Then, just after the war, they had sunk back down again. It was said that the family had suffered from a series of bad investments, but I didn't buy it. Nobody would say exactly which investments had done them wrong. And it was my experience that men could seldom keep their mouths shut about that kind of thing.

I suspected blackmail.

Boy, was I wrong.

By this point you're probably asking yourself, *What's going on here? Who hired private detective Dick Delaney to take photos of these two guys anyway? What's his angle?*

As always, follow the money.

I'd been hired by Vincent Toomey, the president of the Canal Street Bank of Maine, which held the paper on about a half a mil in Ormiston family debts. Not surprisingly, Toomey wanted some extra security on the Ormiston boys. Not just evidence that they were spending money that was no longer theirs, but any kind of material on any crimes, illicit affairs, shady deals, or anything else that might prove useful.

I'd followed them hoping for gun running, illegal drugs, or an orgy. The shovels had surprised me. But digging up a grave seemed promisingly dirty all the same. What were Arnold and James up to, I wondered—pulling the rings off a corpse and using them to pay off the interest on a couple of loans?

The corpse belonged to an ancestress of theirs, a woman named Marie-Jean Ormiston. Her heyday had been all the way back in the 1830s; she had died exactly a hundred years ago, in 1849.

The good people of Portland, Maine, still remembered her as a witch. They said she held Black Masses and ate the flesh of virgins as a restorative. Her house, until they tore it down back in 1932, was *that* house, the one that parents warned about. Little kids crossed the street to avoid it. Big, abandoned, and with the floors collapsing from rot. Dangerous.

Haunted.

I had a personal beef with that house. The reason they tore it down was that six kids had gone into the house on Halloween night on a dare, and only one of them had made it out alive. The survivor, a kid named Ted Germann, had claimed that the ghost of the old witch had murdered the rest of the kids, one after another, with an axe.

Turned out it hadn't been an axe. You guessed it. The killer used a mattock.

First the police suspected poor Germann of having killed all the others. But Germann was right-handed, and, from the angles of the wounds, they were able to determine that the killer had been left-handed, and, incidentally, about six inches taller. Germann had been only five feet, four inches and probably weight a hundred and ten pounds dripping wet. The killer had taken the kids down with brutal efficiency that Germann just didn't have the muscle for.

The police checked the rest of the suspects, listened to their alibis, and decided it had been a drifter. Some crazy who had spotted the abandoned house in the heavy mist and set up camp inside, only to go berserk when some idiot kids decided to join him for the night.

No sign of a drifter was ever found, but what else could it have been?

It couldn't have been the ghost of Marie-Jean Ormiston. She had been five feet tall, and the historians were pretty sure even now that she'd been right-handed.

In the end, they tore the place down, burned the wreckage, then dug up the ash and hauled it out to the dump. Then they backfilled the whole area with clean dirt. The place is nothing but an empty lot these days, a big gray patch in the sod they laid over the spot. The grass never grew. The gray patch in the grass just lingers there, marking the edges of rumor and death.

What makes it personal is that my older brother George was one of the kids who'd been killed. I'd even begged to go along with him to the bonfire that he was supposed to be going to with the rest of his football team. No dice. Nobody wants a little brother hanging around, especially when you and your best friends are sneaking off to an old haunted house to make out with girls.

So instead of getting killed, I ended up getting hired by the Orm-istons to babysit their bratty twins for the night. My parents were going to the same party the Ormistons were. My doom was sealed.

Kind of ironic, the way life had taken me full circle, from the Army and all over Europe, back to my home town and watching over the same two brats as before. I took another photo of them trying to dig through century-old oak roots.

What did they think they were going to find in that grave? I wondered what was going through their minds. Weren't they scared?

They'd been young, though, when it had happened. And I'd always wondered how much they'd remembered, that night.

The hours toiled on. I drank coffee laced with whiskey from my thermos, but I didn't smoke. The scent might have carried.

I found myself remembering George.

When I was a kid, I'd worshipped him. Star quarterback on the team, back when they still wore helmets made out of leather. Handsome, confident, tall, and, to my younger self, wise. Now I can only think of him as the idiot who lied about going to a public bonfire. The easiest alibi in the world to break. What else did he expect but trouble?

Ted Germann had always maintained that George and his girl-friend, Louise Trinward, had been the first ones to die. George had died trying to shield Louise's body from the attack. Later my pop found a wadded-up note in George's room, him trying to find the words to say that Louise was pregnant and they wanted to get married. I remember the look on Pop's face when he found the note, which I'd already read and wadded back up again.

And I remembered Ma screaming at the Ormistons. "You murdered my son!"

It didn't make sense at the time, but later I wondered: Had they? Really?

But the Ormistons had been at the same party as my parents had. Having the father of one of the dead kids vouching for your presence is one heck of an alibi.

I squinted into the mist rolling in off the river and idly came up with a hare-brained scheme to fit all the facts. In my version, someone had found out about some Ormiston family secret and had started blackmailing the Ormistons with the information in 1929. Then the Ormistons had somehow taken revenge in 1932; for example, maybe a cousin had come into town and done it while Mr. and Mrs. Ormiston were conspicuously providing themselves with an alibi. But now, in 1949, the tables had been turned again, and the Ormistons were in serious financial trouble. Blackmailed again. Would there be another killing, to "redress" some terrible balance?

What can I say? I was bored.

The original secret...now, let's see. The old witch had died in October 1849 of scarlet fever, but let's say she was poisoned. One of the great-great-whatevers put arsenic in Old Mother Ormiston's tea, and down the old witch went, swearing that one of her descendants would exact revenge eighty-five years later, in 1932.

That's where it fell apart in my mind. Why not a hundred years later? Why 1932?

And why George? Our family had only moved to Portland in the 1920s. Before that, we'd been Canadian. We didn't have any part of this.

I was just about ready to run back to my car—it had started to rain, the flat kind that rattles when it hits the pavement—when the twins both swore loudly into the night and jumped out of the hole they'd been digging.

The rain slapped onto the tarp they'd laid out on the grass to hold all the dirt they'd dug up. In the light of their little kerosene lantern, their faces looked terrified. I took a quick shot of them with the camera.

I heard the unmistakable sound of something moving around in the dirt. Something flopping around and hissing, or slithering.

Great, I thought, the two brats must have dug up a badger's nest. Gruesome place for it.

Then both men shuddered and took another step backward.

Arnold, who was the slightly older of the two, cleared his throat. His next words came clearly to me through a gap in the rain.

"Well, *one* of us has to get it."

They looked at each other.

Then James dropped down into the grave. I heard a grunt and the sound of a scuffle. "Help me!"

Arnold said, "Get your hands off him, you filthy beast," and jumped down into the grave after him.

I could have sworn I heard the sound of a fist hitting flesh.

I stared at the grave through the telephoto lens for a moment, remembering all the time those two brats had made my life miserable back when they were still in short pants. After my brother George's death, I rarely saw them again. Understandably, the Ormistons had to get a new babysitter.

I cursed and jogged over towards the grave site.

The two men weren't fighting a badger but were struggling with a seven-foot-tall *witch*. Rotten flesh, clothes in rags, eyes shining like a pair of unnatural blue sapphires from her eye sockets.

And covered in gold and silver jewelry. Pearls. Gemstones.

It was like watching some kind of weird parlor trick. Not quite real, or at least I couldn't believe it, even though it was right in front of me.

Like the fool I was, the first thing I did was take a half-dozen photographs of her trying to kill the Ormiston boys. Then I tossed the camera aside under the boughs of a tree, picked up one of the fallen shovels, and raised it over my shoulder.

Those two boys were six feet tall if they were half an inch. But the dead witch was taller. I gave the shovel a swing.

Home run. The back of the old witch's head smashed like an eggshell, and she went limp.

And fell on top of James Ormiston, who had one hand up to protect his face from the old witch's claws, and the other fisted in her jewelry.

The old witch dragged James down to the mud in the bottom of the grave. James started screaming.

"What's going on there?" roared a voice from behind me, as a bright white beam of light threw my silhouette over the grave. Then a curse was added as the police officer stepped forward to look at the chaos below.

The rain came down flat and hard and steady.

What was there to say, really? A dead corpse was lying on top of James. James had a fistful of gold, pearls, and gemstones sparkling in one fist. Arnold leaned against the side of the pit, breathing hard.

And me, I was holding a spade covered with gray hair and unidentifiable sludge where the back of the witch's skull had stuck to it. A camera with a long telephoto lens lay to one side.

It all seemed pretty self-explanatory to me.

"Dick Delaney," Arnold said slowly, finally registering my presence. "What brings you here this time of night?"

"Oh, you know me," I said. "I saw you two boys at work and thought I'd stop by to help out. I'd ask you what brought you to dig up Great-great-great Grandma Ormiston, but it seems pretty obvious. Strapped for cash?"

"Shut up," James said, "and get this thing off me." He was still trapped underneath the witch's corpse.

Arnold heaved himself away from the side of the pit and started to untangle his brother.

"I don't care if she is a relative," the cop said, his voice shaky, "The three of you are under arrest for trespassing, if nothing else."

I protested. "I'm not trespassing. I'm providing aid and succor. It was an emergency."

The cop eyeballed me. "What?"

"That corpse," I said. "It jumped up out of the grave and started beating the snot out of those two men. At least, that's the way it looked to me at the time."

"Uh-huh," the cop said. "Where were you?"

I pointed to my hiding spot outside the cemetery wall, then at my camera. "I'm a private detective, officer. I've been hired to follow these two around and find out what they're up to."

"You d—ed spy!" James shouted. "I should have known! You were always a liar."

"Who sent you?" Arnold asked, his expression steely now.

I didn't answer until the cop repeated the question.

"The bank," I said. "Arnold and James there are almost half a mil in debt at the Canal Street Bank. Although I doubt that the old broad has that much on her. Maybe a couple of thousand in gold, that's all."

The cop whistled.

Arnold had finally pulled the corpse off James. James scrambled out from under her, then kicked her in the shoulder.

The cop said, "Pretty good condition for a corpse from the 1840s, wouldn't you say?"

"There's an old family legend," Arnold said, holding a hand out to me, "that Marie-Jean was a witch. We're looking for her lucky necklace, a set of disks on a long, gold chain. If we could get that back…"

He didn't finish his sentence. Maybe he'd realized how nutty it sounded.

I helped pull Arnold out of the pit, then he turned around and helped his brother out. For a moment, all four of us looked down at the corpse lying there. The earth and roots looked like they had been blasted out. The pine coffin was nothing but shreds of sawdust.

And I swear in the predawn light that the witch's flesh was *green*.

James shoved his handful of jewels into his pocket.

The cop cleared his throat. "You're going to want to drop those back in the grave," he said, putting a heavy hand on James's shoulder. "Otherwise I'm going to have to add theft to the charges you're racking up tonight. Come on, let's go."

James dug the jewelry out of his pocket with obvious reluctance. As far as that kid was concerned, the treasure was *his*. He held his arm out stiffly and let the slinky gold chains and strings of pearls slip slowly out of his hand to fall back down into the grave.

"What about him?" he said, pointing to me.

"He didn't do anything wrong," the cop said.

"He's going to steal the treasure!"

The cop looked me straight in the eye. "He's going to stand guard here while I call for backup. And then he's going to go home for the night. He'd going to keep his hands off that stuff, lucky charm or no. Otherwise he might lose his license."

"Yes, sir," I said. Not a muscle twitched in my face. I didn't even blink.

The cop led the two men out to his patrol car, parked on the other side of the fence. I stood at the edge of the open grave, looking down at the dead witch lying at the bottom.

Like I said, she was tall. Seven feet at least. Dressed in the silk rags of some old-fashioned silk party dress. The back of her skull had caved in. It was like looking down into a void smeared with rotten sea weed. The rain had started to come down even harder. Now when it hit the ground, it bounced back up again. I was wet through to the skin. I didn't like to think about my camera, either. I turned to pick it up. I intended to shove it under my jacket lapel and race with it back to the car.

I could hear the sound of the cop calling it in, playing it completely straight. I glanced over toward the street and found that I couldn't see much other than the cop's headlights, in the thick of the rain.

I glanced back into the grave.

That's when I saw it. The necklace.

I had been expecting, I don't know, a gold chain with a bunch of gold washers strung on it. But that wasn't it at all. It was a kind of sphere made out of interwoven gold rings that seemed to move under the dull light from the lamp on the far side of the grave.

Lucky? It almost seemed magic.

"I found it!" I shouted. I couldn't tell whether they'd heard me or not.

The bottom of the grave was filling up with water. Soil was crumbling down from the sides of the hole the boys had dug.

The twisted roots seemed to writhe through the bottom of the grave, reaching for the necklace.

In a few minutes, the mud was going to cover it up. And then, I somehow knew, it would be gone. So I hopped down inside and picked up the necklace.

It came up in a tangle and caught in the witch's fingers, which were half bone and half green flesh. Her arm rose as I tried to untangle it, dangling shreds of wet silk.

I cursed and reached into my pocket for my penknife. I pulled it out with my free hand, then scraped open the blade with my thumbnail. The cops were going to be mad when they found out, but the thought of letting that necklace slip away, lost forever, when those two kids needed it…it seemed like the wrong thing to do.

Knife outstretched, I started to saw through a string of pearls…

Then the old witched moved her head, slowly rolling it around on her shoulders to look at me.

From a throat destroyed by time, she growled, "You know that curiosity killed the cat, don't you?"

She reached for my throat. I stumbled backward into the wall of the grave and started to scream.

She grabbed for my throat and *squeezed*. Her hands were cold, yet sharp. My scream cut off and I started choking on my own air. I tried to knock her arms aside. It was like smacking my forearms against iron bars.

The edges of my vision started to gray out. Then I saw the disk necklace, the lucky one, hanging from around the old witch's neck. I grabbed the disks and felt them dig into my palm.

The last thing I remember thinking was, *Why me?*

—

When I came to, everything was in black and white and kind of hazy. I was in an old Victorian-style house that had fallen to pieces. At the time, I was confused about what was going on, but from my perspective now, it was perfectly clear that I had gone back to the past.

The floor didn't creak underfoot, and I seemed to float over the missing stairs and sunken holes leading down through the living room floor to the cellar, like some kind of ghost. I tried to pick up a few dusty, spiderweb-crusted objects still lying around, but my hand passed through them.

The sun was setting. Across the street, I could see the flickering lights of jack-o-lantern candles burning inside their carved pumpkins. Every single house had several in front, staring like unshakable guardians at the house I was in. The gray light in the sky faded to darkness. A layer of clouds covered the stars, and the wind picked up, rolling leaves down the gutters.

It was then that I realized where I was. 1932.

"Don't come, George," I said. "Don't come tonight."

I felt like I was fourteen again, the fourteen that had happened to me after I found out about my brother.

The police reports said that my brother and his friends had broken in through the back door; I left the front of the house and drifted to the small kitchen window to wait.

It didn't take long.

Several shadowy forms climbed over the back fence from the alleyway and dropped silently into the grass of the back yard, which was long and full of weeds. The boys caught the girls and lowered them down.

I counted six figures...

Then another one climbed over the fence.

Seven.

Ted Germann had said there were only six: my brother, Ted, another friend of theirs named Bucky Belanger, and their girlfriends.

So who was this?

In the darkness, I couldn't tell.

My brother was the first to reach the back door. It was locked, but its window pane was busted. He reached through to unlock the door. I could hear their breathing as they entered, but it sounded muffled and distant.

The last one through—the stranger—closed the door behind them and locked it. By then, my brother had found the cellar door and had opened it.

There was a spark of light as he switched his flashlight on.

In that strange vision, the images brought up by the light seemed flat and distant. My brother's and Louise's faces looked like still photographs rather than living people.

"George!"

He didn't hear me. None of them did. They shuffled forward down the stairs, following the glow from my brother's flashlight.

I watched the last figure's face, trying to pick out its features. Male and big, that was all I got. Bigger than George, who was a quarterback on the football team. One of his teammates, maybe. But I couldn't get a clear look at his face. He grasped the handrail with his left hand, but took it off again, wiping it on his pants. The spiders had been thorough. A moment later, he scratched his face. Again with his left hand.

Was this man the killer? If so, why had Ted Germann covered up for him, all those years?

Down and down they went. They crossed the cellar, circling the fallen beams from above. On the far side of the cellar, my brother handed his flashlight to Louise and took a jingling set of keys from his pocket. He had reached a door.

A door that had never been mentioned in *any* of the materials I'd researched on the case.

It was a heavy door, made of rough-split oak trunks and iron banks. It looked out of place. My brother unlocked it and it seemed to swing toward him before he could even touch the handle.

On the other side was darkness so black that not even the flashlight was enough to penetrate it. Whispers echoed in my mind as it opened, but none of the others seemed to hear.

George grinned back at the others. "This is gonna be seriously cool. Make sure nobody follows us down here, all right?"

"Sure, chief," the seventh figure said, in a voice that sounded suspiciously familiar.

One of the girls said, "In there?"

Louise looked over her shoulder and hissed, "Afraid?"

"Yes," the girl said.

Yessssss.

The whisper seemed to hiss through time itself.

My brother ducked through the doorway and went inside, Louise following wordlessly after him. The flashlight seemed to have been swallowed up. Outside in the cellar was a faint, reflected light that seemed to come from just around some corner or other. But past the doorway was only darkness.

Bucky and his girl followed after Louise; then came Ted and his little mouse of a girlfriend, clinging to his side.

The seventh figure didn't follow them but stood guard outside the door. In the dull gray light of the cellar, I was finally able to get a look at his face.

My jaw dropped. It was Vincent Toomey, the president of the Canal Street Bank. The man who had hired me. He'd grown up here in town, had been on the football team, and was only a year younger than my brother had been.

He was unmistakable. He has ears like batwings, a big broken nose, and eyelids that couldn't seem to lift themselves past half mast. Toom the Doom. He had been a fullback on the football team. I was sure it was the same guy.

So...why had Germann lied?

Toomey almost seemed to lock black-and-white eyes with me, then ducked through the doorway, closing it after him with a thump. I tried opening it, but my hand passed through the door-knob. If that's how it was going to be, I thought, I'd just walk through the door. No dice. I slammed into the door. It was rock solid. Didn't hurt walking into it, though. It was more like I just bounced off.

I waited, caught between knowing what was had to happen and praying it wouldn't.

The door creaked open, but nobody emerged. I tried to enter but was again rebuffed, this time by the open doorway. A shadow moved on the other side, and then Toomey backed out, holding my brother's body in his arms.

George's eyes practically bulged out of his skull. His mouth was wide open, and his chest was hitching in shallow pants that were almost like hiccups.

He was still alive.

"George!"

He didn't hear me. I tried to pick him up but my arms slid right through him.

Meanwhile Toomey had gone back inside the doorway and returned with Louise, whom he lay next to George. One by one, Toomey carried out all the others—including Germann—and laid them out on the cellar floor.

Then he moved a pile of junk to reveal a mattock, which he hefted and lay over his shoulder. It only took a swing or two before I knew enough. Too much. Toomey was definitely left-handed. I turned my head to the side until the sounds had stopped. Not a scream or a plea for mercy came out of any of their mouths. He went right down the line.

When it was done, Toomey sat down on a fallen beam and rested, panting. Some job he'd been up to, all right. A lot of hard work. He rubbed a hand across his face to clear the blood and sweat away. Then he stood up and kicked each of them, checking to make sure they were each dead.

Then he went up the cellar stairs, taking the mattock with him.

There was nothing else I could do in that cellar. I followed him.

He led me over the back fence and into the alley, then down the alley and across a couple of blocks to his car, which was parked under an old oak tree, the same place I'd had my car parked the night of the gravedigging, in 1949. I'd never before noticed just how close the old Ormiston place was to the cemetery.

He tossed the mattock in the trunk of his car, then staggered toward the cemetery wall. In moments he was beside the old witch's grave.

At the headstone, Toomey stopped. "It's done. Are you happy yet?"

Then he spat on the grave and walked away.

I couldn't understand any of it. Why had Toomey killed my brother and his friends? Why go to Old Mother Ormiston's grave afterwards and ask her if she was happy? Why, years later, had he hired the younger brother of one of his victims to investigate the last heirs of Old Mother Ormiston? Had he known that they would have to dig up her grave?

Why was the old witch's corpse so tall?

Two things seemed pretty clear to me, though. One, I had seen irrefutable proof that Toomey was left-handed as he swung the mattock, and two, that Old Mother Ormiston's lucky necklace was valuable indeed. I had no doubt that what I had seen was the truth, if maybe not the whole of it.

I'd forgotten something. Germann had survived the night. And yet when I'd glanced at him down in the cellar, I was sure he'd been dead.

I raced back to the Ormiston house. Already a police car had pulled up in front, and two officers were climbing down into the cellar, flashlights turning the scene bright, but unnaturally flat. Germann was climbing down after them, shivering and covered with black blood stains, but basically in one piece.

The three men reached the cellar floor and found the bodies.

This time, there were only five of 'em. No sign of Germann's corpse at all.

I came to with the old witch's hands around my neck. However, her head lolled loose on her shoulders, and her hands slithered off my neck and down my chest as she fell in a heap at my feet.

I looked up. The Ormiston boys were looking down at me, Arnold holding a shovel in both hands. The police officer was not far behind, eyes wide.

I held up my hand, still clutching the necklace. "Found it," I said.

James grabbed it from me. The rain had slowed somewhat, but it was still to slippery to climb out of the grave on my own. I held out a hand, and Arnold put down his spade to help me climb out. I was covered with mud, front and back.

"Did you...?" he said.

"I saw something," I agreed. "What, I'm not sure. But I think it went back to 1932."

We looked down at the witch lying in the bottom of the grave.

"That's not Great-grandma Ormiston," Arnold said.

"I don't think so either," I said. "But if not her, then who?"

James stumbled suddenly, took two steps, and went down on his knees. "That *bastard*," he said. "That *bastard*." He must have popped back through time and seen what I had seen.

The four of us looked each other over.

Then the police officer took the two brothers and their strange necklace to the police station, while I rescued my camera from under the tree. It was a grim prospect. After the backup arrived to take charge of the scene, I took the camera home, then rewound the film in my dark room. The camera itself was shot, completely ruined. But I saved the film, which I cleaned and developed.

The camera's lens sees the world a little differently than the human eye. The witch showed up on the film all right, but changed in a way that gave me a little *aha!* moment.

The witch wasn't a witch at all, but a kind of tied-together construct, a set of bones assembled like a hand-puppet with some loose skin, hair, and silk rags thrown on. A trail of dull-looking mist trailed behind her in the half-dozen pictures of her that I had taken from above the grave. The mist led downward into a dark spot in the dirt.

It had been some kind of arcane *puppet*, not old Marie-Jean.

Which kind of explained the way that, when the other pair of police officers arrived and we looked down into that rain-filled grave, all that remained to be seen was busted roots, slivers of pine, and a few pieces of antique jewelry.

I needed to question two people: Germann and Toomey. Either or both of them could be dangerous, perhaps even supernaturally so. I decided to start with Toomey. He had the higher chance of still being human.

Back in 1932, Toomey had been seen at the football bonfire. But by the actual time of the killing, the coach had been plastered and the chaperones had more or less wandered off. Several other football players, cheerleaders, and their girlfriends had sworn that Toomey had been there the whole time—but then they'd sworn that my brother and his friends had been there the whole time too.

Toomey's house along the coast was definitely a banker's house. It had a too-small, fussy feel about it. It had pride of place, the feeling that it had elbowed its way onto the perch over the cliffs, and it asked no more of life than that. The gray shake siding seemed to mutter in the breeze and the dark. The water sucked at the pebbles along the edge of the bay.

Sssss, said the waves, as they retreated off the beach.

I knocked on the door.

"Mr. Toomey? You home? It's Delaney. You need to see what I just got on the Ormiston boys."

Nobody answered. The car was still in the drive. Eventually I worked my way around to the back of the house and slipped the lock on the back door.

I left two hours later, a wiser man.

Vincent Toomey was going broke. He was being black-mailed—by Ted Germann. Among his financial papers I found a note. *Remember 1932 and donate accordingly. Ted.* But there was a smudge on the paper; it might have said 1832. I couldn't be sure. The note had been torn up and tossed in the fireplace, which had gone out.

Vincent Toomey was down in his storm cellar. At least, he wasn't anywhere else in the house, and the body that lay on the floor down there looked like his. But there was a door just barely ajar on the far side of the cellar, filled with impenetrable black-ness, and by then I had grown to doubt the evidence provided by common sense.

Was the thing that lay down there human? It stank of human-ity, you might say.

I heard something slithering on the other side of the doorway, and left promptly, cleaning up after myself and wiping up any possible prints.

My skin crawled, waiting for *it* to climb up the stairs and come after me.

I always knew that something nasty lay just under the surface of everyday appearances. I just hadn't realized my suspicions were so *literal*.

That left Ted Germann. He was easy enough to find, right there in the phone book on the table by the phone, but I dragged my feet for an hour or two, drinking coffee and looking through old photograph albums. *Did* I have a photo of Ted Germann from after the attack? The old newspaper clip-pings I had all cut off at his feet or above, all the better to focus on the young man's face. What I wanted to know was whether he was the same kind of puppet that the witch in the grave had been.

I dawdled until about one in the morning. If I were a little more dramatic, I'd say my soul crawled with horror at the thought of confronting him. But mostly I felt the kind of bone-tired you get when you've been in a war for about two years too long. *People.* Sometimes you just get sick of the sheer stupidity of them.

Then I remembered there was at least one more box of albums downstairs, in my basement.

I went down there with my flashlight in one hand and my mattock in the other. No mysterious door in sight, which was a relief. I found the last box and brought it up with me.

Flipping through the photos was painful. These were the last photos of my brother, the album that my mother had been putting together for George's graduation. The album had changed with the night of the murders, and had become a collection of evidence.

Mom had saved several photos of Ted Germann. One in particular caught my eye. It was one from his younger days, with George's arm over his shoulder. The best of friends. Neither one of them was some kind of occult puppet. And I didn't find anything else useful in that album, except memories. There were a couple of blank spots where she had pulled the photos of the Ormiston boys out of the album. She had *never* forgiven that family for the death of her son.

I found one of my old cameras in the bottom of the box, which I took to replace the one I'd ruined. I took it into the darkroom and loaded it with some film. I couldn't put it off any longer. It was time to go.

—

Ted Germann lived in an apartment, one of those buildings with two up and two down. A miserable, cheap kind of place. Not the kind of place you'd pick out for a successful black-mailer. But then again, maybe it was just right—the IRS would never suspect a thing, living in a place like that.

It had started to drizzle again. I parked the car and walked to his apartment, holding the mattock in one hand, the flashlight in the other, and the camera strap around my neck.

Germann had the downstairs right-hand apartment. I busted the lock and went in. The chain wasn't on the door. All it took was a little prying with the mattock.

A quick search showed that Germann wasn't on the main floor. That left the communal basement.

I found the door to the stairs, opened it, and went in.

Slowly, one foot after another.

Down and down...

I could already hear the hissing sound, the sound of *it* moving in the darkness. I should have turned around and run, turned around and left a trail of burnt rubber straight to Nebraska.

Instead I kept walking forward until I reached the basement floor. I swung my flashlight around. It was a bunch of cement, two-by-four framing, and pipes running overhead.

Ted was waiting for me, grinning.

"Delaney," he said, turning my name into a joke.

"Germann," I echoed sardonically. "Or whatever you are."

"Now, now."

"What the h— is going on?" I asked. "None of this is making sense."

"Doesn't it?"

"No."

"I'm not Germann," he said. "This is just my Germann suit."

"Who are you, really?"

"Oh," he chuckled, "I don't think you need to know that. I'm not exactly *authorized*. All you need to know is that I'm the imp that makes people forget things. Except for a few people...I make them remember. Painfully so. A devil has to eat, you know."

I squinted at it. "You killed my brother." It was a testing kind of statement. Somehow, that didn't feel right. Whatever Germann was, he wasn't a killer, not like that. I just couldn't feel it.

I'd been through Poland in 1945. If a man was a killer, I could feel it. It was just that there were a lot of us killers walking around those days. It confused the issue.

"Oh, no," Germann said. "That was Toomey. Who is dead now. I'm sorry, little Dick. You're all out of revenge."

"Why?"

"Why is Toomey dead? Because his little plots were becoming unraveled, and I'd already drained him almost dry."

"You killed him?"

"No, I just...left a door open."

"What killed him, then?"

In a sing-song voice, Germann said, "Oh, just...that thing that comes out of the dark places."

"What is it?"

"Something so old it doesn't have a name anymore. Something exactly as old as humanity." He chuckled again. I could have done without it.

"What's it trying to do, take over the world? Destroy the world?"

What can I say? I read too many pulp magazines, back in the war.

Germann grinned. "What makes you think," he chortled through needle-sharp teeth, "that it hasn't already?"

The hissing grew louder. It was all around me.

"The witch summoned it," Germann said. "With her greed and her hate and her anger, she prayed for it to come and kill… oh, well, more than one person. She prayed for it to make the path ahead of her easier. She asked for the wisdom of the stars. She asked for power. She asked for money. In 1832 it came and answered all her prayers."

Germann giggled. Clearly he was enjoying himself.

"Then it moved on to her servant, Toomey. He hated. He hated the old witch. And when he had prayed hard enough for it to kill her, it was able to answer *his* prayers, too."

"What is it, a god?"

Its scales hissed on the cement floor.

"Maybe so, maybe so," Germann said. "Maybe it's something made out of leftover bits of human nature. And maybe I am its prophet."

As far as I could tell, Ted Germann had started ripping off the Ormiston family in 1932, saying that he had recognized Mr. Ormiston, the twins' father, that night as the murderer. The fact that Mr. Ormiston had been at the same party as my parents could be conveniently ignored, because Mr. Ormiston had, at one point, stepped into another room to take a long phone call that occurred at approximately the same time my brother and his friends were killed.

I'll tell you who made the phone call in a moment.

But now I knew that Ted Germann had died that night in the massacre and been replaced by a sneering imp.

Later, I looked up Toomey's family records. They led backward to a foundling, a child who'd been left at Marie-Jean's door in 1832, and whom she had adopted after the death of her first husband. The child's last name had originally been the anonymous "Smith," but was changed later to "Toomey," after one of Marie-Jean's servants, who became the boy's mentor.

His family had served hers until 1914, when a pair of Toomey brothers went off to war and one of them came back with enough money to set himself up in the banking field. The other one came back in a coffin and was buried somewhere else out in the cemetery. You win some, you lose some. My guess is that the surviving Toomey boy said a few foul prayers and sacrificed his brother in exchange for something that wasn't worth it.

But I promised to tell you about the phone call.

The person who called Mr. Ormiston that night in 1932 was none other than yours truly. The twins had heard something outside of the house, and it had scared the h— out of them. Their panic had spread to me. I'd locked the doors, closed the curtains, and gone upstairs to the twins' bedroom with a garden tool in one hand, waiting for someone to try to break into the house and kill us all.

It sounded like the thing had come into the house through one of the windows—one of them must have been unlatched—crawling through the hallways, looking for something.

The boys lay under their beds and I stood over them, you guessed it, with the mattock I'd grabbed out of the mudroom by the back door as I'd locked it. It slithered along the wood floors, tentatively touched the knickknacks on the shelves, opened and shut the closets. It ran what sounded like a fingernail across the back of the boys' door.

We waited, shivering, for an hour. Then the sounds retreated, and finally we heard a downstairs window close.

I crept through the hallways, d—ed near jumping out of my skin. I reached the phone and called the party.

My father answered; I talked to him briefly, saying that we thought someone had tried to come into the house. He questioned me about it, and I lied and let him talk me into believing it was a teenager playing pranks on us, that the Ormistons would come home and see their front yard covered in toilet paper.

He did tell me not to leave the house, not for any reason whatsoever.

"Boys will play pranks," he said. Then he handed the phone over to Mr. Ormiston.

We talked, and he called me a brave boy, and a credit to my family. He said he would rather that I had panicked and defended his sons than I had kept my calm and let them walk into danger. He told me he would pay me extra, and that he would ask the police to drive around the block a few times. After he hung up, I went through the house, cleaning up every trace of mud, disturbed dust, and little things being moved that I could find.

The only problem was the scratch on the back of the boys' door. I found a can of paint out in the garage and covered it up. I'd tell the Ormistons that the boys had gotten a little rowdy while they were playing, but that it was all taken care of.

As I was putting the paint away, I heard another slithering sound like before, coming from outside. I looked out the window and watched the fallen leaves turn in the breeze, slithering across the grass in a trail that led away from the house and toward... well, toward the old Ormiston place, and the cemetery. The new house wasn't that far from the old one. That's the thing about these neighborhoods. The roads twist around on themselves so much that you can't tell how far one thing is from anything else unless you start cutting across people's back yards.

Then I went back inside the boys' room, carrying a pair of mugs of hot cocoa. But they were already asleep.

I was never sure how much of that night they remembered. In fact, I had forgotten most of it. Until I started speaking to Germann, or whatever he was, that night in the basement.

The hissing sound seemed to tighten, coming in closer. Coming in for the kill.

I thought about swinging with my mattock. But I didn't see what good it would do.

"Pray to it," Germann urged me. "Pray and it will give you your heart's desire. Otherwise, it will kill you."

In a flash, I could see the whole arrangement: pray to it for money or pray to it for the end of fear, it didn't matter. All you had to do was give it permission to enter your soul.

Like a vampire, only more intimate.

This was no kind god, nor a stern one. It was a god of greed and hate and jealousy.

And fear.

Oh, that mattock was coming out. But as a talisman, not as a weapon. But first…

I raised the camera, set the flash, and slipped off the lens cap.

The world turned white for a moment.

Then, as it faded, I almost saw it. It was larger than universes. It consumed itself. It was creation itself, that which creates itself in misery, eats itself in woe, and grows in suffering daily.

I dropped the camera and raised the mattock.

I had to get over to the jail. To the Ormiston boys.

—

Don't ask me how I got out of Germann's basement. I did, although my legs ached for days afterwards, as if I'd been out mountain climbing. When I emerged, the sun was just beginning to rise. I got in my car, panting heavily, and drove to the jail.

Wide-eyed and uncommunicative, they let me in.

I was too late. Arnold was dead, strangled by his brother James as they had spent the night in the holding cell. Even now he was muttering to himself.

"That thief. That *thief*. That bastard. He's a liar. He lied to me…"

"James," I said. My throat ached from having to say it.

James glanced up at me, did a double-take, then launched himself at the bars, snarling and foaming at the mouth, like a man with rabies.

Then there was a cough behind me. Germann had followed me in, or else he'd just appeared there, like the demon he was. He snapped his fingers and James fell silent, leaning up against the bars, so slack in the jaw that he drooled. His eyes closed and he slid down to the floor, where he curled up on his side.

"Now, he forgets," Germann said. "Later, when he has money, I'll let him remember."

I shook my head.

"You don't approve. How delightful," Germann said. "Would you like to forget, too?"

"No thanks," I said. I was remembering the twins on the floor under their beds, fast asleep. I was remembering my brother. I was remembering the look on Toomey's face as he carried the others out of that doorway and hacked them to pieces.

I remembered the film in my camera. I turned, raised the lens, and snapped a photo from the hip. The lighting in the jail wasn't bad, what with the dawn and all.

Germann gurgled, rubbed his eyes, and said, "Screw you, Delaney."

"Screw you," I said. "I got your number."

"Let's see what good it does you," Germann hissed.

As it turned out, not much. The film was melted inside the camera, I never did get paid, and I had to answer a lot of questions about a couple of fingerprints I'd missed in Toomey's house.

But when I went downstairs into my darkroom, it was never a black doorway leading to nowhere. And that has always meant something to me.

That necklace is in a Plexiglas box at the Maine Historical Society now. The rest of the jewelry was sold off to help pay for James's lawyer. I may have thrown in a couple of bucks myself. But it was a doomed effort. James had killed his brother. And he owed half a million dollars to a bank whose president had just wound up dead.

If you want to know what's really going on, all you have to do is follow the money, after all.

All the way down to that black place under the dirt.

About the Author

DeAnna Knippling is always tempted to lie on her bios. Her favorite musician is Tom Waits, and her favorite author is Lewis Carroll. Her favorite monster is zombies. Her life goal is to remake her house in the image of the House on the Rock, or at least Ripley's Believe It Or Not. You should buy her books. She promises that she'll use the money wisely on bookshelves and secret doors. She lives in Colorado and is the author of the A Fairy's Tale horror series which starts with *By Dawn's Bloody Light*, and other books like *The Clockwork Alice, A Murder of Crows: Seventeen Tales of Monsters & the Macabre*, and more.

Find out more about DeAnna at:
WonderlandPress.com

It Came Out of the Swamp

Ron Collins

The first people killed were Kevin Shay and Kylie Mendel, kids from maybe five miles up Highway 94, kids who were probably doing what young lovers do in the dark cypress at the edge of the swamp, which is, of course, where the monster came from.

No bodies ever turned up, though. No bones either.

Not that anyone really looked too hard.

I mean, some puzzles don't take a *summa cum laude* to put together.

Kevin's rust bucket was abandoned there, after all, and the stink of the creature was ground into the upholstery so deep that the vehicle wasn't good for anything but landfill afterward.

So, yeah, the first people killed by the Swamp Beast were Kevin Shay and Kylie Mendel.

That's how I planned to start the book, anyway.

I was twenty-five, living in Philadelphia, and using freelance gigs for a news outlet to put food on the table. It was working I guess, but I was restless. There had to be more, didn't there? High school, then college, and now…I didn't know. I felt restless, like I was missing something. I wanted to do more than drop 250 words on what Alderman McGary moved at the city council meeting last night, but I had no idea what that could be and no idea how to go about finding it.

Until I thought about the dust-up that happened over the Swamp Beast story back in the twenty-aughties.

Dr. Yglasias used it as a case study for one of my Truth in Journalism classes a couple years back, and it stuck with me.

The monster was impossible, after all.

I mean—it was exactly what you would expect from a swamp beast, right?—a hulking mass of mud and swamp gas that smelled of decomposing moss. It was roughly humanoid in shape but awkwardly huge. They say it rose up like some kind of movie prop, and commenced destruction like it was a mini Godzilla. When it moved, people said it made a slushing sound that was thick and sluicy like someone digging deep into your guts to search around for a while.

Think pig slop.

Its eyes blazed gold or yellow, or crimson—though the number, size, and location of them varied by witness. It wasn't reported to have teeth, at least not that anyone could tell. Just a mouth that hung open and a body that could flow like a mass of swampy lava, suffocating its victims, no matter how big, and digesting them down to so much compost.

It was big enough to rip a man in two, angry enough to pulverize a wobbly shack to the ground.

Then it was gone, burned to bits, never to rise again.

Pretty much anyone paying in the area at the time knows that part of the story: how Dred Davis used a home-hacked a flamethrower to burn the creature to such a crisp that no scientist could study it, and that no intellectual would even agree it was real despite the swath of destruction it left behind.

I would title the book *My Trials with the Swamp Beast*, or some riff off one of the headlines of the time.

Mindless Monster Mauls Hundreds.

Swamp Beast Terrorizes South.

Scientists Doubt Sci-Fi Horror.

It could be a big book. A journalistically sound examination of the beast, or at least a serious look at the *legend* behind it. The whole thing would be from the beast's point of view. No one else had thought about it that way, had they? *Swamp Beast Meets Mr. America*. I could see sections on Sasquatch and Bigfoot and a few others from Native American mythos interspersed with the truth of the Swamp Beast.

The more I thought about the idea, the more I liked it.

It also happened that I needed a break from Philly.

Hana Lethem, my girlfriend of the last two years, had just dumped my ass for no apparent reason, and I didn't think I could handle running into her again without putting my brain through a brick wall.

Hell, maybe in writing this thing I would even stumble over some big-assed corporate coverup, find a loose-lipped local with a whiskey-sotted conscience who could open a new can of worms about bio-engineering or the dumping of radioactive waste.

Happened in Watergate, right?

And, let's face it, a corporate cover up was a hell of a lot more reasonable explanation for this kind of thing than some kind of crazed Swamp-a-Beast that no one could prove existed. If I found that kind of thing down in the heart of the country, I could write my own ticket.

Wouldn't that put a kick in Hana's metaphorical teeth?

So that's why I finally pressed a couple days of shirts into my saddlebags, strapped on my helmet, and kicked my motorbike down to where the swamp monster frenzy first happened—a place deep enough in the south of Georgia that Florida came up to meet it, a bit west of the Okefenokee National Park, and a bit east of a great big patch of nothing.

The first thing I came to understand when I decided to take this trip is that the "town" the monster ransacked isn't even on the map.

Never has been.

I missed that before—even in class I'd looked past the fact that the reports came from "South Georgia" or "the Georgian swampland," rather than a place with an actual name.

That bothered me all the way down.

Had I ever questioned it? Had I ever wondered where these people were from?

The oversight made me angry in that uncomfortable way I got when I used to step past the crazy people living under the overpass down the street from my first apartment.

I came to no conclusions as I rode south, but my brain kept circling back to the idea that I needed to get in with the locals.

So, I asked a guy at a station up in Valdosta if he knew anything about the area. Told him I wanted real flavor. He smiled and said, "Gatortail Tavern," then gave me directions. Having done my homework, I knew close enough where he meant. It was just down the road from where everything ended.

"Perfect," I said.

As I arrived, the day was getting dark.

It was also Georgia in the dead of summer, which meant I was drenched in sweat, sucking humid air like it was covered in cellophane, and barely able to see through the bug juice that covered my visor.

The rumble of my bike faded into the night as my tires crunched through the gravelly parking lot. The tavern was nestled in the silence of ash, cypress, and dark oak, its thin parking lot half mud and all overgrown with timothy and crabgrass.

Right then I saw the road for what it was: a forgotten strip of asphalt that was crumbling away against a barrage of neglect and heat. It had probably been a proud road at one time, a road built by hard men and that families took to go on vacation, or just to visit each other—probably even a Sherriff's speed trap before interstates stole away its stream of rolling profit. Now it was just a place where desperate people put up desperate walls while living out the rest of their desperate lives.

I removed my helmet and was hit by a wall of barbecue aroma and the low screeching of cicadas gearing up for a symphony.

Thin strains of raw country music came from inside the building.

Under it all, my motorbike pinged and popped after the hard workout.

The bike was small as they went, a Suzuki that was more college student savvy than Hell's Angels hog. It smelled of motor oil and melting rubber.

My thighs hurt as I climbed off. My ass felt like it was on fire, and I suddenly realized just how hungry I was.

The tavern itself was barely a shack, but it had the aura of having been there forever. The walls were mostly warped wood that was watermarked and splintered and seemed to be held together by friction more than by nails. A dust-covered, neon orange Budweiser sign glowed in the dimness from one window. The words gatortail tavern ran over a weather-beaten placard nailed onto the roof. The lettering had been red at one point, but sun and time had beat it up pretty good.

If the guy in Valdosta hadn't told me to look for it, I would've missed it, easy.

Fighting intimidation, I stepped through the doorway.

The floorboard squealed under my weight, and two voices came to an awkward halt. The room was dark and smelled of tobacco and mold. The music was tinny and seemed to come from a corner behind the bar.

An old man sat at the bar smoking down the butt of a cigarette. "Looks like you got a customer, Doyle Bob," he said. Three crumpled cans of off-brand beer sat on the counter before him.

"What can I get you for?" the man I assumed was Doyle Bob said from the other side of the bar.

He was big and balding with biceps that bulged from under a rumpled black T-shirt, more flabby than built, but still suggesting power. The T-shirt had a silkscreened pattern that was worn and peeling.

"Got any barbecue?" I said, tightening the grip around the helmet I realized I was still carrying. "Smells good."

Doyle Bob smiled.

"Twenty dollars," he said. "Comes with a beer and big fries."

"Awesome."

Other than the bar itself, the place had three mismatched tables, each surrounded by an equally mismatched assortment of wooden chairs. I took one and put my helmet on another as the guy went to the kitchen to dish up.

I saw more of the place then.

The taxidermy and the bumper stickers. Mildewed posters of old movies. A dirtied-up Confederate flag hung down from one dark corner, and a Jolly Roger from another. There was a rusted-out motor of some kind beside the bar, and a cooler on the floor split down one side, maybe still functional and maybe not. A big-assed box fan blew air from a window behind the bar, the sound rising up between songs.

I don't know if there's a time in my life where I ever felt more northern.

"Where you headed?" the big man said when he put a plate and a beer can in front of me.

"Here," I replied, trying to sound nonchalant.

He laughed. "Hear that, Scat? The kid says he come lookin' for us."

The man at the bar had lit another cigarette and gotten himself another beer. He was thinner than Doyle Bob, scrawny and wrinkled in a harsh, alcoholic way.

"Dumbass," he said, combining the word with a smoky exhale. His voice was as rough as his skin.

"What can you tell me about the monster?" I said before shoveling pork into my mouth.

Doyle Bob straightened, then grunted for show as he headed back to his post behind the bar.

"Looks like we got us a reporter," he said.

"Been awhile," Scat replied.

"I'm not a reporter," I said. "I'm writing a book."

Neither replied to that, so I ate more.

"Crap, this is really good," I said, not lying. Sure, I was hungry, but the barbecue was amazing, and the beer hit it better than perfect.

"Been cooking all day," Doyle Bob said.

Johnny Cash played while I ate. Scat smoked.

"So, what can you tell me about it?" I finally pressed.

The two passed a glance as if deciding what to say, then lit into a talk that felt half practiced and half in-joke. It was clear even then that they'd been through this before.

They talked about Kylie and Kevin, Nettie Mae—the old woman whose house was the second in the monster's path—the Deakyman, and several others I'd heard about before coming to the climax with Dred Davis and the little girl he saved. I got the whole schtick, a standard rundown of the swamp monster's entire run through what they called "the Lane."

That's the one thing I learned new—how the people called their home "the Lane."

And I learned something else, too.

I'd read and re-read all the articles, and I'd seen pictures of the place and its people—grainy black and white images of Davis and the Deakyman, one white, the other black, but both hollowed out and ghostly, played up in varying parts of the press as either veterans of the desert wars or wayward hobos. I'd read about Nettie Mae. Seen pictures of the destruction.

But between the cracks of Doyle Bob and Scat's stories I heard things I hadn't heard before—how people like them and Nettie Mae and the Deakyman just seemed to show up here, almost like they seeped up from the swamp. And that they live in it. Find ways. Scrounge a few dollars here, or trade a found tool there. I learned then and there that, for a lot of people, the Lane is something more than home.

"A person comes here, they don't never leave," Doyle Bob said when he was talking about Dred Davis and the girl he saved.

"Not 'less the swamp takes 'em," Scat added with a five-toothed smile.

I thought about the little girl Dred Davis had saved as I watched them riff off each other.

She'd been what, nine? No one knew for sure.

I'd watched her one and only public interview several times now. Her name was Kewana, but she didn't have a family name and there had been no birth record. As far as anyone could tell, the girl had come straight from the swamp as much as the monster did.

The authorities found her a home when she was saved, but I knew she'd left it. Just disappeared.

I didn't know much else except that at the end of the interview, Kewana said she had been trying to talk with the beast when Davis showed up.

"It couldn't say anything," Kewana said, holding the new cushy doll the network had given her and looking up with those brilliantly wide eyes that made audiences melt. "It was lost and I thought it was crying," she said. "I wanted to help."

I was looking for fresh facts, though, not retread human-interest stories. My book needed new truth, actions, details, or other things that people who came before had missed.

"I want to get under the skin of the monster," I said in the middle of the Doyle Bob and Scat show, but they were on cruise control and just grinned as they told stories they'd told a hundred times before.

I settled in, bought another beer, and listened.

I left the place an hour later filled with barbecue and knowing I'd heard everything they'd wanted me to hear—and just as certain there was more where that came from. How to find it, though. That was the question, right? I smelled the swamp as I straddled my Suzuki, feeling more than ever that the full story was out there somewhere.

Five miles east of the Gatortail I found the motel Doyle Bob pointed me to.

Surprised myself by being so tired that I slept through the night.

The next day I went to where Kevin Shay's car was found.

I used pictures to convince myself I was standing in the exact place, then turned and looked deeper into the swamp. It was later in the morning than I was hoping for. The sun had already baked the morning off.

The patch of ground where the car had been found was off the highway and down a winding path far enough back that I couldn't see the berm at all. You likely wouldn't hear a car up there unless the wind was just right.

I stood in the clearing in my jeans, riding boots, and a sleeveless shirt with a Grass Parade logo on it, which was an indie band I'd been following. For some reason it had seemed right. It was worn and had an acid-washed red tone to it that matched the clay here.

The heat was stifling. Sweat beaded on my shoulders and trickled down my arms. The smell of the swamp was thick and organic.

I shielded my eyes and peered into the morass.

My plan was to tell the story a chapter at a time, following the path of the creature as I went: start with the kids, move on to Nettie Mae's, see the world from the monster's eyes, and tell the story of the Swamp Beast at each stop. I'd read the old comic books and watched the old movies. I had pictured the resulting book as an entertaining mix of old pulp and hard-nosed journalism, but something about the silence of this place was making me think about things differently now. There was something here.

An emptiness, maybe. No, not emptiness. Something slippery like a ghost or some other wraithlike kind of phantom. It made me itch inside. It made me wonder about Kevin Shay and Kylie Mendel.

They had an assigned part in the story, right?

Slasher movie kids.

Young and lusty, naïve and self-absorbed, getting it on while the Swamp Beast sucked them down. It was a simple trope. Immediately relatable. Funny in its own way.

But Kevin and Kylie weren't actors.

After the flick was over, they were still dead.

Standing at the edge of the swamp, I began to wonder who they were. Why did they come here? I mean, beyond the obvious. What did they dream of? Who would they be now? Were they really in love?

A splashing came from somewhere in the swamp, and my heart lurched.

I took an instinctive step back, then laughed at myself.

Despite hairs raising on the back of my neck, I did my best to forget that moment where primordial instinct screamed out that the monster was still alive, or that there could be another one—a brother or sister, or worse, its enraged mother.

"Get a grip," I said aloud.

No swamp monster was going to spring out of the muck to get me.

I understood then, however, that this story did not start at the car.

If I was going to write from the Swamp Beast's perspective, I needed to start where it came from, and it came from the swamp.

So that's where I went.

I stepped into the shade of the bog's canopy and kept going, ducking brush and low branches that reached down with a snakelike presence, crossing sawgrass, slogging through boggy peat that sank an inch or two with each stride, stepping over dead trees and matted leaves.

I found a place at the edge of the muck and climbed into a thick cypress tree. The bark was corky and rough, covered with Spanish moss. Some of the bark peeled as I climbed it, and for the first time ever, I thought about the scar I was leaving on the land around me.

It would heal.

As long as I didn't kill it, the tree would make it on just fine.

How long does a cypress tree live? Longer than me, I'd guess.

I sat back against the bark.

At first there was nothing but stagnant silence, but slowly the sounds of the swamp came back: the rustle of wind in leaves, calls of birds and frogs, a deer picking its way through the bog, nibbling greens and lifting its feet gingerly as it went.

I sat without motion, feeling oddly connected to the world around me.

Branches swayed in the hot wind. Leaves fell into the wetlands. Currents of the water flowed silently southward.

I closed my eyes and imagined I was the beast rising from the muck.

Feeling the place under its feet. Hungry. Needing to feed.

It was made of the swamp, a true nature's child. And since nature is hard, it would have to be hard. Nature is Darwin on crack, right?

So, you're a swamp monster, and you've just been born.

If you are the Swamp Beast, what do you know of the world except that you need to eat? Where do you go? How do you feel when you hear a car rolling up to the headlands?

How do you rise up, silently so as to not scare it away?

How do you move?

What path do you take?

Can you split yourself? Are you one creature, or many? One cell or infinite?

The sun was well past midday when I left the swamp.

I felt drained but invigorated.

I got back to the motorbike and ate a pair of granola bars, then left on foot again, following a path west toward Nettie Mae's.

—

Later that night over another plate of Gatortail barbecue, I described the feeling of being at Nettie Mae's. Doyle Bob and Scat sat quietly through most of it, both drinking, Scat smoking. Occasionally they would nod or look over at one another.

They knew the score better than me.

Knew Nettie Mae's was the first of the Lane to get a visit.

"I saw the foundation," I said of Nettie's place, nearly shivering as I recalled the distant sense of power that came over me as I stood there.

I'd seen the old reports, heard about the wailing that came like a dire horn and the waves of fetid rankness that rolled off the monster as it waded through the Lane. Heard about the monster's strength, how it had torn buildings to bits, pulverized plywood walls, destroyed kitchens, and blasted furniture into so much kindling.

Standing on the overgrown sheet of concrete that had been the foundation of Nettie Mae's place had been like being at a funeral, but different. A person had lived and died here, and I felt it in the breeze and the humidity that wrapped me up like a blanket.

"Nothing really prepares you for it," I said, trying to explain.

I talked about the barren platform, about imagining the walls, and seeing a few shreds of rusted tin that were still wedged in a bed of rock nearby. I talked about how I stared for too long at the half-gone woodstove that was the only thing left after the swamp monster took her, how the woodstove sat there alone and steady on the foundation like nothing but the rain and the wind had touched it since the days slaves had last lived there.

"You can't help but feel her," I said, killing a beer. "It's like she's sitting there watching."

"Nettie was an ornery cuss," Scat said. "Got off two shots, they say."

I paused. "Didn't know she kept a gun."

The codger ground his few teeth together and took a pull on his beer, sharing a glance at Doyle Bob that got returned in an offhand way.

"Ain't no one wants to die," Scat finally said.

I nodded. "Heard all she left behind was a bloody stump of a foot," I said.

They were done for the night, though, and all the prying did was make me for a hick reporter. That was fine, though. I had more about Nettie Mae in my brain now than I'd had in years of reading about the swamp monster. Instead of pushing my luck I bought another beer and listened to them talk. Told them a little about Philadelphia, but it felt hollow. What did anyone care about a big city up north?

When I was done, I went to the motel and slept, dreaming about Nettie Mae and her gun, and Kevin and Kylie, and the swamp monster rising up like the heart of the earth to take them all.

I started earlier next morning, this time at the Deakyman's tree, which was east of Nettie Mae's place and across from a boggy creek bed. They called it the Deakyman's tree because that's exactly what it was—the place he lived in, the place where every night he climbed up and found his refuge. In class that fact always carried an edge of humor. Crazy guy who lives in a tree, right? That's funny. But it didn't feel funny now.

It didn't, however, feel sad either.

Instead, it just felt there. Real.

The tree was a low cypress with wide branches the Deakyman must have figured were just high enough to keep him safe from gators, bears, and pretty much anything else.

"Guess he didn't take into account swamp monsters," I said to Doyle Bob late that night.

He laughed. "Reckon not."

"The Deakyman was never one to take a lot into account," Scat added.

I climbed up the tree, though, and I sat in his spot, looking out the direction the swamp monster must have come from. Who was the Deakyman? Where had he come from? The question brought back the gaze Doyle Bob and Scat shared before saying the swamp seeped up people like this. Maybe I was starting to understand.

Had he been asleep when the swamp came to take him?

Had he been drunk?

Nothing in this tree said anything about what the Deakyman did that night, but I discovered a rusted can opener wedged into the tree, and, higher up, an equally rusted shaving kit that held a military medal that also was corroded to the point that I couldn't make it out well enough that Google was any help.

Farther up the tree, I found three nooks with views where a man could sit sentry. They made me think of late nights in a uniform, staring out over a bombed out desert city.

I'd never served.

How would it feel to be the Deakyman? How would it really feel?

I climbed into the spots and looked over the treetops, feeling oddly like the Batman peering over Gotham.

I stayed later at the Gatortail that night.

Bought them both a third beer that Doyle Bob didn't take money for.

From pictures in the papers I knew the Deakyman was a thin black man with what appeared to be gray shot through most his hair. His cheeks seemed hollowed out. When Scat got to talking that night, he added in that the Deakyman had fingers that moved like spider legs, and that he was mostly quiet, but that sometimes he'd laugh and it was always a dry sound. Doyle Bob said he talked once or twice about the army, but otherwise just found a few bucks for a bottle most every night and went to sleep up his tree.

As I left the tavern that night, I flashed on the image of those three sentry posts and thought about home.

I felt odd. Like a part of me was empty almost.

My life was good, wasn't it? I had a job. Or at least a little money coming in. Enough, anyway. I had my bike. I was writing a book about a swamp monster that should be pretty cool. What more did I want?

My mind kept asking questions I couldn't answer.

Why did the Deakyman come here? Why did he stay? Why did seeing his tree make me feel like this? And why, when Doyle Bob and Scat talked of these people, was there no remorse? Why was there never a tone of loss?

My sleep was restless that night.

I woke up early.

I came to the final scene on the third day.

The swamp felt different now. I was comfortable in it, if not familiar with it.

I stepped into mire and mess without hesitation.

I grabbed big branches and stepped over land with a stronger sense of confidence, continuing long into the day until I came finally to the overgrown clearing deep in the sucking heat of the swampland.

Sweat beaded my skin. Brine covered my lips.

Last night Doyle Bob talked about Native Americans who had lived here. I could feel them now: the Apalachee, Chickasaw, and Creek. As he talked, I'd come to understand I had work to do before I could tell the story of this swamp creature. I had history to learn, things to understand. There were Spanish here for years, then cotton growers up north.

No one stayed, though.

Doyle Bob had said it was like this patch of land belonged in a different place or a different time.

"More like a different dimension," I replied.

I'd been thinking about Philadelphia, the lower side where no one goes. They nodded, though they didn't know what I meant.

People live in that lower side, though. They make lives there in Philadelphia just like these people make lives in the Lane. Places like this are different worlds. Shadow dimensions that operate alongside the one I live in, but never quite touch down. A guy dies on a street corner and the city just swallows him up like the swamp swallowed up Nettie Mae and the Deakyman. He's gone like nothing ever happened and if he's lucky he gets a rusted woodstove as a tombstone.

Maybe that man'd been happy, though.

Maybe he had a family, or kids, or a set of friends to drink a bottle with.

One earth, multiple dimensions.

Talk about your weird book.

Now, though, I was standing in the only place in the whole story that most everyone would know about—the clearing where Dred Davis came upon the swamp monster. Just the mental picture of the hypervigilant, hooch-drinking, ballcap-wearing militia man strapping on the World War II-era flamethrower he'd tricked out to use kerosene for fuel was enough to make a dent in your brain.

Probably stoned out of his gourd, some said at the time.

Just another whacked-out vet with a hero complex, others added.

Kinder folks commented about PTSD and mental help.

Whatever you think of him, though, the facts are that Dred Davis had been in the military for five years before coming home from the Middle East, then found himself without a job or family. Buddies from his unit say he retreated into the swamp. Some say he lived happily on his own until the day he went ape-shit with the flamethrower.

Maybe he snapped.

Maybe he had a flashback. Maybe he saw the little girl and just went into savior-complex overdrive.

He could have been defending his country.

He could have been blasted on dope or high on pure adrenaline.

Who knows what goes through the mind at times like that?

He lumbered into the clearing I was now standing in to find the beast hunched over the little girl, and commenced to deliver a hail of whooping profanity and flame throwing that left the creature incinerated and the child quavering.

We also know, from police reports and from that one interview Kewana gave, that the beast screamed and burned, and that Dred Davis suffered a similar fate when the flamethrower's compression tank exploded behind him.

"There was less left of the guy than there was of the Swamp Beast," one late night comic said. "Here's your Darwin Award."

Despite the humor of the situation, much of the country hailed Davis as a hero, which I suppose he was.

The government flew flags at half-mast, and newsfeeds were full of stories about missions Private Davis had been a part of. Men and women of his unit were asked for comments, which they gave. He was given a burial at Arlington, but no one he knew came forward.

I sat on a mound at the middle of the clearing and thought about the girl.

I closed my eyes and felt the insects call.

Frogs burped. Bugs droned.

I felt the monster around me as sure as I'd felt Nettie Mae and the Deakyman before. I felt Dred Davis, too. Does a beast leave a ghost? Was there even a beast? Had the swamp creature really taken the lives of these people, or did the swamp itself just reach out and do what this world does to a person?

So many questions.

I came here for information enough to write a simple book, but all I really managed to find were more questions than my mind could answer.

I saw my ex's face then.

The moment when Hana left me, the expression of vacant disquiet when she tried to explain why. I understood now. How do you explain to someone that they're just not all there? How do you tell someone that they don't know what's going on? They're just writing fool news stories as a way to just play along?

"Grow up."

They were the last words she said as she walked out of the coffee shop we'd been in.

I breathed in the heat of the day, and as I exhaled I felt the pressure of eyes on me.

Slowly, head down, I opened my eyes.

Across the way I saw a woman wearing a blue T-shirt stained in sweat.

She was older now. Maybe twenty.

Her hair was razored short, her muscles toned and wiry, her face sharp and focused. She was squatted down beside an ash tree whose roots were dark from soaking up stagnant water. Her eyes were unmistakable, though, her lips rounded but closed.

Yes, it made sense. The little girl who ran from her foster family returned to the only home she knew.

"Kewana?" I said.

Her eyes half-closed and her head cocked to one side as if she was asking herself a question.

I wanted to talk to her, then. I wanted to ask why she was here. What was her life like?

She was the only living survivor of that night. The only person who knew what it all meant.

More than anything I'd ever wanted in the world, I wanted to hear what this woman who had been pulled from the swamp as a little girl had to say.

She bolted.

Without thought, I followed her into the swamp, pursuing her as much by the rustle and splash of tangled thatch and boggy mire as by sight. My boots sank into the mud. The smell of fern and moss was everywhere. The stagnation of the swamp felt like it was part of me. My breath came harder, and the image of a gator hole filled my brain.

In the distance I saw a treehouse, complete with hammock. There was a couch of some kind there. A broken bookshelf maybe. The roof was off-kilter sheets of aluminum and wood.

I was closing.

Another few steps…

A moment later we came to a grassy clearing I could climb on.

"It's all right," I said to Kewana, panting. "I don't want to hurt you."

This is when the earth moved.

She stepped back into the bog and the swamp shuddered with a tearing sound so low and so powerful that it made my stomach clench and my chest feel like it might explode.

A dark morass rose from the mire, huge and bulky, made of clay, algae, and mud. It writhed with snakes and swamp grasses shot through by rivulets of gritty water. The beast gave a growl like two snapped trees grinding together.

Arms sprouted from its body and flailed toward me.

I fell to the ground like I'd been hit with a baseball bat, frozen in fear.

The ground shook as the monster rose to its full height and levered itself from the swamp. Swamp water drained over me as it spread its body above mine, pinioning me with tendrils that bored into the ground to make cage of living mire.

It grunted then, expelling methane and algae.

A series of eyes sprouted from its underside, blazing with crimson heat.

Kewana came to where I could see her. She was tall and proud in her way, her shoulders thrown back, breathing hard of her own exertion.

"What are you doing here?" she said, her voice low and husky.

I looked up at the swamp monster.

"It's alive," I said.

"You cannot kill the swamp," she replied sharply. "What are you doing here?"

"I wanted..." I licked my lips, worried that telling the truth would be a problem. Then, in a way that my Truth in Journalism class could never teach, I realized that telling the truth would always be the only thing that really mattered.

"I wanted to write a book," I said.

"A book?"

I nodded.

"About what?"

I swallowed hard.

Above me, the monster grew more fetid every moment.

I reached to touch its underbelly. It was slick and slippery like seaweed, but warm like the earth. I felt Nettie Mae's orneriness there, the Deakyman's sense of calm. The tone of Doyle Bob and Scat's words filled my mind. I put my other hand on the swamp monster, feeling the grit of its soil between my fingers. I thought about Philadelphia, about my job selling news bits, and the feeling of grime under the veneer of the city.

I pulled my hands from the monster, then glanced to Kewana. She chewed the corner of her lip.

"I thought my book was going to be about the monster," I finally answered. "But now I think it has to be about something bigger."

"Bigger?"

"Yes," I said, rolling mud between my fingertips. "I think it needs to be about seeing people for who they really are."

She took a breath, then gave the Swamp Beast a nod of conviction.

The monster rose, then receded into the morass, leaving behind a deep sucking sound and then silence.

I stood up, not bothering to brush away the mess that coated my body.

"That's a good thing for a book to be about," Kewana finally said.

"Yes," I replied. "I think so, too."

I glanced in the direction of the highway. It would grow dark soon. The trek back would be long, but I knew the way.

Suddenly I was hungry.

"Would you like to talk?" I said to Kewana. "I know a place with great barbeque."

She smiled in the gloaming.

About the Author

Ron Collins is an Amazon best-selling Dark Fantasy author who writes across the spectrum of speculative fiction.

His latest science fiction series, *Stealing the Sun* is available from Skyfox Publishing.

His fantasy series *Saga of the God-Touched Mage* reached #1 on Amazon's bestselling dark fantasy list in the UK and #2 in the US. His short fiction has received a Writers of the Future prize and a CompuServe HOMer Award. His short story "The White Game" was nominated for the Short Mystery Fiction Society's 2016 Derringer Award.

He has contributed a hundred or so short stories to professional publications such as *Analog*, *Asimov's*, and several other magazines and anthologies (including several editions of the *Fiction River* Anthology Series).

He holds a degree in Mechanical Engineering, and has worked to develop avionics systems, electronics, and information technology before chucking it all to write full-time–which he now does from his home in the shadows of the Santa Catalina Mountains.

Find out more about Ron at:

typosphere.com

About Amazing Monster Tales

Dawn of the Monsters is the first volume in the *Amazing Monster Tales* anthology series. Follow us on Facebook or our website, *AmazingMonsterTales.com*, to be notified about new releases.

You can never have enough monsters...

About Borogrove Press

Borogrove Press is a partnership between editors DeAnna Knippling, of Wonderland Press, and Jamie Ferguson, of Blackbird Publishing.

Amazing Monster Tales is Borogrove Press's very first project.

Other Collections

Other speculative fiction collections are available through Borogrove Press' cousin, Blackbird Publishing.

As always, this story is dedicated to Lee and Ray, without whose love none of this would be possible.
DeAnna Knippling

Thanks to Jo (aka Mom) for listening, and to Jasper for keeping me company.
Jamie Ferguson